BETTER THAN A REST

BETTER THAN A REST

Pauline McLynn

HEADLINE

First published in Great Britain in 2001
by HEADLINE BOOK PUBLISHING

10 9 8 7 6 5 4 3 2 1

ISBN 0 7472 7460 6

Typeset by Letterpart Ltd
Reigate, Surrey

Printed and bound in Great Britain by
Clays Ltd, St Ives plc.

HEADLINE BOOK PUBLISHING
A division of Hodder Headline
338 Euston Road
London NW1 3BH

www.headline.co.uk
www.hodderheadline.com

For Dominick McGrath without whom
things might well fall apart . . .

ONE

It is surely a given that a hairy big toe is not an attractive feature, on a man or a woman. Cats and dogs get away with it, as do otters, rabbits and what have you. Humans, no. That's what I was thinking at 12.30 a.m. as Michael O'Donoghue let himself out of another woman's house and set off for the southside of Dublin city where he lived with his wife, Miranda, and, occasionally, their two teenage children, Tara (15) and Ben (13). That's how scintillating the evening's mental activity had been, how interesting covert surveillance can get at times: hairy big toes.

I followed at a discreet distance. Sadly, not all of the motorists abroad that night had their full quota of discretion on board. As the O'Donoghue Mercedes slowed to a stop at traffic lights, and I began to do the same, a red banger hurtled out of a laneway, smashing into the side of my dark green banger. There was a sickening crunch, and my innards lurched as the cars scuttled sideways. After some

1

moments of a macabre metal waltz, we screeched to a noisy stop and I realised that my journey this evening was just about over. In fact, I was going nowhere, fast.

As soon as I could, I extricated my trusty steed from the mess, and pulled in to the verge. I counted to ten, then calmly got out and walked over to the offending vehicle. The ninny in the other car was blubbering. She became incoherent when she saw the motorcycle cop who had appeared, *as if by magic*. They really do have the ability to fall from the sky. Black streams of mascara ran down the woman's cheeks, and saliva bubbled from her lips. If she hadn't messed my night up so badly, I might have felt some pity. I handed her a tissue as the policeman joined us. We had enough people for a small cheese 'n' wine do now. Worst of all, Michael O'Donoghue reversed to join us, and got out of his car with the immortal words, 'I'm a doctor, is there anything I can do to help?'

The crying heap shoved her face further into her hand-kerchief and began to pace up and down behind her car. The young Garda took off his helmet. He was just a kid, and could barely muster sideburns. When you've begun to think that teachers and the police look like babies, you know you're getting on. I was thirty now and felt every day of it. At least I wasn't old enough to be his mother, I thought. Or was I? I wondered with a shudder. No, biologically that wasn't possible. Even in these days of technological advancement. Surely? A nagging doubt lingered in my mind.

Michael O'Donoghue ascertained that his professional services were not needed and, lacking an inclination to involve himself in any other way, sped off to the south. I envied him. Unfortunately, he was now familiar with my face and my car, although he did not know that I had been following him that night, and for the previous three, on the instructions of a worried and suspicious wife. I would need a major rethink of this case, no thanks to the stranger in the red car. And, inevitably, it would cost money to get back to the status quo. Money was in short supply. But then, what else was new?

My dance partner gathered herself sufficiently to begin the tedious exchanges that typified motoring in Ireland, April 1997. I didn't know the Garda, which was a relief. Many of his colleagues, who knew me all too well, would have relished a chance like this to put me on the spot to see how I reacted. When asked my occupation, I simply answered 'self-employed', and he was satisfied with that. For mischief, others might have pushed for a more detailed description, just to see me sweat. He was happy enough with the name Leonora Street, spinster of number 11, The Villas, Dublin 3. I could have offered 'insurance adviser', and it would not have been a lie; a lot of cases I work on involve insurance fraud. Equally, I might have given myself the title 'marriage consultant', because infidelity is the meat and drink of my trade. Only one thing was for sure, I was never going to admit to the real description, private investigator. Life was always easier when I avoided mentioning this.

When all of the relevant insurance details had been exchanged, the females of the group promised to stay in touch like the good friends we would never be, and the little party broke up. We all went our, now, separate ways. I headed back northwards, along the coast road, with a heavy heart and a limping, rattling car. I would need someone else to follow Michael O'Donoghue, at least in the short term.

The problem was not so much that he'd seen me – a wig and glasses would have taken care of that. But I had no quick access to new wheels and the risk was that he would recognise my car now, with its distinctive, and unwanted, dent. I was going to need a new body with fresh transport. Best have a good night's sleep and tackle the problem with a clear mind in the morning.

I wasn't too worried about what my subject would get up to the following day during business hours. That was as predictable as my own moodiness coming up to a period. Michael O'Donoghue was one of the country's leading obstetricians, and held a clinic in his practice on Merrion Square on weekdays between nine and two. Then he had a quick lunch, usually a sandwich at his desk, before strolling across to do his daily round at the Fledgling Clinic, behind the National Maternity Hospital in Holles Street. The Fledgling also dealt in childbirth, but aside from that any similarity between the two institutions was hard to find. The latter was run by a private trust as a lucrative business and boasted a fertility clinic amongst its assets. It was a very expensive, and exclusive, facility with a clientele of the rich, the famous and the bankrupt. Michael O'Donoghue was one of its star attractions – in the medical sense, that is. Now, without our old friend 'the unforeseen circumstance' turning up, I had until tea time to find someone else to continue surveillance on him.

Noel peeked his cheeky face through the curtains as I hiccoughed my jalopy over the speed ramps and clanked to a halt outside my house. It was one of a series of triangular dwellings, all in a row, known locally as The Toblerone. The lights of the front room were on and I could hear music being played on the stereo. I didn't think that Noel or Bridie or Snubby was responsible for the noise. They were cats. That left me with Barry, my live-in boyfriend. Unless it had been No. 4, who was partial to the Divine Comedy, the group I could hear singing about Daddy's crashed car. Here comes Mummy with her version, I thought, as I followed my cloudy breath up the pathway and let myself in the front door.

Barry Agnew was draped lazily along the couch, smoking a joint. Nothing unusual here. Barry had lived either on the bed or on the couch since he had moved in with me, three years ago. The only addition to this familiar sight was the figure lolling in the opposite armchair: Coleman Pearse, another actor. They favoured the term 'wandering minstrel' to describe their profession. I was beginning to prefer 'meandering wastrel'.

'Leonora,' exclaimed Coleman, in deep theatrical tones. 'What an unexpected surprise.'

'Coleman, I live here. But what an expected surprise to find *you* in situ.'

'Of course I am, dear heart. This house of yours is an oasis of the finest hospitality imaginable to a poor thespian.'

'Nice diction, Coleman,' I congratulated him, my voice lightly iced with sarcasm.

'Now, now, Leo,' said Barry, from the deepest reaches of his lair. 'Coleman is a guest, so play nice.'

'Okay, okay,' I agreed. 'Sorry to be a grouch, Coleman, but someone tried to take the side off my car tonight, and they very nearly succeeded. It's in a right mess.'

Coleman nodded his head sagely. 'All part of the derring-do of your profession. The risking of life and limb. Very brave of you, Leonora.'

This 'Leonora' business was beginning to get to me. Only my family used it with any regularity, and then it was usually reserved for occasions when they were angry with me, or winding me up for some reason. In them it was occasionally endearing, in Coleman I found it overly familiar, something I could not abide in a casual acquaintance. Coleman was very casual, particularly with my beer. And my food, for that matter. Oh, yes, and my spare bedroom, when he was too trashed to make it home to his own house.

Barry and Coleman had become the best of friends some weeks ago when they began work on the Dublin Literary Tour and Pub Crawl. They took to the job with marked alacrity, principally because it involved lots of thunderous oration and the drinking of, at least, one glass of stout in each of the many pubs they visited on the Crawl. And then getting properly shit-faced afterwards with the punters. It had been their vocation fulfilled. They finished most of these evenings with a brace of takeaway lagers, and smoking a load of dope. At my house.

Coleman liked to put it about that he was a cousin of the late Padraig Pearse, the Irish writer and revolutionary. I thought it more likely that he was as related to the famous Pearse as I was, which was not at all. But according to Barry, the boast worked a treat for pulling women, and Coleman was never short of a bedfellow in the shape of a foreign student, au pair or American tourist. That's when he was not bunking over at mine. I drew the line at him keeping company there, using the place like a brothel and giving me, effectively, another mouth to feed and water.

'Anyone for a beer?' I asked, foolishly.

'Did Rose Kennedy have a black dress?' replied Coleman.

I opened the fridge and saw two tins of Czech beer with an unpronounceable name. This brand was obviously the cheapest available locally; neither Barry nor Coleman believed in paying much for their drink, if they were using their own money. It didn't take a genius to figure out that three into two did not go. I announced as much.

'Well, you drink wine so,' suggested Barry. 'Anyhow, that lager is a terrible ring-stinger, and you'd regret having it as much as I'm going to tomorrow.'

'You're all heart, Barry, do you know that?' I said sweetly. 'And I would be delighted to drink some wine, if there were any. If seems the wine mouse has been to the fridge again, and had the lot.'

'Bad, evil, wicked wine mouse,' he slurred.

I looked back into the living room, saw the two languid beauties and made a decision.

'You've both been drinking all night, and now you're smoking your faces off. You don't need any more booze, so here's my revolutionary plan. Why don't I have *both* the cans that are left, and that way everyone is happy? Particularly me. Now who's a clever girl!'

The cream of Ireland's young actors looked shocked, but knew better than to argue; it was my house. As I closed the fridge door I noticed that the cat magnet poetry was getting more and more puerile, with overuse of the words 'pussy' and ' lick'. Kick rhymes with lick, I mused idly, and remembered that 'doggerel' is the word for bad verse, though it didn't seem appropriate in this case. As I made my way over to a chair, I looked around uneasily. The power of poetry had triggered a thought in my brain. Something was bothering me about the domestic set-up; something was missing. No. 4 was nowhere to be seen. He had come to live with us as a bizarre by-product of a case I'd worked on in Kildare. At that time I had been chosen for, perhaps even by, No. 4.

'Barry, where's the dog?'

'Oh, he's upstairs in one of the bedrooms. The cats and him were killing one another all evening, so I had to separate them.'

'Well, I hope you let him out for a pee before you banished him,' I said.

Realisation clicked behind his eyes, and I knew that he had not.

'Oh, for God's sake, Barry, can you not be trusted with anything?'

As I rushed up the stairs, I heard Coleman ask, 'Do you think that was the kind of green boat that the owl and the pussycat took?' followed by hoots of laughter. I opened the bedroom door and a yelping white-black-brown blur whizzed by and made for the cat flap from the kitchen into the back garden. It was still swinging to and fro when I got back downstairs.

'Doggone!' Barry hooted. Coleman enjoyed this and showed it noisily.

'Tossers,' I murmured to myself.

When the little Jack Russell had discharged his business, he returned and covered me with licks, before boisterously making friends with the bewildered felines.

After that I took great delight in cracking open the second last tin of lager in front of the lads. They looked on longingly as I slowly sipped the ice-cold brew. I gave a contented sigh and said, 'Barry, I don't know what you're talking about. I think this is delicious.' Then I squeezed on to the couch beside him so that he had to adjust his comfortable slouch to accommodate me. This was shaping up nicely, I thought.

We sat in silence for a while, and Barry rolled another joint. Then he and Coleman smoked it. I didn't partake. I never did. In a way there was no need. Unlike Bill Clinton, however, I did inhale. It would have been hard not to in the fumes that filled the air in the tiny room. I noticed that the cats, myself and No. 4 were like the Bisto Kids, our noses slightly upturned and inhaling the wafts of smoke though this was a different joint from the one the Bisto Kids would have been involved with, I guessed. We were all smiling although on No. 4's face this looked a little like a snarl. The expression on blond-haired Coleman Pearse owed more to Harpo Marx, but in a spirit of peace and reconciliation, I refrained from mentioning this.

'Leo, you'll love the latest standout advertisement we've found in the *Northsider News*,' said Barry, reaching for the local free paper. 'Myself and Coleman are very tempted to apply. We'd be just right for the job.'

In the Situations Vacant section, a drawing of a truck headed an ad declaring: 'Wanted – articulate drivers. Experienced HGV licence essential'.

'That old devil, the roving "d",' I laughed.

'If only I'd heeded me mammy and taken the heavy goods vehicle test,' wailed Coleman, dramatically, 'life would have been so different.'

'Yes,' I agreed, solemnly. 'You're only half qualified. You may be articulate, but you don't have the driving licence.'

'And your experiences may be of the wrong kind anyhow,' added Barry.

'Oh, I don't think so,' grinned Coleman. 'Trucking, and all that.'

The two actors began to discuss the finer points of a play we'd seen at the Abbey Theatre the week before. This amounted to a fair bit of bitching about the younger members of the cast. Both Barry and Coleman had been up for parts, but had not been successful. As a result, they had long ago decided that the female director of the piece was a lesbian. I had enjoyed it very much, particularly as it starred my friend Maeve Kelly. She assured me that the director was as straight as ourselves, and married to a stunning, filthy-rich businessman.

I looked at Barry as he waved his arms about, explaining some complicated notion he had about the leading actor's lisp, which I had found charming in the extreme. Barry's long, square-jawed face was animated and therefore at its best. As he smiled dimples appeared in each olive-skinned cheek; his vivid blue eyes sparkled and crinkled good-naturedly. Every time he jerked his head, masses of black curls bounced up and down. He was gorgeous.

I had met him, and his friend Maeve, at a party in a house in Glasnevin on Dublin's north side. There was a catholic mix of people, ranging from air hostesses to brokers to teachers, with showbiz represented by actors and solicitors; a very good party. I ran into Barry, Maeve, and some more of their cronies in the kitchen as I foraged for beer. Of course, Barry had appointed himself Keeper of the Fridge, so I had to speak to him to cajole my way into the ice box. One sentence led to another, and when the night was winding to a close I found myself bundling him into a taxi and taking him home with me for a night of raucous sex and laughter. I called him Larry for the entire evening, having misheard his name in the noisy kitchen. He corrected me, gently, over a breakfast of beans on toast the following morning. He moved in three weeks later. There would be times over the next three years when I would miss Larry.

I had heard of a seven-year itch, but begun to think that Barry and I were going through a three-year ditch; some sort of a trough at any rate. Everything had become awfully routine. Sex was all too rare and drunken, and most other intercourse involved rows about hoovering and bill paying. The fun and adventure had disappeared, and somehow we had both grown too lazy and careless to rekindle those essentials. But at least Barry was working steadily again, even if he still hadn't had his big Hollywood break, and that meant he could run to his habits and social life without having to borrow money from me. He was also handy for transferring the shopping from the supermarket trolley to the boot of the car. Occasionally he gave me a contribution towards the mortgage, but suffice to say it wouldn't have amounted to rent in even the smallest bed-sit imaginable in the area.

For all that, life was okay. We still had laughs, and rarely a dull moment. I met lots of people I would never have come across without Barry, including Maeve Kelly, whom I adored. The cats liked him, in their cat-like way, and when No. 4 had joined the household unexpectedly, he had adjusted fairly well. Barry, that is.

I had never lived with anyone before, apart from my family, so I had no comparisons to make, if these are ever a good thing anyway. I had had boyfriends, of course, but none had stayed over for more than a weekend at a time. Barry's moving in, although swift, was a gradual process. His clothes turned up in the wash pile, a toothbrush appeared in the bathroom. Then people started to leave

11

messages for him on the answering machine, and he began to invite his friends around. Before I knew it his dole office had shifted him to my area, and demands for payment of his credit card began to plop through the letter box.

It took my family slightly longer than me to figure out that he lived at number 11, The Villas. And that was probably a good thing. I had two brothers, Peter and Stephen, respectably married to Anne and Angela respectively. Between them they had four children, all happily born into wedded bliss. My parents, who were by no means small-minded, would still have preferred their only daughter to be formally and legally hitched to the man she was living with. But that was glossed over quickly, and Barry became a regular fixture in the Street household, much to the delight of my teenage niece Lucy, who had a crush on him the size of Texas.

'Training, shmaining,' I heard Barry say, dismissively. 'If he hadn't gone off to London and got those letters after his name, no one would bother their arses with him. All he learned over there were fuzzy esses and a big attitude.'

'Agreed, agreed,' agreed Coleman. 'But,' he raised a forefinger significantly, 'you know yourself . . .' His face drooped, but I felt that this had more to do with the grass he had been smoking than the perfidy of the Irish theatre world. The discussion would probably go around in circles from here.

As the two actors' melodious voices dissected their peers, I pondered my work problem. It was not unheard of for a private investigator to get someone in to help on a case. It happened for a variety of reasons. You might simply not have the time to do all of the leg work yourself. Or you might have been spotted, as I had been, although Michael O'Donoghue would not have known that I had been following him at the time. So, there was no disgrace in any of this. The problem was that I ran a very small operation of one, me, and avoided drafting in extras. I was moderately successful, but could ill afford to have another dependant on full pay. I racked my brain for a suitable replacement. And then, in a Road to Damascus revelation, it came to me; I actually slipped off the couch a bit as a name formed in my brain. I thought of Ciara Gillespie.

She had been part of our gang of four on a cookery course I had taken earlier in the year, a teenage minx who was driving her parents around the bend at home. Ciara was bored, aimless and full of mischievous intelligence. She was young, quick-witted and capable – I should have been writing her CV for her. I could train her in on this straight-forward case, and she would be very useful in the future. She would also be cheaper than hiring another pro, and money was a consideration. Ciara would be perfect. If it had not been so late, I would have put the call in there and then. But the Gillespies had enough to contend with in Ciara without some strange woman rambling at them in the wee small hours about a less-than-average job opportunity.

I was so delighted with myself that I opened the last can of lager without even teasing Barry and Coleman. I had gulped back half of it before I remembered to ask if there had been any messages for me during the evening. Coleman had to be cut off in mid-flow of his treatise on Irish Theatre For A New Millennium as his rapt audience reported that my mother had phoned to remind me about lunch the following day. I was looking forward to this. It would involve the Street women: myself, my mother, her mother, my two sisters-in-law, and our special guest Rose street, who was the latest addition to the family, and who would be mewling and puking at her mother's breast for the occasion. Angela, the mother in question, had even promised them both a glass of champagne; she would drink it, and Rose would have the filtered benefits.

I checked my watch and saw that it was close to 2 a.m. I hoisted myself into a standing position and announced that it was very late and probably bedtime for all of us.

'A lovely invitation, Leonora, my dear,' said Coleman, 'but I'm sure that Barry would prefer you all to himself.'

I looked at him, gobsmacked. Did he really think that I had been suggesting a threesome, or was he taking the piss? I caught Barry's eye and we both began to laugh.

'I'll just shuffle away,' Coleman continued.

Now I was very taken aback. Was he going home? I looked to Barry again. Huge tears were pouring down his cheeks.

'No need to be so sad,' slurred his cohort. 'I'm not going far.'

With that he made a lunge for the door, and before I could bid him goodnight, I heard his footsteps clumping upstairs to the spare room. Coleman might not have been going home, but he was certainly making himself at home.

As Barry wiped the tears of merriment from his face, he remembered something.

'Oh, yeah, there was one other call,' he said. 'Some man wants you to phone him tomorrow. I don't think he left his name. It'll be on the machine still. I'm off too, Leo. See you above.' He got to his feet and staggered slightly. 'Jeez, that latest dope is really strong stuff. I'm wrecked.' He stopped at the door. 'Have you seen my lucky underpants anywhere?' he asked.

Barry was as superstitious as any other actor I'd met. If he had an audition or an opening night, he had to wear a certain pair of Y-fronts. They were a bluey-grey from countless boilings and colour runs, no doubt a difficult shade to replicate if one had a mind to. I truthfully denied all knowledge of their whereabouts. He continued his unsteady progress to the stairs where he murmured what sounded like 'love ya, g'night', and disappeared. I could hear him bump softly off the walls of the stairwell at regular intervals before throwing himself on to our bed.

I slugged back the last of my beer as I pressed the 'play' button by the telephone. A deep and sexy voice said, 'Leo Street, you owe me and I'm calling in the favour. Ring me tomorrow.' He didn't identify himself. He didn't need to. I knew who he was. My heart gave an involuntary leap. Andy Raynor had called.

TWO

I could not remember a time when Andy Raynor had not been around. He was older than me by a year, which would have made him Peter's friend initially, but since no one could remember when 'initially' was, he was just subsumed into the family as a friend of all of us. He had grown up across the street, and was in all of the photographs we had of children's parties, Holy Communions and Confirmations. And even if we were not running a social occasion at our house, he would be there. He was part of the Street furniture, and I treated him like that. Actually, I treated him as badly as I treated any member of my family. And in turn, he treated me as badly as one of his.

And then, in adolescence, something strange happened. Andy shot to his full height long before any of the other boys in the area, but without any awkwardness. He just blossomed. Gone was the pug-nosed rapscallion who was forever in some scrape or another, to be replaced by a suave ladykiller who charmed every parent for miles around, and was allowed free rein with their offspring. Or so it seemed to me and the gaggle of girls I hung around with, on corners and outside chip shops.

He was captain of his school's rugby team, and a crucial winger on the soccer team. He could also turn his hand to hockey, athletics and, God help us, *chess*, if required. He was a top debater both in Irish and English, and we were often pitched against one another as I was the captain of both of these teams in the girls' school. It was galling one year when they won the Dublin Regional Final of an Irish debating competition after an impassioned and totally baseless summing up by him, and we, the hot favourites, were left with our arms dangling by our sides. We were robbed. I could not be gracious in defeat, and did not speak to him for a month. I was never sure he even noticed that at the time; he was too busy fending off female attention. Or rather marshalling it, so that he was never without some stunner on his arm.

But busy as he was with his amours, he seemed to spend most nights in our house. Sometimes he would help me with mathematics, for which I had no aptitude and never would have. Or else we'd listen to the latest LP he'd bought and have some major difference of opinion about music, mostly just for the sake of it. I would deliberately champion the Police so that he could praise the UK Subs; I'd vote Madness, he'd say the Clash; we would agree on some common ground like the Specials and Thin Lizzy. I loved all of them and so did he; it was our game, these were our shared references. Sometimes he would just sit and watch telly with the family. If I was feeling particularly poisonous, I would ask if the Raynors' own television set was broken, but he would always laugh me off. That's how he handled me, he laughed. It worked as well as any other way with the teenage Leonora Street.

But something else had changed between us, and I was the last to realise it. We became attracted to one another. Maybe we always had been. But this physical longing upped the ante considerably. I never trusted it. How could someone so cool be interested in me? I was a heap. My hair was too greasy, my face was too spotty, my bottom was way too big. I was moody; even I knew that. I had nothing to recommend me, I thought. My parents were horrified when I would go into one of my rants about how ugly I was. They couldn't understand how they had instilled me with so little self-confidence. I think, in fairness, they had just forgotten how awful and bleak it can be to be a teenager. One day my mother, close to tears, burst out with, 'It doesn't say much for myself and your father, does it, if we made you and you've turned out to be so hideous? Don't you think it's a bit of an insult to us?' So I toned things down after that. But I could not figure out what Andy Raynor wanted from me when he could have his pick of anyone in the area and beyond.

One early-summer's evening I was sitting in our back garden in quiet despair. It was nearing exam time and I was worried that I might not do well. I liked school, and I was academically sound. But I wanted to be one of the best because I wasn't much good at sport and felt I had very little else to recommend me. I was all of sixteen years old. I had also had a shaggy perm done in town the previous Saturday, and I wasn't sure that it was me. Andy came out for a breath of fresh air. I stuck my nose deep into the book I was studying, and ignored him. I tried so hard to read what was in front of me on the page but all I could see was a jumble of letters, and the light was a bit dim for reading anyhow. I could feel him close by and began to shake.

'Are you cold?' he asked.

'No. And anyway, even if I am, what's it to you?'

'Just asking. No need to bite my head off. I was going to offer you my jumper if you were. No big deal.'

No big deal? I would have died at that moment to be swaddled in Andy Raynor's jumper. I began to shake even more violently at the thought of being so close and intimate with something that had touched him. What to do? I would be lynched at school the following day if I confessed to messing this opportunity up.

'Maybe I will take it, if you don't mind? I am a bit chilly.'

He took off the grey V-necked sweater and held it up for me to climb into. I did. He stayed right there beside me and said, 'It suits you, Leo. And, by the way, I like your hair.'

I was so sure he was lying that I began to cry. It came up on me from nowhere. Suddenly his arms were around me and he was saying urgently, 'Oh, please don't cry, Leo. What have I done? Please don't cry. What's the matter? Tell me.' And all the time he was stroking my hair, and its vile shaggy perm.

I sobbed into his white polo shirt for a while, and only stopped when I felt exhausted. He continued to hold me, then pulled back and asked, 'What's the matter? Did I do something to hurt you?'

I shook my head, fairly violently, and managed to stammer, 'I'm a bit worried about my exams, that's all.'

'As long as you're sure it's nothing that I've done,' he said. 'I couldn't bear that.'

I looked into his beautiful hazel-green eyes and smiled,

shaking my head again, a little more gently this time. He magicked a handkerchief from somewhere and wiped away my tears. Then he held it to my nose and said, 'Blow,' and I obeyed. Then he leaned down and said, 'Kiss,' and we did.

We had an unspoken, unofficial arrangement after that. If we were in a group, we would oscillate towards each other. He would buy me chips at the weekends, and I would get him the *NME* if I thought I'd got to the newsagent's before him on the day it came out. These were blissful summer holidays, with no worries and nothing to do. We went swimming in a gang. We would go into town, or to the pictures, in a gang. But each evening Andy would come around to my house, sometimes to leave me home, sometimes to spend time in, always kissing me goodnight, at length. We grew hungrier and hungrier for one another. But with it came desperation on my part. As I fell deeper and deeper under this spell, I became more and more distrustful of it. I still could not believe he wanted the ugly duckling when there were so many beautiful girls in our group of friends.

I started to let my insecurities show. It began in little ways. I would tease him gently about how Karen Grealish looked at him, or ask him why he had never gone out with Maria O'Grady when she was so gorgeous and obviously had the hots for him. He gently brushed all of this aside. But I would not let up, and eventually he broke one night and told me that the teasing was boring now and would I please stop it. I accused him of being bored with me. He denied that he was. In retrospect, who could have blamed him if he had been? And then, like the lemming that I was, I declared one day that it might be better if we had a break from each other for a while. I meant it to be a test, and he should have said 'no' and convinced me that it was a bad idea and that

21

we were meant to be together forever. But he was so worn out by my shenanigans that he thought I genuinely meant it. And, reluctantly, he agreed. I took to my room and cried for a week.

My family did not know what to do with me. I couldn't sleep. I wouldn't eat. I could not stop crying. In the end, they left me to my splendid isolation. I played every mushy track about love and loss that I had, over and over again. I waited hour after hour for a visit from Andy. Every time the front door opened, I was sure it was him. Each time the back door slammed, I felt certain it was in the wake of his arrival. I was wrong, each and every time. He did not visit my family, and he did not come to see me. I later found out that he had been so convinced by my assurances that separation was what we needed that he really felt he was not wanted anymore in my life. He respected my space; he left me to it. He genuinely hoped that we could be friends again at some stage.

And by the time I re-emerged into teenage society he had an arrangement with Belinda Farrell, and that was that.

Life settled from torture into bearable torture after that. Another academic year came and went, and my parents deemed it acceptable for me to be allowed to go to the local youth disco. My brother Peter would keep an eye out for me, but I was never to know that. Of course I did. It made me feel both angry and safe, having a big brother to look after me. Weekdays were spent in feverish discussion of what to wear on Saturday night. Hours were spent trying on outfits and experimenting with make-up. Nothing was ever perfect, but by 9 p.m. on a Saturday evening, a compromise between fantasy and reality would have been reached, and the girls would be ready to descend on the

Youth Centre. I would see Andy in the distance, chatting easily with both the males and the females of his group. We were on speaking terms again, actually quite friendly, after our old style, before romance had ruined everything. Which was to say that we had many sparky arguments, and were vicious to one another when pushing a point home. It was almost like the old days.

Then one balmy evening, Andy Raynor took me to a nearby field and showed me that kissing could be applied to more than the mouth area, and I was lost all over again. This time I was prepared, and, fall as I did, he never knew how bad my longing for him was. I even took a boyfriend, a lovely lad called Liam. Liam could not believe his luck with some of the things he was allowed to try out. I couldn't believe some of the things that I had learned.

When it came time for the young ladies of the Holy Faith Convent to have a Debutantes' Ball, excitement reached fever pitch. Liam and myself had parted company, but he still expected to be asked to this, the top social event of the school calendar. However, I knew that Andy Raynor was at a rare loose end, and decided to bide my time before pouncing. Everyone knew that this was my plan, including Andy, I suspect. But my timing was off, and I left it that tad too late. It was so close to the event that he assumed I had asked someone else. I had kept my cards so close to my chest that no one could confirm, or deny, his suspicion that I had intended invite him. Imelda Phelan saw her opportunity and made good with it. Liam was granted his wish and accompanied me on the worst night of my young life.

I was the picture of gaiety, of course. I looked great, because I was so miserable that I had lost at least a stone in weight. And my mother had bought me the most beautiful, classic gown. It was a long, flowing number in deep crimson, bias-cut, with an ever so slightly plunging neckline. She had also insisted on a special makeover in a salon in town. The Mammy did me proud. Andy and Imelda sat at the same table as Liam and me, and we all laughed and joked the night away. But I knew that it was all wrong, and so did Andy. Each time Imelda touched him, I died a little. She gazed into his eyes, she fed him morsels of her food, she even wore his bloody bow tie at the end of the evening.

He brought me out for a slow dance three-quarters of the way through. I shouldn't have gone, I knew it would be agony. But I had to grab any chance I could to be with him, no matter how painful and traumatic. As we swayed to the music, he told me that I looked lovely. I thanked him.

'You seem to be having a good time,' he said.

'Yes, I do, don't I?'

'Liam is a good bloke. He likes you.'

I made some sort of non-committal sound.

'Leo, I have something to tell you.'

My heart stopped beating, and my body wanted to fall to the ground. This did not sound good. He was solemn. Oh, sweet Jesus, please don't let him say that Imelda is pregnant and he has to marry her, I thought.

Or even if she is pregnant, please let him not marry her. If she is pregnant, please let him take me outside and make me pregnant too. Anything. But don't let him be taken from me so comprehensively. As it happened, he was taken away, but not by Imelda.

'You know I've been wanting to go to university,' he continued. 'Well, a place has come up.'

'That's great, Andy,' I murmured. 'Well done you. So, which one is it, Trinity or UCD?'

24

'Neither, I've decided to go to Galway.'

My world had ended. It was only marginally eased by the fact that he was not going to marry Imelda and become a father. At least if he did that, I would know where he was and what he was up to. This way, I felt sure I would never see him again. He would live the high life in Galway, sampling exotic delights that Clontarf could never offer or contend with. And I knew no one in bloody, bloody Galway; I couldn't just turn up out of the blue, and magically bump into him. I was out of the picture. I had ruined my life, by my own stupid, hormonal teenage hand. I was hollow with grief.

Andy did go to Galway to study for four years. We kept in touch. Every so often, during term-time, a postcard would arrive, usually a lewd one. I suspected that these delighted my mother every bit as much as they did me. Andy was always a favourite of hers; of all of the Streets', truth be told. And I did see him again, on a fairly regular basis. He returned at vacation time, and then we would go to the pictures, or to a gig. And we would argue, and kiss and make up. But never with abandonment, because that would have meant a commitment, and neither of us was in a position to make that. And neither of us wanted to upset the delicate balance it had taken us so long to find.

When he returned to Dublin to find work, I had started my apprenticeship as a private investigator and was more than a little preoccupied. After a few months of bunking out at his parents' house, he found his feet and moved to a wonderful bachelor pad near the Merrion Gates, right on Sandymount Strand. My mother assured me that it was the best place on earth to live, and that every woman in Dublin was queuing up to get in there with Andy Raynor. I didn't doubt it. The only thing that made her shut up going on about it, was when I accused her of being one of the women who had their sights set on it. And she'd only shut up then because she couldn't think of a good enough retort. Not, I suspect, because what I had said was untrue.

Andy moved in different circles. I tended not to move in any discernible circle at all, because of my work and the covert nature of my job. Oddly enough, once he moved back to Dublin we started to drift apart. In a way, because we could or might run into one another, we made less effort; if we did, it might acknowledge something that we could not sustain. *À la recherche du temps perdu*. It was, and would have been, too serious, and we had no real footing for that anymore.

I contacted him whenever I needed information that I thought he might have. He worked as a journalist and part-time lobbyist in the Dáil. He kept his finger on the pulse of government and politics. My job often took me into that milieu, and if he could, or wanted to, he'd help.

Now that I lived with Barry, I felt that Andy and I could be proper friends again. As long as he didn't mention the stupidity in Kildare earlier in the year. I had slept with him, by accident. I was hardly even party to the event, given my unconsciousness through alcohol at the time. Andy assured me that my virtue was intact. He had been worried that I might come to some harm because of the state I was in, and had taken it upon himself to look out for me. It didn't count, but I still didn't mention it to anyone. I had been living with another man for three years now, and I was sure that Andy respected that. Even if he had little time for Barry.

So why was my silly heart so excited at the prospect of paying Andy Raynor's forfeit?

THREE

It was doubtful Barry even noticed that he and I slept in the same bed that night. We had recently rallied ourselves in an effort to return to the heady, early days of our romance, and had been moderately successful, but things had fallen away again when he got distracted by the Pub Crawl. It seemed that he couldn't keep up with every option for pleasure at the same time. In the choice between a sex life with his girlfriend or paid fun and games with other thesps, I came off worst. But at least I had been moderately satisfied, even sexually, for a goodly number of weeks, and was no longer looking rabidly at any lengthy, bulbous thing that crossed my path. It had whetted my appetite, however, and now I was left with an amorphous notion that sexual activity should be a touch more regular. Swings and roundabouts, really. I wanted more.

The following morning started well. For once I didn't have to prise my face off the pillow. If I go to bed too knackered or too smashed to take off my make-up, it tends to act as a glue between me and the bedclothes. And if there's been a lot of alcohol involved, my saliva turns into Bostick too. Snoring can also enter the equation, and it's bad enough that Barry is talented in that area without our playing a duet. I hopped out of bed quite briskly, full of the joys. I was looking forward to the day ahead. This had a lot to do with one particular telephone call, but I resisted making it; at 8.30 a.m. it might have seemed a little needy.

A fresh hairball of cat vomit in the middle of the floor took some of the shine off my breakfast. The three lined up beside it as No. 4 pranced by. 'I know he makes you sick,' I said to them, 'but I'd really appreciate it if you could stage the protest outside from now on.'

If there is anything good about catchuck, it's that it doesn't smell and is relatively easy to clean up. That said, the day is always better without it.

I had a leisurely breakfast of cereal and coffee, taking good care to leave only just enough milk for one other person to have a hot drink. I knew this was a petty meanness, but giggled to myself as I sloshed the milk into my second cup. Perhaps it would help to strengthen the friendship between the two actors if one of them had to make a tiny sacrifice for the other. I giggled again. Honestly, it didn't take much to amuse me.

Maeve Kelly was on the radio telling me to buy a new brand of dishwasher tablet, but, persuaded as I was by her dulcet tones and brilliant delivery, I could not oblige; I didn't have a dishwasher. After some infectious pop music, I was treated to helpful home tips from a bouncy young Australian woman. She wanted to know if I was worried about fleas on my pets. And occasionally I was as they're a seasonal nuisance. She said she understood my reluctance to put chemicals on their fur, or to have it introduced into their bloodstreams, but those fleas were still a problem. Well, no more. The natural solution was to use a little urine, apparently. My own. I looked at the small menagerie in the kitchen, and decided that none of the creatures there would be at all pleased with that particular homeopathic remedy. Back to chemicals it was. Besides, I really did not think that any of them would stand still long enough for me to pee on them. And I wouldn't have known where to look while I was about it. All in all, both advice and marketing were wasted on me that morning.

I showered and dressed, humming all the way, then I set about the task of feeding the furry members of the household. As a dog, No. 4 felt it incumbent upon him to eat everything in sight. This habit, or *raison d'être* as he might have it, was beginning to piss the cats off mightily. If he had bothered to read the tins involved, he would have known that three-quarters of the food on offer was manufactured specifically for cats, but that was of little interest to him. After my third peacekeeping intervention, I separated them entirely by way of doors, and decided to bring the dog with me to work. A United Nations-style buffer zone would only work if it was in situ, and as I was that zone, and in situ, it seemed best to divide and conquer.

I rang the Gillespie household to hire Ciara. Her mother answered in a frail and weary voice. I explained who I was, and reminded her that we had met some weeks ago at the end of the cookery course Ciara had taken with me in Kildare. She relaxed a little then, but became agitated when I asked to speak to her daughter.

'Well, I don't know now. She doesn't like being disturbed

too early in the morning. She's not really, you know, em, a . . . a morning person. And she was out late enough last night. So.'

Ciara pulled the wings off parents and toyed with them for sport. I could understand the poor woman's reluctance to waken her. I tried reassurance.

'Oh, believe me, I do know, Mrs Gillespie. But I may have some work for her. And if she does it, you'd be rid of her for hours on end each day.'

That did the trick.

'Really? Right. Here goes so. Wish me luck.' I could hear her walk slowly off to rouse the kraken.

Five minutes later a gruff voice said, 'Make it good,' into the phone. I did. Ciara agreed to be in my office in an hour's time.

Outside the weather had brightened, and a late spring was . . . well, springing. Miniature daffodils smiled and waved from every corner of my garden. I began to walk on air; that is what the colour yellow does to me. But air-walking is a tricky business, and after faltering above several of the concrete steps leading to my front gate, I reluctantly decided to stick to a more solid footing. In the confusion of righting myself I careered into the ancient, rusty fence and snagged my tights. Curses! Mental note: buy new pair and put on before meeting family, particularly mother and mother's mother. With family, details are everything. So much for my grand gesture of wearing a skirt and blouse for them, rather than my usual jeans and jumper.

While No. 4 was busy de-fleaing the grass and hedge, I took note of the other types of yellow flowers blooming on my little patch. Dandelions were having something of a field day, as they tend to do. We called them 'pissy beds' when we were kids, because they were supposed to make you wet yourself if you slept with them under your pillow. Why you would want to do that in the first place was always lost on me. All of the weeds living in the garden were flourishing. I sighed. I'm under no illusion about who's boss out here. Slugs, snails, slaters, creeping buttercup, spiky thistles, velvet nettles, dandy lions, docks, they're in charge. I'm like a student tenant, very low on the evolutionary ladder.

Our street busybody, Marion Maloney, was standing vigil over my car.

'That'll cost you,' she murmured, inspecting the damage. She tut-tutted as she inserted her fingers into the grooves. St Thomas wasn't a patch on Marion. Did she really think the dents weren't there if she didn't touch them? If only. I thought of a question Barry was fond of posing of late (he was also fond of just posing): is the grass still green when you've got your back to it? I looked beyond Marion and saw that it was. Then I whipped around to check my own lawn. Even taken by surprise, it was one of the forty or more shades.

'No use looking for the culprits,' Marion said. 'They're long gone.'

'Oh, no, don't mind me, I was just checking something else.'

She gave me a look which confirmed that I had sprouted another head.

'It happened last night,' I explained. 'Someone ran into me.'

A silence stretched between us. I realised I would not be released until more information was forthcoming, so I glossed over why I was where I had been when the incident

31

occurred, and gave her the low-down on the other woman and her car, even offering the make and registration number. Getting blood from a stone was second nature to Marion, no bother whatsoever. To be thorough, and Marion was nothing less than, she would probably check these details with the police. Finally, she was satisfied and returned to her lair. I was exhausted. I looked at the newly laid speed ramps on the road and wondered if we would make it intact to the corner at all.

'To the city and beyond,' I announced to No. 4. The engine *roared* into life (but not as we know it) and off we went.

The traffic lights were with me all the way, and I made excellent time from my house in Clontarf southwards to the city centre. Normally, this would have made me a little apprehensive, on the grounds that if something good happens, the inverse is lurking waiting to get me back. I'm nothing if not a fatalist. But with Dublin glowing in a faint April sunshine, and healthy greenery popping out of every amenable crack in the concrete, it was hard not to grin. I passed hotels and office buildings and car parks, and found it hard to tell the difference between them most of the time. This morning that didn't bother me at all. I passed a shop called 'Inspiration' which was having a closing down sale, but even that didn't dampen my mood. Was it that phonecall to Andy Raynor, just waiting to happen? I laughed out loud at my girlish whimsy and dismissed the notion.

The car really was making a racket. Passers-by were staring, and every so often No. 4 would shoot me the look that said, 'Knock it off on the noise, okay?' I reckoned that the jolt the previous evening was responsible.

'It's sporty,' I told him. 'No mufflers, or squifflers, or bloofers, or . . . whatever,' I added, blinding him with automobile jargon.

He was mightily unconvinced.

My office was in an old building in the newly trendy Temple Bar area of Dublin. At one stage, the crazed municipal plan was to turn all of this 'Left Bank' into a giant bus depot, but a new spirit of Europeanism had put paid to that. Now we had coffee shops, craft outlets, *trattorie* and lots of pubs and hotels; themed or neo-traditional, spruce and expensive. I had managed to talk my way into a parking spot on a disused lot two streets away from base. It was only a matter of time before it was built on, and the word was that it would house a multimedia gallery space, cyber café, three bars, two restaurants, a bookie's and a dentist. All solar-powered.

For the moment, it was guarded by a gnarly old codger named Malachy, who could be kept sweet with a noggin of whiskey 'for the rheumatics', and £25 a week for the car. This is not to suggest that Malachy had any official capacity on the site; it was my opinion that he had happened on to a good thing and simply hung on to it. He had an entrepreneurial spirit, and good luck to him. I suppose whoever did own the place thought there were worse things that could be happening on it. Malachy, or Molly as he was also known, did a huge trade in the evening in theatre punters and restaurant goers. So much so that he had to enlist help in the form of a 'younger' chap called Gerry, who took this job very seriously and wore a peaked cap and changed his rolled-up newspaper daily. The paper was used as a pointer, along with the words 'lock hard, lock hard'. Gerry bore an uncanny resemblance to Molly, and as Molly was a bachelor boy all his life, rumour had it that Gerry was a lovechild. Romance is everywhere, and in all lives, you just have to know where to look.

'Grand day for it,' Molly said, by way of greeting. As this seemed to cover everything, I agreed with him. He shuffled over, all Sean O'Casey play, right down to the fingerless gloves.

'I heard you crossing O'Connell Bridge five minutes ago in that thing. You'd want to watch out, I think it's against the law to make that much noise in a car. Unless you're the President, maybe. And who is this little chap?'

'Malachy, I'd like to introduce you to Number Four. Number Four, this is Malachy.'

'No need to be formal,' he said to the dog. 'You can call me Molly.'

No. 4 was delighted with himself, and popped his front paws up on Malachy's knee so that the old man wouldn't have to bend down too far to pet him.

'They're grand company, aren't they?' said Malachy. Then he spotted the left wing of the car and shuffled over to inspect it. 'You've been in the wars since I saw you last.'

'It's a bit of a mess all right,' I acknowledged.

'Oh, it is that. And it'll be worse if you don't have it seen to a.s.a.p. If the rust gets in there, you won't be happy at all, at all. It's worse than the rheumatics, is the rust.'

I'd been treated to the long list of his ailments on many previous occasions, so I knew to nip this in the bud.

'Actually, Malachy, I'm just running off to ring the mechanic now about that. I'd need to hurry and get him before he books in a load of other jobs for the day.'

'Oh, you would. A mechanic is a hard man to find these

days. Or a plumber, or a carpenter. There's no trades anymore, d'yeh see?'

Ailments and trades, a deadly combination of obsessions with Malachy. I had to run, quite literally; it was the only way to get away from him. I waved back and shouted 'see you later', then legged it with the dog. It's amazing how many obstacles have to be overcome before the working day can begin. And I wasn't past all of them yet.

My office building was once a Home for Indigent Chimney Sweeps, and given when it was originally built, those sweeps must have ranged in age from three to thirty. At that ripe old age, which I had attained myself recently, they would have been expected to die, having lived such a hard life. Well, life's still hard, there's just much more of it, I thought, as I decanted the mail from my post box. I turned hopefully to the elevator, reluctant, as always, to climb the many flights of stairs to my office. I know that it's all good cardiovascular exercise, but at that time of the morning, I just couldn't be arsed.

The lift was straight out of a thriller: an open-plan cage with latticed metal doors which accordioned open and shut. Unusually, it was ready and waiting, and not stuck on another floor full of the cleaner's equipment. Mrs Mack, the woman who 'does', likes to keep the lift for her own personal use, and you would need to be up very early in the morning to thwart her on that. I was delighted with myself, but Mrs Mack had a surprise ally up her sleeve. Or more accurately on my leash. No. 4 was terrified. Try as I might, I could not persuade him to go in. He whimpered, he cried, and when I went to carry him, he lay heavily on his side and whimpered and cried some more. I tried being cross with him, and he leapt to his feet and barked back. 'You cheeky pup,' I said, with some accuracy. He began to run around my legs, until they were well and truly bound. I spun around to free myself so fast I nearly turned into Wonder Woman. Leaning against a wall, I waited until the stairwell stopped reeling. Then I tugged on the leash once more to pull No. 4 into the elevator, but, as if instructed by Gerry, he locked hard on all four legs and began to howl loudly. I took the hint, and cursed just as loudly as we started up the stairs.

We were making a lot of noise at this stage, and several doors opened to check on the commotion. When we had all calmed down, and everyone had established that I was not being cruel to the dog, we set off again. In a knot of self-righteous indignation that anyone would think, even for a moment, that I might harm one hair on his disloyal little head, I caught sight of Mrs Mack looking down from her lair on the second floor. She was beaming with unexpected triumph. No. 4 was now dancing along merrily, his little claws scraping rhythmically on the wooden floor. 'Traitor,' I growled through gritted teeth. Hard to imagine that he was in league with the enemy on Day One of joining the firm. As someone once said, life is just one damn' thing after another.

I explained to No. 4 that he would have to behave himself in the office, as it was a place of work. He cocked his head from left to right, as if paying attention, then trotted over to the desk and cocked his leg against it to have a wee.

'Oh, no, you don't,' I said. 'No need to mark this territory, Mister. Anyhow, you went before we came in, so don't try it on.'

I began to have the inkling that inkles to you that you're

behaving like a crazy lady. Or perhaps it's confirmation that you've become one. Here I was, talking aloud to an animal who probably didn't understand English, or even if he did, really didn't care what I was saying. So who was I trying to impress or convince? I rummaged in No. 4's bag, and took out his favourite ball and squeaky toy for him to play with. While he got to work with those, I fitted a box up with a blanket in which he could have his frequent snoozes, and wished that I had someone to do the same for me. This cur was a sharp operator; all of this was achieved without any overt instruction from him. I felt a conspiracy theory about mind control coming on, and decided to save it for a coffee break later in the day.

I was about to choose between calling Andy Raynor or retrieving my messages from a furiously blinking answering machine when a fierce kerfuffle in the hallway caught my attention. Like the canine incident earlier, it attracted the notice of the whole building. This time the voices in the stairwell were more or less human, two of them. I glanced at my watch: 10.06 a.m. and already we'd had major action at the Indigent Sweeps' place, so nothing poorly about that.

It was, of course, the Arrival of the Queen of Ciara. And small surprise that Mrs Mack would try to shoo her from the building. Today's sartorial ensemble was Vampire, with a suggestion of drug-crazed thief thrown in for good measure.

'I'll have the cops on you, so I will, if you take one step further,' warned Mrs M.

'Listen, hag,' drawled Ciara, 'cut me some slack or face the consequences. I work here.'

'What?' shrieked the divine Mrs M.

'Yeah, you heard. I'm official. And if you don't let me

37

pass, I'll have your sorry ass fired, OK?'

No one, and I mean *no one*, spoke to Mrs Mack like that. Every worker in the place retreated slightly into their respective doorways in order to enjoy some more of the sport, while it lasted. We all shared a common unspoken certainty that Ciara would suffer for this outrage. But for the moment it was bliss. And it seemed wrong to rob a young person of such a life-shaping experience, even if it would subsequently be filed under 'Learning the Hard Way'. It is hard to explain the gist of an argument when it's all gist, and this one was. After a few parries and thrusts, including a splendid 'you were dragged up, not brought up' speech from Mrs Mack, I decided it was time to intervene. Not for any noble reason, I just wasn't sure how far things could go before Mrs Mack did actually call the cops.

'Ah, you're here,' I shouted to Ciara, as I leaned over the banister. This passed into legend as one of the most unnecessary observations ever. But, in a roundabout way, I felt it could be used to strengthen and underline my deductive powers as a private investigator, even if I was unlikely to list it as a career highlight. I bounded cheerily down to the combatants. They were pulling an enormous black bag to and fro between them, and growling like two Rottweilers, though Mrs Mack looked like a beige poodle and Ciara resembled a dark Afghan hound with an unfortunate hair cut.

'Mrs Mack, I'd like you to meet my new assistant, Ciara Gillespie, and vice versa. I'm sure you two will be the best of pals.'

They gave me a long look of disdain that was united and terrifying. The older woman let go of the bag. Then, with almost ceremonial formality, they turned to one another and bowed their heads, ever so slightly. Time out. Mrs Mack fixed a steely gaze on me and said, 'Miss Street, I'm not sure that you're allowed dogs on the premises.' Before Ciara could thump her, I hurriedly interjected a 'she doesn't mean you' and swept her up the stairs. 'I'll have to check the rules,' warned the Mighty Mack. I shivered; I was in *such* trouble.

'You are in *such* trouble,' Ciara confirmed.

FOUR

'WHOAH! This is *so* retro . . . *man*!' Ciara took in the office; black-and-white-tiled floor, sturdy oak desk and battered leather chairs. It even had frosted glass in the door bearing the legend 'Leo Street and Company'. When you came in, you expected to meet Humphrey Bogart and a glamorous but down-to-earth, heart-of-gold secretary. They rarely turned up for work.

'Coffee? Tea?' I asked. Ciara nodded to both. Snap decision: coffee. 'It's not retro,' I explained. 'It's the real thing. It was like this when I arrived.'

'Yo! So *old*.'

No. 4 took time out from chasing his tail to dispense licks and love. Mmn, nice.

'It's cheap too, in comparison with the rest of the build-ing,' I explained. 'The rent goes down the more steps you have to climb. I think the landlord must know that the lift is not an option. Because of Mrs Mack,' I added, darkly.

Ciara had now made herself comfortable by sliding sideways on to the big old brown chair opposite the desk.
Clients had a choice of this or a slightly more modern
upright, and the more uptight chose the upright, while
those trying to appear cool, or business people about to nail
an employee, usually perched or lolled in the armchair,
with the cools perching and the nailers lolling, respectively.
Ciara's head rested on one arm; her legs swung over the
other as she addressed the ceiling. I'd never had a client
choose that option.

'So, Streetsky, *meine kleine maestro*, what's the story?'

'Ciara, don't take this the wrong way, or do, whichever
you like, but I hope you're not intending to keep this banter
up all day? It really is enough that one of us in the office is
barking.'

No. 4 duly obliged. Fair play to Ciara, she could nearly
take a hint, however short-term and half-assed.

'CooLeo, *chill*. So who's the Spectre?'

'Oh, Mrs Mack. Well, she's officially the cleaner, but that's
pretty much an honorary title. She doesn't believe in
imposing herself or her cleaning products too much on the
building. She sort of sprinkles disinfectant around, but stops
shy of washing it in or out. It's some sort of weird illusion-
of-cleanliness fetish. And far less work, of course. *But* she
does actually run the place, so beware.'

'Too late for that now, boss. Duly noted, though. I wasn't
referring to the Licence to Spill babe, who the fuck is that
scary fucker?'

I followed her eyes. Ah, Mick. From the large photograph
on the wall behind my desk a face hewn from rock, and
thatched by a shock of wiry grey hair, glowered down at
me. At both of us.

'Everyone is answerable to someone, and I'm answerable to him,' I explained. 'That's Mick Nolan. He's my boss, you could say. He trained me, and I worked for him for a few years. Now he's a kind of silent partner, I suppose, though not half quiet enough for my liking. He follows me around, giving me advice and berating me whenever he thinks I need it. He can be a right pain in the ass.'

All of this was true. Then I remembered a pertinent point.

'Oh, and he's been dead for a few years.'

Ciara had shifted out of her seat and was walking around the office, watching Mick as she went.

'That following thing is weird. No matter where I go in the room, his eyes are on me. You go over there, I'll stay here, and let's see how he manages that.'

I did as I was told, and sure enough, he was looking at both of us.

'Spooky,' I said.

'Yeah. *Man*, I never even met the guy and he's on to me already. You're gonna have to have words with him about that, boss.'

'I'll try, but I can promise nothing.'

I knew then that Ciara was exactly the right woman to join the firm, however short-term; she hadn't batted an eyelid at the prospect of being tailed by a ghost, and didn't seem to think it unusual that he was constantly on my case.

'Okay, let's get down to business. When do I start, what do I do and how much will you pay me?'

Succinct, to the point, my kinda goil.

'I need help,' I said.

Ciara began to laugh. 'Everyone knows that the minute they meet you,' she teased.

'Ha-ha. I mean, professional help.'

43

'Again, that's obvious, boss.' She laughed even harder.

'I need someone to take over a job for me, temporarily, you wagon.'

'And that's me. You've made a brilliant decision there, O, Streetwise one. Reveal the legend.'

On second thoughts, maybe I would just throttle her.

Instead, I told Ciara about Michael O'Donoghue, and his wife Miranda's fears of an affair. 'These are the cases I mostly get. Not glamorous at all, so you'll be starting at the bottom. I rarely do computer fraud, because I'm a turnip with technology, and I'm not brilliant with gadgets either.'

'I am, though,' said Ciara. 'When I've got this ordinary shit figured out, we may have to diversify as a company.'

'Steady on. I only need you for this case.'

'So far,' she interjected.

'I prefer to work alone, so don't get your hopes up.'

'You're not very good at delegating, are you? You don't trust people, do you?'

'What's with the hard philosophical questions?' I exclaimed. This whippersnapper was putting me on the spot. 'I see a lot of the darker side of human nature, so no, I don't always have a very good opinion of people. I'm a realist, that's all.'

We were getting side-tracked here, and in territory where I didn't feel comfortable. I wasn't particularly proud of the fact that I spent my days and nights trying to find people out in lies rather than saving the earth. I was in the grubby end of the PI's world, but hey, it was a dirty job and someone had to do it.

'Enough of the farting around,' I said, reaching into a drawer for pictures of Michael O'Donoghue, his wife Miranda, and his friend, special or otherwise, a Mrs

Bernadette Flood, resident of Raheny on Dublin's northside.

'How did you find out the friend's name?' Ciara asked.

'I approached the postman while he was delivering one morning and asked if the O'Briens lived in number twenty-seven, and he said no, Mrs Bernie Flood lived there. She's a widow, her husband Joseph died last year.'

'Simple as that?'

'Yep, simple as that. A question is usually good for an answer, maybe eight times out of ten. Use your common sense and you'll be fine.'

Common sense is something that has always intrigued me. In a way it's an oxymoron. There's nothing all that common about sense, for one thing. And for another, is it one word or two? Or put it this way, should it be one word or two?

'The postman told you all that?'

I snapped back to the present. 'No, I also checked the electoral register, and births, deaths and marriages.'

'Wow, life is so formal.'

'Death too,' I pointed out.

'What if you ask a question and the answer is a lie?'

This girl was smart all right. 'Good point. Even if you don't get the truth, the form of the lie can be telling. It's up to you as a detective to establish the truth. That's what you're hired for.'

She gave an imperceptible nod, which was my signal that she understood and I was to continue.

'Let's see . . . yes, when in doubt, lie.'

'There's a lot of that around.'

'Yep. It's the three Ls really: Look, Listen and Learn.'

'Oh, so we just ignore the fourth "L", the Lie. Or do we count that as "F" for Fib?'

45

'Ciara, let's not get sidetracked so early. Now where was I? Oh, yes, never presume anything, just deal in facts; that's all we want, proof, not theories. And stay on the right side of the law. Okay?'

'And which would be the right side again?'

'The one that doesn't get you put in jail,' I explained.

'Riiiight. So, don't get caught doing anything illegal?'

'Mostly, yes. Also try not to do anything illegal either, if you know what I mean.'

She took a moment to contemplate that can of worms, then, sensibly, moved on. This girl was shaping up to be a natural, if there can ever be such a thing in a PI. It's not exactly a genetic trait to want to be in the grey area between law and disorder; to snoop furtively around other people's lives without any hope of a medal of honour or a public commendation at the end. And with no real power to back you up. Not much back up at all, to be honest. It's just you and the power of nosiness to the nth degree, with a tough stomach for lies, corruption and abuse. Oh, and no state-supplied uniform either, which some might argue goes on the plus side for private dicks, and on the minus for public ones.

'What made the wife suspicious in the first place?' Ciara asked.

'Well, you'll see for yourself, this guy is very much a creature of habit. He keeps to an orderly timetable. But recently he's been coming home late, hasn't been where he says he was, or not for as long as he'd like her to believe. So, she confronted him, and he gave her a speech about how she'd have to trust him for the time being, that he'd explain everything soon, and there was nothing for her to worry about.'

'Now *that* would put the wind up anyone.'

'Exactly, and that's where we come in.'

I took her through the rudiments of my stills camera, the video, and the sound equipment she was to use. The latter was a directional microphone, which could be used to listen from a range of, say, a car parked close by. The essentials were point and record, though I could have dressed it up in more flattering terms. 'This and the camera with telephoto lens are good, because you won't be trespassing on the property,' I explained.

'And we'd never do that,' she teased.

'Nnnno. Or mostly never.'

I brought her up to speed on Michael O'Donoghue's clockwork routine during the day, and said that for now she might like to check that out herself, before beginning the more pertinent evening surveillance. The only half excitement I encountered was when he gave a colleague a lift to her car. She was a petite thing with a dark Cleopatra bob. Nothing incriminating, but I took a photograph and I'll let you have it when it's developed.' His wife, Miranda, visited the clinic a few times, laden down with designer shopping bags. Looks like she knows how to spend money.

There were a few other details I might have mentioned, but I felt it more important that Ciara should ground herself in the mundanities of this case before progressing to some of its quirks, which I myself was not yet certain were relevant.

'One last thing. You'll need to be a bit less conspicuous than you are at the moment. Nosferatu is a noticeable look in the daytime.'

'But at night I am Princess of Darkness,' she pointed out.

'Actually, I'm ahead of you on that, I've brought a change.'
She indicated the black bag from the tug-of-war with Mrs
Mack.

'Why go to all that trouble?' I asked, somewhat naively.

'If I left the house dressed as a normal person just one
morning, I'd never hear the end of it from my mother.
She'd expect it every day. I can't let my rigorous standards
of torture slide.'

'Sometimes, Ciara,' I said, 'I wonder where the good twin
is.'

And then she genuinely surprised me.

'Oh, that eejit Ronan. Goody-goody is at college. He
wants to be an engineer, for God's sake. I mean, how square
can you get? See you in five.' She left for the loo.

I mulled over the Gillespies' plight: two Ciaras. Still, at least
not identical girls, which would literally have meant a split
egg. Ronan would have been a completely different one, if I
remembered my biology correctly. There was, therefore,
some hope that he would stay good and true, and, bless the
mark, become an engineer.

I still had a strange feeling of wellbeing, which was
bothering me. I should have been feeling all guilty about
going into a supervisory capacity, as I now was. But I was
not feeling guilty. There were in fact a few other avenues of
Michael O'Donoghue's life to root around in, and now I had
the time to do that. This assuaged my professional guilt. But
I think I was relieved to find myself at one remove on this
case. I was sick to death's door of pettiness. I was tired of
the ugliness of cheating. And I was fed up with the paranoia
that surrounded suspicion. Now it looked like I was going to
get some distance. However, it didn't quite qualify for a

victory dance around the room; for all I knew, some bags would walk in the door and offer me another job, and in truth I was in no financial position to refuse it. Subdued joy and a nascent smugness were the order of the day for now.

I thought of the other things I hadn't shared with Ciara. Last time I counted, there were upwards of sixty private detective agencies listed in the Golden Pages, or Yellow Pages, or Buttercup, or Sunshine . . . whatever you're having yourself. And that's before we even got to the 'security experts', another fertile area for ex-cops and private eyes who have hit lean times. I've been a bouncer in my day. I've collected 'bad' debts. I hate having to do that sort of work, but sometimes you're left without a choice. And you try telling a house full of cats that you can't afford their food and that you're on a diet yourself anyway; doesn't always wash. You takes what you gets sometimes. And often it sucks. Welcome to the real world.

Some agencies are listed as members of various Federations. In Ireland, where two or more of us are gathered together, a Federation can be founded. And like the seasons, they come and go regularly. I'm going out on a limb to say that a lot of those who advertise are chancers. And as I fall to the ground on my broken twig, let me also say that we all have our areas of expertise. I'm a people woman, so I've made that my remit. Big remit: the world is full of people. What I mean is, I'm best at observing, and I'm not great on the technicals. I'm not comfortable with technology. I prefer the worn shoe sole, a pen and paper, the dusty certificates that chart a life. And talk: conversational and inquisitorial. I do know my way around a bug, visual and aural, and the basics of an electronic search. I get by.

I also have a rule about death. I like to see as little of it as possible. I once heard a man on the radio say that when he is setting up a big business venture, he asks himself two questions: will anyone die if I do this, and will anyone go bust? If the answer to both is 'no', he goes ahead. I like those questions, and what they stand for. Unfortunately, when I take on a case I cannot know the answers, but I've been lucky that no one I've confirmed bad news for has felt so murderous about it that they've taken to fatal violence. So far. And, you know, so far so good.

I wondered if I should have talked to Ciara about the little I have learned during my time as a detective. Should I have mentioned that the truth and what you believe are often two different things; that people tell you what they want you to know, no more; that sometimes they tell you stuff which they believe to be true but which is completely false; that we are bred to lie and to cheat and to mould our morals to suit our situation of the week? If I had said any of this, I don't think Ciara would have been disillusioned; she doesn't seem to expect much of the human race.

Just as well.

FIVE

Staring at the walls of my office often leads me into a reverie, and sometimes from there into a doze. I decided it wouldn't look good if Ciara returned to find her new boss asleep, so I used the time to review the beginning of the O'Donoghue case in my head.

Miranda had arrived at my office on a filthy, rain-soaked afternoon, punctual for her four o'clock appointment and untouched by the weather. Even her coat appeared dry. She was composed as she described her problem, her voice a hypnotic, quiet monotone. Her steel-grey eyes considered me as casually as if I was an incidental, hardly there at all. Her coldness made me shiver, accompanied as it was by the howl of a late-spring storm outside. A deadly calm settled on the room.

She was a strange-looking woman. Her dark, shoulder-length hair was lustrous and expertly cut, framing features which didn't quite seem to match. Taken singularly, they appeared to be placed too high on her face, but together they gave the lie to that first impression. She was thin, painfully so, but this gave her a gaunt haughtiness, like a spindly aristocrat in the grips of poverty but too proud to admit it. A sharp nose descended from eyebrows held permanently in an arc of disdain. Cheekbones jutted out above a slender, fine jaw. Her mouth was surprisingly full, though she stretched it into a mean line as she spoke. If she had ever carried any weight on her spare frame, I imagined it had softened this harsh image. Here, in an uncompromising April light, she was frightening, formidable. But she was beautiful, too, and high on her high cheekbone was a magnificent scar, small and geometric. She wore it in the way a pirate would an eyepatch. 'I did that with a diamond ring,' she said, dismissing any further mention of the mark.

She did not loll or perch on the client chair, she inhabited it. Her story was told economically. Salient information, I felt, was that the O'Donoghue children, Tara and Ben were weekday boarders at Saint Columba's in the mountains.

'In that case, Miranda, I don't see why you can't follow your husband yourself. It really would save you a lot of money and waiting. You know him so much better than I do, you wouldn't have to go through the familiarisation I would. It makes sense.'

There is a certain school of thought which says that doling out this sort of advice is business suicide for a single woman with so many dependants. But I felt that it needed to be said, so I did just that. Dismissive was the kindest word for the look she bathed me in. I seemed lower than the lowest crawling thing on earth, which at last check was any government minister of the old guard.

'It is not appropriate,' she said, curtly. This was the closest to emotion she had come. An angry light almost manifested itself in those extraordinary eyes. Then she was back to the beauty and composure of a Renaissance Madonna. 'Money is not a consideration, Miss Street. I do not need to justify my decision on this to you. You will either take the assignment or not. I would appreciate a speedy answer. I cannot abide time wasting.'

Every nerve in my body said 'don't do it', while my brain reminded me that I needed the cash. I was on board. She handed me a five-hundred-pound advance in crisp, new banknotes, and told me she would forward her husband's mobile phone bills, which were now all handily itemised for the cautious and the curious alike. Then she shook my hand and made to leave. Her clasp was indifferent, but afterwards it burned on my palm.

Later, I reasoned that there are many ways of dealing with a problem. So Miranda O'Donoghue was not a shouter; she preferred to turn chilly and clam up. Who was I to say whether this was a bad or a good thing?

She stopped at the office door and turned back. 'Oh, yes,' she said, calmly, 'one last thing: he's been receiving death threats.'

I was agog. 'You didn't think to mention this before?' I gasped.

'Well, no. If you knew my husband and his business, you wouldn't be too surprised either,' she said. 'I'm sure it's nothing to worry about.'

'And I'm sure it is,' I protested. 'Have you informed the police?'

'Oh, there's no need. Michael deals with a lot of emotional people in his work, it all blows over eventually.'

'What form do these threats take?'

'They seem to be of two types. Sometimes he'll get a letter in the post, made up of newspaper or magazine clippings; you know the sort, very popular in television dramas. At other times, a woman's voice makes dire predictions on the telephone. But they've been going on for some time now, and we don't pay them much heed anymore.'

'Do you have any of the letters, or the envelopes they came in?'

'No, no. My husband has taken them. I won't have them in the house.'

'I really do think this is a matter for the police,' I reiterated.

She laughed then, hollow though it sounded. 'I think you're over-reacting, don't you, dear?' She gave a limp wave of her hand, as if the gesture was beneath her somehow, and left.

Death is a big word, and a bigger event. So, if persons known or unknown threaten another person with it, this can quite reasonably be considered a serious situation. But I had not mentioned Michael O'Donoghue's *billets-doux* to Ciara. I justified it by telling myself that I didn't want to overburden her in these initial stages. Perhaps the truth is that I needed her help, and wasn't prepared to look elsewhere: a crazy mixture of laziness and penny pinching without any regard for the outcome, no matter how potentially dangerous.

At the edge of my vision, and consequently my attention, a light was blinking hard enough to induce an epileptic fit. Real time was intruding. Basically, my answering machine was hopping mad that I had not consulted it to hear its treasures. I took a pad and pen and pressed 'play'.

Maeve Kelly wanted to know would I sell her mother some of my home-made bread. I laughed out loud. I am a terrible cook. In fact, it would be more accurate to say that I cannot cook. But I had recently taken a course in Kildare whilst on a job, and it was there that I had found both Ciara and the ability to make delicious bread. There was no scientific explanation for this, I just had 'the knack', like dowsing for water or being able to tell cars apart by the sound of their boots closing. Things had come to a pretty pass when I was selling something to Maeve, rather than her persuading me from my television or radio set.

'You would be the latest thing for my mother. There's *huge* competition between the Ladies Who Host Lunch to have a new and *marvellous* discovery. I mentioned you to Mum and she was *very* excited. *Do* say yes, and she'll pay *handsomely* for your wares.'

I wondered how many noughts there were in *handsomely*. Sold, to the lady with the golden tones, and her affluent mother. I phoned Maeve to tell her as much. She was delighted to hear from me, for more than one reason. 'There is another little matter I need your help on,' she continued soberly. This was obviously serious. Maeve never usually spoke without sprinkling theatrical emphases liberally throughout. Now her voice was quiet and uninflected.

'I've been having crank calls, and they're beginning to get to me.'

'Right, don't panic, and don't let this sad fuck rile you, whoever it turns out to be. You're not alone, these calls happen to a lot more people than you'd think, unfortunately. Have you contacted the police?'

'Well, no. I didn't want to bother them. I assumed they'd take no notice anyway, just regard it as a nuisance.'

'Mmn, they might initially, but they will deal with it if things get out of hand.'

Maeve gave an involuntary cry.

'No, no, we'll nip this in the bud before it gets to that,' I reassured her. 'Do you have Caller Display on your phone?'

'No, I don't.'

'Right, I'll give you a handset that does. If we're lucky, this idiot won't have screened his or her number and we'll trace them that way. I'll bring something over to record the calls and that'll help give us a clue as to what we're dealing with here. One last thing, are you in the phone book?'

'No, I'm ex-directory. I thought that would ward off creeps. I was obviously mistaken.'

'What happens when you get one of these calls?'

'Nothing much, that's what freaks me. I suppose there's a bit of heavy breathing, but no obscene remarks or anything like that. I wait for a few moments, in case anything else happens, but it never does, and then I hang up. If a few calls come together, I take the phone off the hook for an hour or two. If someone wants me on business, they'll get me on the mobile.'

'What sort of sounds are in the background?'

'Not a lot really, maybe a television or radio, something like that.'

'Okay. I'm going to my parents' for lunch, so I'll drop off the stuff on the way. Don't worry, we'll get the sad bastard.'

By now Ciara had returned and was looking curious. So was I. I hardly recognised her. Gone were the chains, the rings, the piercings, the paraphernalia of the Goth. She had changed into a plain blue polo neck and jeans, topped by a black leather jacket and an ordinary, wispy hairdo, not the usual rock-solid hedgehog. Her face was naked, but for a sprinkling of freckles across her nose. She looked positively pretty.

'Don't mention the freckles,' she warned. 'I hate them.'

No. 4 began to bark and run at the door. Ciara opened it to reveal Sammy the Sandwich, who leapt back with a yelp.

'Call it off,' he cried, referring to the dog, we hoped.

'He's harmless,' I said. Sammy presumed I meant No. 4, and Ciara assumed I meant Sammy. Everybody happy. I introduced them all to one another.

'Have I got news for you?' said Sammy, reaching into his wicker basket. 'Not only did I manage to take the lift up here today, but look . . .' He flourished a cellophaned munchie. 'Dadah! This is our latest. It's a kind of Peking Duck in a three-grain baguette. It shouldn't work, but it's just so crazy – it does!' Then he sighed. 'These are the days that make this job worth living for.'

'Sorry to disappoint, Sammy,' I said. 'I'm off to The Mammy's for lunch. But perhaps Ciara can be tempted.'

'Damn' right I can,' said the youngster, diving in.

'What's with Mrs Mack today?' I asked Sammy. 'The elevator has been available to all.'

'Eshep mee,' Ciara pointed out, dribbling some masticated cucumber.

'Except you,' I acknowledged.

'It's sinister,' Sammy said. 'She's obviously looking for something.'

A chill ran through my body. If I had been religious I would have crossed myself. As it happened, religion was the right ball park.

We didn't have long to wait to find out what Mrs Mack's 'something' was. A light knock came on the door, followed by the All Powerful One herself, in hat and coat. The effect was all cream and off-white, and it was hard to make out where her face was.

'I hope I haven't disturbed you with a client, Miss Street,' she said, referring to Ciara, who was trying her best to disappear into the depths of the leather armchair. Mrs Mack darted looks, henlike, round the office. 'Is the other rip gone?' she asked. 'I didn't see her leave.' In fairness to Mrs M, she is as effective as Closed Circuit TV, so I had to let her off the hook.

'This *is* Ciara, she's cleaned her act up a bit.'

'Well, not before time,' said Mrs Mack, primly. 'I suppose there's hope for us all yet,' she added. Rather cryptically, it seemed to me. Isn't that one of those nonsense phrases people use, which means nothing really but presents the illusion of wisdom?

'What did you want?' I asked.

'Oh, yes,' she said. 'I'm knocking off early today because I need to go and get a few things for my pilgrimage. I'm off to Lourdes for a few days.' She hung her head in a suitably pious pose.

I'd been around long enough to know that this meant she would expect some cash to bring with her; sterling, francs, traveller's cheques, diamonds or gold bullion, all were acceptable. Now, if we'd been talking an appropriate bonus for work done, the amount would be nil. But this was Mrs Mack, and hard currency would have to change hands.

'Well, do make sure to call in before you go,' I said. 'Who'll be taking over from you?'

'That'll be a treat for everyone. My husband Kevin has agreed to dep for me. And he's a hoot, so he is. You'll all enjoy him. He's great *craic* altogether.'

With that happy thought she left us. My heart had now

frozen over. If there's anything that frightens me rigid, it's people who are 'great *craic* altogether'. We obviously had a rocky trip ahead.

'I'm packing it in for the day,' I said to Ciara. 'I can't take the excitement anymore.'

'Now, now, Sarky,' she chided.

Of course, there was one excitement I could have treated myself to. I could have phoned Andy Raynor. But I didn't want to appear too eager. And, admittedly, I didn't want to do it with Ciara around. She would be on to me like a hot snot if she smelled any kind of intrigue. And though I knew there was nothing more than teasing going on between myself and Andy, I couldn't be sure that he'd be entirely the gentleman with me, and I didn't want to be caught in an inappropriate reaction or situation. I was The Boss now, and had to maintain my dignity.

'You've a huge ladder in your tights,' The Staff said, on cue, deflating my managerial bubble. 'It's been travelling in both directions all morning. That doesn't look good for the firm, so you might want to clean your act up.' No. 4 barked in agreement. I resisted the urge to kill them both, but only just.

I could feel Mick's eyes bore a hot hole in my back as we left the office. Ciara was getting the same treatment.

'Does he get out much?' she asked.

'Depends,' I said, grimly. Mick Nolan was far too free-range for my liking. He had been impossible in life, and death hadn't changed him all that much. I could hear him muttering darkly about how it would have been just as easy to borrow a car as it was to get in help. I ignored him. I was heartily sick of his moaning, and the ugliness of other people's lives.

We parted at Malachy's billet, with Ciara promising to check in later with a progress report. I loaded No. 4 into the car and said my goodbyes. Just then, Malachy had a coughing fit and hawked up a huge, green gob of phlegm on to the gravel of the makeshift car park. Good Golly, Miss Molly.

SIX

'Legs Eleven,' was Maeve's greeting.

I had to set her straight. 'It's an optical illusion, I've only got the two.'

'And do I spot a deliberate mistake?' she asked, as I hauled myself, the dog and my equipment into her luxury apartment.

'If you're referring to the ladder in my tights, I can only presume that it won't work as a fashion statement.'

'Oh, *no, far* too grunge, *particularly* for a family lunch. *No*, not even close. *However*, help is at hand. I have a new pair that should do the trick, *and* lift that outfit all in one.'

Reasons To Be Nervous, Part 1.

Maeve disappeared into her bedroom, which housed her frighteningly extensive hosiery department while I installed her 'new' telephone and tape recorder. No. 4 had a good old sniff 'n' root. When she re-emerged, a glint in her eye made me uneasily prudish. I had erred on the side of conservative dress for the four generations of Street women gathering today; keeping a low profile and all that. Well, it was what I was used to in my line of life and work. Maeve had a slightly different notion of the look I was going for, and it was embodied in the sparkling gun metal grey item she now brandished above her immaculately coiffed head. My thighs in shining armour, as 'twere.

'A bit flashy,' I demurred.

'Exactly. Live a little.'

'I don't suppose I have a choice,' I chanced, tentatively.

'Correct,' was the firm reply.

I went all obedient and struggled out of one pair of tights and into the other. Maeve Kelly was, and remains, mistress of the age-old art of timing, and as I was hauling the twinkling gusset into place, she made good her opportunity to ambush me.

'That handsome friend of yours, Andy Raynor, was in to see the show during the week.'

'Oh, yeah?' I said, diving behind the couch to fiddle with some cable.

'Yes. He stayed for a drink afterwards.'

I stayed by the skirting and tried to sound cool. 'I suppose he had some gorgeous woman on his arm?'

'Two of them, actually, one older, one younger. *Very* charming.'

I let slip a mewl of disappointment.

'*Ooh,*' Maeve purred, delighted with herself. 'And do I detect the merest *hint* of jealousy?'

I stayed down by a socket. 'Oh, don't be ridiculous. I've known Andy far too long to care what he gets up to.'

'And *that* would be why you are now a delicate shade of fuchsia?'

How could she tell from where she was standing?

I took a few breaths to calm myself. I did feel a bit hot. And bothered. I weighed up my options. There are times when you can win, and times when you can not, and this seemed the latter to me. So I gave in a little, and it was almost pleasurable to admit, 'Well, I am supposed to meet up with him soon. I guess I'll hear all about it then.'

'He *did* mention that I should tell you to phone him,' she said. 'So I am now *officially* reminding you to do just that. Oh, and by the way, he is *gorgeous* so why the delay?'

'It's a neighbour thing, nothing more,' I protested.

'Yeah, *sure*.'

'Look, Maeve, I know far too much about Andy to take anything he says or does seriously. He is so unreliable. And untrustworthy.'

'And gorgeous.'

'If you like that sort, yeah, I suppose.'

'All right, I can see that you *refuse* to be drawn so I'll tell you that he was with his mother and some other bit. *Fluff.* Not a patch on you.'

It was kind of Maeve to be loyal, and loose with the truth. Andy always had beautiful women hanging off him, I just wasn't in the same league. And, as he liked to remind me regularly, I was a huge pain in his butt. Before my heart could sink too visibly, I changed the subject.

'How is the show going?'

'Grand so far, we're all getting along. *But* Teddy Buckley, my father in it, is inclined to be a bit *fresh* with the younger ladies of the cast. Apparently, he was a *notorious* swordsman in his day, shagged everything and everybody. And he's *very* eager to prove that he's still active. There were fears for some panto ponies a few years back.'

Maeve let a silence descend, and fixed me with one of her looks. I knew what she was up to, and distraction was futile.

'Okay, okay, I'll phone him later,' I said.

There was a pause, accompanied by the Kelly gimlet eye. 'Promise?'

'I promise.'

'Atta girl.'

It was high time we got grounded again. 'These calls,' I began, 'you say you never get them on your mobile?'

'Not that I know of,' she answered, back down to earth too. 'If it's switched off people leave messages, and there have been no blanks, or silences if you could call them that, like the ones I'm getting on the landline.'

'Right. I don't want you to get overly worried about this, Maeve. Together we'll sort it, okay? Now, I suppose I'd better freshen up before facing the Street Tribunal.'

The bathroom in this apartment is where I want to live when I grow up. It is huge, with a claw-foot enamel bath in the middle of the floor. The sparkling steel taps are on the side, so as not to inconvenience the one or more persons who might be relaxing, or washing, or whatever. For those in a hurry, there is a power shower tucked discreetly in a corner beside a tower of towels, robes and fragrant fol-de-rols. It is lit by a huge, frosted window which manages to capture light all through the day, and is covered by a royal blue blind at night. Above the sink is an enormous mirror which bounces the light to any spot that nature finds hard to get to, and all of the ones on my face which don't need highlighting. And here on shelves are the unctions and salves of the modern girl. I swear that Maeve Kelly has enough to do a good mummification. And no matter what man is in her life, she manages to keep their presence discreet, if not invisible. Actually, she never lets them move in, perhaps that's her secret. That's the difference between Maeve and me. She's a serial dater, I'm more live and let live in.

If there is one feature that makes me nervous, though, it is the toilet. It's one of those modern jobs with no stem under it, so it juts out from the wall at an angle. I can never relax on it because I'm convinced that it will snap off while my large arse is enthroned. If there was a safety apparatus like, say, a seat belt, I'd be that bit more at ease. Still, I can change this when the time comes.

I noticed that one of the bubble baths had a quote on the label. I moved closer to read it. 'My hopes are not always realised, but I always hope,' it said. Fair enough. Then I noticed who the quote was from; Ovid, no less. What was the world coming to when these pearls of ancientness were turning up on mass-produced bath products? Still, maybe Ovid would be pleased that, although his genius had been reduced to a slogan, the message was reaching out to the wider populace who might not normally feel the need to check him out. The bubble bath was called 'Well Being'.

As I was surreptitiously dousing myself in a glorious Jo Malone cologne, Maeve knocked on the door and announced coffee, to fortify my spirits and make me just hyper enough to make a good entrance at home. 'I've given the mutt some water,' she added, ever the perfect hostess. As I joined her she said, 'More lippy, and toss your hair up a bit. That Jo Malone is divine, isn't it?'

'Em, yeah, I hope you don't mind?'

'Not at all. It's not mine, it's Mark's.'

Aha! In the past six months, Maeve had dated a copy-writer, a cameraman, a Formula One racing driver (it made the tabloids for three days running, and she swears she's now allergic to champagne as a direct result of the excesses of that escapade), and a magician who specialised in children's parties, much to his own chagrin. I did a quick totting up and discovered there was not a single 'Mark' amongst them.

'A man leaving something in your bathroom? That is *so* serious. Tell all.'

Maeve was the cat who got the cream and had the t-shirt to prove it. She curled up on her designer sofa and stared dreamily into space.

'He's a lawyer or something. Whichever one does the theatricals in court.'

'A barrister then.'

'I suppose. He did that murder thing recently.'

The penny dropped in the amusement arcade of my brain.

'You mean, Mark Rolands? Only the most famous man in Ireland at the moment. The one who got Sara Fingleton off the charge of murdering her husband, even though she was as guilty as the prison day is long?'

'Yes, that Mark Rolands. He's divine.'

'*And* you've let him leave stuff here?'

'Worse than that, he's got his own key.'

'You realise you're going to have to kill him now?' This was as serious as a hardened criminal letting you see his face.

'I know!'

'I never thought I'd see the day, Maeve.'

'Well, in truth you haven't, yet. You know me and men,

it may come to nothing. But I have to admit that I wouldn't mind with this one, he's special.'

'And he can defend me when I finally get nabbed by the law for something shady.'

'Which reminds me, *why* are you not at work? Are there no more bills in your life? Has Barry lost the *run* of himself and decided to support *you*?'

I laughed at the notion.

'No, I've had to get someone to take over for a while. I came face to face with the man I was following, so I'm having a change, which I hope will be as good as a rest.'

'Or, in *your* case, better than *arrest*.'

'Doesn't matter now, I've got a direct line to Mark Rolands. Hang on to him, Maeve,' I pleaded, dramatically. 'I need him.'

She beat me with a cushion.

'Let me know when you have something on these phone calls, and I'll hang by and have a listen,' I said.

Her mouth twitched, and I knew that she was putting up a braver front than she had in her store.

'Maeve, the law is on your side. Making malicious calls is considered a criminal offence, and we'll involve the cops if we have to.'

Another twitch.

'Which we won't. Okay?'

She nodded and then she smiled. 'Ooh, but you're *forceful* when you want to be.'

'All in a day's work, ma'am,' I said, in a woeful American accent. 'Now don't you go worryin' your purty little head 'bout nothin', ya hear?'

She was still nodding as I hitched me up ma dawg and made fer ma wagon. Time fer this pilgrim to hit injun country.

★   ★   ★

Although our family name is Street, we live somewhere else entirely, the Close, Sycamore Close. I have no idea whether this was far-sightedness on my parents' part or pure serendipity. Whatever, it works for me. There is nary a sycamore in sight, of course. I half recall the helicopter seeds of sycamore trees from my childhood, but it is only a half recollection, and the trees might have been elsewhere, like Larch Grove which is parallel to the Close.

I passed the Raynors' house as I approached Casa Street. It looked a lot like our own, with the small exception that Andy's dad is devoted to hedging, carving it into whatever shape takes his seasonal fancy. This spring was all about Noah's Ark, it seemed. Two of everything, though the every-things were a little hard to identify. And I was certain that there were three unicorns on display, possibly to make up for the ultimate fate of the beast. Last year's effort had gone awry somewhere between idea and execution. He had intended giant acorns around the periphery of the garden, to make some complicated horticultural joke about oak trees, but the result was a phalanx of green penises, which his wife, Breda, quickly vetoed. Mind you, gardens are all about sex and reproduction so the scheme was perfectly sound thematically, and some might even have said a joy to behold; I guess it's all to do with the eyes that are beholding.

Frank Raynor was inspecting his handiwork as I drove by. He raised a head and waved, and I returned the salute. Andy has his father's dark, handsome features, coupled with his mother's fierce wit and way with words, graced by sparkling eyes that are all his own. A formidable combination. God, I wanted to make that call. But I held on to my dignity. And creamed myself.

★ ★ ★

I parked in a space opposite our driveway as my grand-mother, Mary Ellen Doyle, rounded the corner, dragged by Fanny and Margot, two dogs who shared five hundred and thirty-one breeds between them. She was dressed in a red fleece, which she'd teamed with a knee-length emerald skirt and some very funky patterned tights. I complimented her on the latter.

'It's two pairs, the holes are in different places, so there's no need to waste them.'

My gran was a pioneer of recycling. On her back was a knapsack of indeterminate colour, for piccaroonying wherever she went; you never knew the hour or the minute when a top relic would present itself to be brought home. She was having a bit of trouble controlling the dogs, and had a look of Ben Hur about her.

'Did you forget your chariot?' I asked.

'Piss off,' she replied.

My granny had recently started a campaign of plain speaking, particularly with her family. She thought it was hip and modern, but I suspect she also enjoyed mortifying us all, and daring us to pull her up on her 'language'. She was inclined to tall tales of late, too, and again I suspected this was to tease out a reaction, and to worry us that she might be going a bit ga-ga. She loved the attention. In fact, there was nothing senile about this old lady, let me assure you. I could see my poor mother shaking her head, saying, 'She's hanging around with a bad crowd.' And she was. Gran's best pals were renegades, and none of them under seventy-five. They were a mixed bunch who got together to swap spells and potions, and sometimes to play poker for money or souls. Well, the sorcery was only suspected by the families, no one had the guts to tackle them directly on this. You never knew what life form you'd come back as after they'd finished with you.

No. 4, Fanny and Margot were now a tangle of leads and wagging tails. Mary Ellen Doyle handed me her two leashes and headed for the door, saying, 'I'll see you inside.' I tried protesting that I had an important phone call to make, but it didn't even merit a reply. I persuaded the knot of dogs to follow me around the corner of the house, through the side gate and into the back garden, where I unclipped any catch that looked viable and let the hounds run loose. Then I sat on a bench out of sight of the kitchen and rooted out my mobile to call Andy. My hands were clammy with nerves.

A luscious, deep voice answered, 'Andy Raynor. How can I help?'

'You get more mid-Atlantic by the day, do you know that?'

'Ah, Leo, that was quick. I thought you'd leave me hanging at least another six hours to prove how nonchalant you are about me.' There was a distinct merriment in his tone. DAMN! I thought I'd left enough of a time lapse. Well, he hadn't bettered me yet.

'Andy, I'm in a hurry, what did you want?'

'I need an escort.'

'That's not actually one of the services I provide,' I explained.

'I need your body, Street.'

'Mmm,' I murmured, coolly. 'In what way?' And gave myself a mental shake. What the hell was I doing flirting with bloody Andy? He was more trouble than any one woman could handle, particularly a woman living with another man, i.e. me.

'I've got to go to a Rugby Club dinner dance tomorrow night and I need someone along who doesn't crave attention and can look after herself. You may be a royal pain in the ass, but at least you can make conversation with strangers. And it's not a date, which is great, because I just don't have the energy for all that at the moment.'

'You surprise me, Andy,' I said. 'I can't believe you'd consider going out with a member of the opposite sex without the prospect of a shag at the end of the evening.'

'It's the new mature me.'

'And you've been let down at the last moment.'

'You are a very cynical woman, Leo Street.'

'Yeah, well, that's life.'

'So, are you up for it?'

My mind was thinking a hundred thoughts all at once. I was miffed that he didn't see me as a date, while at the same time reasoning that this was a good thing and what I actually wanted. We were friends and occasional sparring partners. It would surely be a laugh, at the very least. But I was insulted to be the last port of call in an emergency . . . or was that a compliment? And how dare he assume that I'd be available at such short notice?

'I'm not sure that I can make it,' I returned.

'Yes, you can, and you know you want to.'

'You are one cocky bastard, Andy Raynor.'

'Yep, and I know how to show a girl a good time, even you. Anyway, you owe me for helping you when you were on that case in Kildare.'

I gagged indignantly. 'I beg your pardon? All you gave me was some information, which was damn-all use anyhow.' I was spluttering now.

'And have we forgotten the little matter of me not letting

you choke on your own vomit, because you were too pissed to know that you were unconscious?'

'That's dirty and low down and you know it. I was caught off guard!'

'You still owe me.'

My mind was racing now. But one fact clinched the deal for Andy, though he did not know it at the time. I knew that Michael O'Donoghue was a member of the same club as Andy, and might be at the dinner. That could yield something. So, it would be a work trip, as well as possibly assuaging some of my rampant hormones with a little window shopping.

'Oh, *okay*, I'll go.'

'I'm delighted that you've seen reason,' he said, laughing aloud now. 'Dress is informally formal, whatever that means. Something short and without knickers should do the trick.'

'*WHAT?*' I shrieked.

'Just joking, Leo. If you weren't wearing panties and your mother found out, I'd have to marry you, and God only knows where that would land us. I warn you in advance that it's a kind of fundraiser for some very worthy cause or other, so it'll probably be dull as dishwater.'

Ain't that the way of the world? Badness is spicy, good-ness bland. I couldn't let it go.

'So it's sub-interest, and you're lining up the B-Team?'

'Leo, Leo, Leo,' he admonished. 'You are a sour woman at times. Choose those scanties, get primping yourself, I'll pick you up at eight. Ciao.'

I found myself staring at the phone with a mixture of horror and delicious anticipation. He had invested the word 'scanties' with such promise that I was in need of changing mine there and then. I made a note to wear two pairs of interlock knickers on the night.

According to Barry, the female equivalent of a hard-on is a wide-on. He can be utterly gross when he wants to. But as I struggled to walk upright to the kitchen door, I began to have an idea of what he meant.

SEVEN

I once saw my four-year-old niece Mary tackle the day. It was 8 a.m. and she had dragged herself out of bed; Mary loves her sleep. She descended the stairs, slowly and gently, flakes of sleep stuck to her eyelids. As she reached the door of the dining room, she stopped, gave a big sigh, then *danced* sideways into the room, shouting, 'Mary's here, Mary's here!' She had to, you see. She was a kid, and that was her job. I was now in a similar situation, and though I had two foot four on her in height, and twenty-six years, the demographics were pretty much the same. I took a deep breath, then bounced into the kitchen, saying, 'I'm here, I'm here!'

I needn't have bothered. There was no one to greet me. Or should I say one member of the family was lurking, but it was not strictly human. Smokey Joe Street, our cat, sat in the middle of the table, and he couldn't give a hang about any of us one way or the other. He chose that moment to stretch a pantalooned leg in the air, and lick his hairy white arse.

'You'd know you were a man, Mister,' I said, as I made my way into the sitting room.

I never did get to make 'my entrance' because as I reached for the door handle a youngster exploded into the corridor and ran for the stairs. It was fifteen-year-old Lucy Street.

'Shouldn't you be at school?' I asked.

'Leo, you are beginning to sound like my mum. Day off. I'll explain in a minute, I'm bursting to go to the loo.'

She bounded up the stairs two at a time, though with her legs she could have managed three steps, no problem. At the top, she turned and said, 'Don't you think you should answer that?' And disappeared.

I could hear the strains of a highland jig, but didn't think that was anything to do with me until I realised it was coming from my bag. How could that be? I hate novelty rings on a mobile, and mine is programmed to the most boring sound available with my model. I fished it out and sure enough it was my telephone making the awful racket. When I answered, Barry's cheery tones yelled, 'Surprise!'

'Brilliant trick, Baz,' I drawled.

'Don't be so square, Leo. Live a little.'

This was the second time I had been told that today. If I'd had a moment I might have paused to give it some thought. Now was not that moment; I was on the cusp of the tribal gathering and didn't need any miscellaneous distractions. Instead I gave the Barry Boy short shrift, but not before he could say, 'Don't forget to get cat food and some milk on your way home.'

'Does that mean that you have no intention of leaving

the house at all today?' I asked, probably a little sanctimoniously.

'Who knows?' he said, airily. 'And I don't mean to excite you, but if I don't, I may not even wash myself.'

'Gee, there's something to look forward to.'

'Sarcasm, Leo. Unattractive in a lady. I will of course release myself into the community later, to bring culture and entertainment to the paying public. I have to do the Pub Crawl. But it'll be no harm if you get some provisions too. See ya later, babe.'

Lucy thundered back down the stairs, and paused long enough to tell me, 'You've a bit of froth at the side of your mouth, could be drool,' before crashing back through the sitting-room door. 'Leo's here,' she announced. 'She's got hose beast tights on.' That was my fanfare. Not the entrance I had intended, but sometimes you have to use whatever gets you to where you need to go. In my case, it was deep into the female bosom of the family, or 'boosum' as my granny likes to call it. She is also given to the word 'picturescew'. So you get the . . . well, anyway, I wiped my mouth with the back of my hand and stepped in.

My grandmother popped a bottle of champagne as I entered, and I'll admit that I felt very flattered. Then she made it all the more special by saying, 'Jaysus, I thought you'd never get here, me brain thinks me throat's been cut. Who's for gargle?' When we'd all been dispensed our fizzy 'poo, my mother raised a glass to Rose and we toasted the little beauty. My gran grimaced and groaned, not her usual reaction to champagne. 'Me poor teeth are dancin' for want of a few fillings,' she explained. 'The cold kills them. And as for the neuralgia . . . oh, now, don't start me. Still, we'll soldier on.'

'Neuralgia?' I hooted. 'I thought that went out with the Ark.'

'No need for that sort of mockery, miss. You'll know all about it when you're my age.'

Angela popped her new daughter into my arms and said, 'This will be great practice for you, Leo.'

'Ah, now here,' I protested. 'I haven't a maternal bone in my body.'

'Oh, I don't know,' she said. 'You look after Barry pretty well.'

From anyone else, the comment might have held a barb, but this was Angela and all she spoke was the truth. I refrained from comment and, unusually, so did the older members of the family.

Rose Street was a dote. She locked you in her gaze with huge azure eyes, and waved her hands as if to tell you some important information. Sometimes, she gave an emphatic downward gesture that seemed to have a warning in it. You ignored her wisdom at your peril. I placed her flat on my thighs, with her feet to my stomach and her head at my knee, where she continued with a leisurely t'ai chi routine. I was as happy as mussels in garlic butter.

'It suits you, you know,' said Anne, Lucy's mum.

'Don't you start,' I warned. But it was too late, my mother was on to one of her favourite subjects.

'You're not getting any younger, Leo. The longer you leave it, the dodgier it gets. And you don't want to miss out. When I see all the attention you pay to those cats of yours, and now that dog, it brings it home to me. It's a baby you should be having, and no more of this aul' nonsense with pets.'

I thought I might try a different tack. Normally I would

argue with her, but now I went for enigmatic and vaguely agreeable.

'Well, you never know. Maybe you're right. Maybe one of these days I'll surprise you all.'

My grandmother snorted. She has a very well-honed bullshit detector. I guess she's heard a lot more of it in her lifetime, being the eldest of us. If she was going to undermine my newest plan, it was time to change the subject.

'Why are you off school?' I asked my niece.

Lucy was trying her best to like champagne, but each time she took a sip her face creased at the bubbles and the nasty taste. I had no doubt that, like her forbears, she would stick with it, and eventually reach a point in her life when she resented her parents for not having the surname Bollinger.

'Sister Mel died, so we got the day off.'

'Oh, no,' I blurted. 'Mel was great, she was one of the good guys.'

'She was?' Lucy's eyebrows were dusting the ceiling.

'Yes,' I insisted. 'I had her for Latin for three years, and then she started doing school plays and running the tuck shop. She was a mad little thing. I could never work out why she was a nun though.'

'I know that,' my gran said. 'She was brought up in the West. Her family owned a pub with a bit of land around it. But Mel was the youngest of two daughters, and there were no sons, so her sister got the family business, and she was sent into the convent. That's just what happened in those days. If she was growing up now I doubt she'd be a nun.'

'No, she'd be a writer or a theatre director or something like that,' I said.

'I thought she was a crazy old bat,' said Lucy. 'We used to call her Old Habits Die-Hard.'

'She'd have liked that,' I laughed.

'Wasn't Mel short for Melchisedech?' Anne asked.

'I hope so,' I said. 'I'd hate to think it was anything boring.'

We all took a moment to remember the dead nun. Except Lucy, who'd clearly decided that we'd all gone crazy. And Rose, who was set to grow up in a world where nuns were becoming obsolete. It didn't bother me that they were dying out, but I had liked Mel, and hoped that she'd got her due reward. That was the deal when you invested your life in the Catholic dream, wasn't it? I was so lapsed that the details were decidedly muzzy. And we had never been a devout household to begin with. *Carpe Dominum*, Mel, I thought, hoping that I'd remembered even a little of what she'd taught me. I added the proviso 'by the balls if you have to, to get what you want' in English, because my Latin studies had not continued to senior level.

Mothers have special powers which seem to come to them by osmosis over the years. They gain the ability to read your mind, as well as your post, they can wrongfoot you, they can make you do things that you don't want to, they can tell what colour underwear you're wearing, and whether it matches, and of course they can smell lust and intrigue at a hundred paces. There's probably a simile in there somewhere, involving a wild animal hunting its prey.

'Did you ring Andy?' was all she asked. But this was no innocuous query. My mother was basically asking, 'What are you doing with your life and when are you going to get sense, or at least see things my way?' I wriggled in the bit between the rock and the hard place. (Amazing the way it's not site-specific, just turns up wherever it's not wanted.) I looked to Anne and Angela for moral support. All I met were grins, and the twinkle of expectation in their eyes. I looked down at Rose. She gurgled and gave me a wave. Lucy was curling up her nose, but this was more to do with a French château than my plight. And the vultures just perched and waited.

I tried, 'Oh, yeah, that, it was nothing.'

'So what are you going to wear?'

'Sorry?'

'What will you wear to the do?'

'Mammy, how did you know about that?'

'I'm your mother, of course I know.'

'This is a set up, isn't it? You've probably been planning this with Andy for ages, haven't you? You are so devious. No, I want to change that. You're evil, that's what you are.' I was on a roll now, so I waxed lyrical. 'He's a philanderer,' I added, summoning up a lorry-load of biblical denunciations, I hoped.

As if.

'Ah, calm down, would you?' my grandmother said. 'Sure he's gorgeous. I'd say he has a lad on him like a donkey's arm holding a child's orange.' There was silence in the room while everyone checked their hearing. Then the pronouncement sank in. I started to choke. Anne and Angela were holding on to one another for support. I'm glad to say that Lucy was bemused. But the look on my mother's face could have frozen peas. She squeezed out an indignant 'Mammy!' I was doubly delighted to know that I wasn't the only one in the house with mother-trouble. Mary Ellen Doyle finally asked me what was so funny.

'Nothing, Granny, I've just never heard it put like that

before.' I tried gulping in some air to calm myself.

'So what did I get wrong?' she asked.

I cleared my throat. 'Well, I think the phrase you were looking for is "a child's arm holding an orange", I explained, not daring to catch anyone else's eye.

'And which of the two would be bigger?' she wanted to know.

'Em, I don't know really,' I had to admit. 'Probably your description.'

'That's what he is then.'

'I'm sure Andy's ears are burning, wherever he is,' my mother said.

'No, Mammy,' I corrected her. 'I'm certain it's another part of him entirely.'

The room fell about again.

There is a deviousness in all mothers that should never be underestimated. I'm not sure if it's an innate talent that's unleashed when parenthood is achieved, or whether it's something that's acquired stealthily over the centuries. Whatever the case, a Mammy can turn any situation to her advantage. Granted, when her own mother is there too, it's a little tricky, but not impossible. Geraldine Street, née Doyle, slalomed on a consonant, then proceeded to display her mastery by dominating the conversation from there on out. I was quizzed high up and low down about what I would wear, what I would eat and drink, and basically what my intentions were towards Mr Andrew Raynor. I eventually heard myself exclaim, 'His virtue is safe with me, for God's sake. You can come along to make sure, if you'd like.' And, do you know, for just a moment she considered the offer, rhetorical though it was. I found myself staring, horrified, as my mother and her mother looked at one another, sizing up the advantages and disadvantages of that particular scenario.

'It does sound like a fantastic night out,' my grandmother said. She was perched like some laughing troll on the edge of her chair.

'I could go with John Senior,' my mother calculated, referring to my father. 'And you could bring one of your cronies.' My grandfather, Nobby, is long gone.

My grandmother shuffled her round bottom forward in the armchair, stretching one leg out, then stretching the other past it, until she seemed on the brink of overshooting the furniture. Her eyes sparkled as she announced, 'We'll make a family night out of it.' To their credit, both my sisters-in-law had the decency to look taken aback. But I was saved by a double-pronged rescue from my nieces: Rose started to cry, and Lucy announced that she was going to be sick. They were both whipped away to be seen to, and I escaped to the kitchen.

Quite honestly, I was sweating by now. What crazed fever were we gripped by? I know that sexual politics is an inexact science at the best of times. There is no practical solution to infatuation, not even consummation. But what do you do when more than one of the women in a family is obsessed with one man, albeit in differing ways? Or what if the ways don't differ that much, just the generations under the grip of the infatuation? It's not only a nightmare, it's chaos.

So is losing your sense of humour.

The harpies followed me into the kitchen, laughing their heads off.

'Leo, you'll never learn. How could you be so easy to rise?' my mother asked.

'What do you mean?' I countered, tetchily.

'We can read you like a short story,' my gran said, shaking her head.

'I don't know what you mean,' I tried again. 'And anyway it's all a bit cruel, if you ask me.'

'Oh, for goodness' sake,' my mother exclaimed, 'would you loosen up and live a little?'

I was becoming entirely cheesed off with being told that.

'Go out and have a whale of a time, why can't you?' she continued. 'I only wish I had half the chance.'

Of course they had a point. I certainly was taking things far too seriously. But why? The frightening realisation was that a Pandora's box in my head would be opened if I admitted, even to myself, that I fancied the rocks off Andy Raynor. And that was not only undesirable but unethical in the relationships stakes. I was living with a man; had been for three years. We had had our ups and downs, but the arrangement worked, and what was commitment if it could be tossed out of the window at the first lusty imagining? 'Barry is not Andy,' Pandora whispered. I switched my brain immediately to neutral. I wouldn't listen to her. I could see the lid on the box lift ever so slightly, and I didn't think that I could deal with whatever was about to spew out.

'Is that your phone?' my mother asked.

We all paused to listen. The opening of Bach's Mass in C, 1997 remix, was repeating itself over and over, not my new and improved highland fling, so I denied it. I was about to do this again and make a liar of myself when it became apparent that it was indeed my mobile making this latest bizarre noise. How had Barry done that? Surely he couldn't have programmed it from afar? My answer came through the kitchen door just then, green of gill and dull of eye. She smiled sheepishly at me.

'Nice one,' I smiled back. The things we do for love . . .

'It's not lemonade, Lucy,' her mother Anne was saying. 'You shouldn't knock it back as if it was. No wonder you were ill.'

'Don't mind her, Luce,' I said. 'We've all been there in our time. As I recall, your mother had more than one run in with cooking sherry, and cider, and other classy tipples like that. Sometimes all mixed together.'

'Oh, do you hear the queen of the hedges herself?' Anne laughed. 'I seem to remember many's the night you found your way home following a trail of orange puke you'd made earlier.'

'It was a system,' I shrugged. 'It worked.'

'I hope to God you're not still using it,' my mother said, with just the right mixture of superiority and mock outrage. She's good at being a Mammy.

'Oh, holier than thou now,' said Über Mum Doyle, who was of course the Mammy of us all, and not to be undone.

'If you breathe a word about what I think you're referring to, I won't be responsible for my actions,' her daughter, Geraldine, warned.

I would have put myself deeply into hock to find out what she was talking about. But I should have known better. They grinned at each other, then settled into *Omerta*. They were shored up sheer, no questioners need apply.

My nose was itching with curiosity, and I had to scratch it somehow. Feeding it information (of any sort) was the only remedy here, so I accessed my message. It was Ciara. Short and to the point. 'I'm in the office. Phone me.' I followed instructions.

'What are you doing back there?' I asked.

'You know damn' well what I'm doing back here. You never told me I wouldn't get bloody parking on bloody Merrion Square. So how was I supposed to case the joint?'

I allowed myself a smile. Had she passed her first test? She was certainly working on the lingo.

'What did you do?' I asked, casually.

'I followed your advice,' she said. 'But in a much more effective way.'

'Of course. And which piece of my wonderful advice was it you remodelled so well?'

'I asked a question *and* told a lie, all at once,' she crowed. 'I telephoned, pretending to be our family doctor's receptionist, and checked on the good doctor's availability this week.'

'And?'

'Jammed solid. So he won't be going any place unusual any morning between now and Saturday. No need to sit on some bench like an eyesore attracting attention, or mess around in a bus shelter pretending to wait for the 46A.'

First test passed with flying colours. I glanced at my watch.

'Shouldn't you be back there now?'

'All in hand. I'll be hot on his tail to the baby factory within the nano-second. There have been some interesting developments in the doctor's life. I suggest you get an evening paper. Talk to you later. Over and out.'

A tingle of relaxation had been trying to establish itself between my shoulder blades since early morning; Ciara was doing well. She had sense, common or otherwise. She also had a sense of what needed to be done. It would be interesting to see this case through her eyes, unjaded as she was by the vagaries of the cheating classes. I say classes because in my experience being unfaithful is not a restricted activity. Anyone can get in on the act. Birds do it, bees do it, et cetera. And I wasn't worried about Ciara being damaged by the experience of spying on the unsavoury; for all her sense, she was not that kind of sensitive soul. Not by a long shot. But she had halted that pleasurable tingle's journey with her enigmatic remark. Instead of relaxation oozing through my muscles, I stiffened from my neck downwards again.

EIGHT

There were signs to be read all over this case. Treat them as
omens, if you like, but that's not always a good road to go
down. I try not to be superstitious because it's nonsense and
you can end up spooking yourself and taking your mind off
the proper focus of the work in hand. Also, it drives Mick
Nolan completely mad, and he's not a man I like to piss off.
But it seems to me that whenever I get relaxed, or even a
little confident that things are going well, bad things are
skulking around the corner waiting to run me down.

As it happens, I did have to run around the corner to get
the newspaper in our local shop. Mrs Bradley had been
running 'The Tip Top' since before I was a grope in my
parents' romance. She still liked to press a sherbet upon me,
and sometimes I didn't even have to pay for it. Today, as I
dipped my liquorice stick into the vile, fizzy, white powder,
I read the headline 'Scandal of Baby Shop', below which
was a grainy photograph of my quarry. As I read the

breaking news, I disengaged my tongue from my palate, where the sherbet had just glued it, with a loud smacking noise.

Department of Health officials today began investigating claims that one of Ireland's leading obstetricians is involved in a 'babies for sale' scandal. Unconfirmed reports suggest that Michael O'Donoghue is at the centre of the latest controversy to involve the beleaguered Fledgling private hospital and fertility clinic. Sources close to those involved say that complaints of overcharging and risky procedures have been received from members of the public. The Medical Council has refused to comment directly on the matter, saying only that Mr O'Donoghue has been a respected practitioner for many years, and that all allegations against him are hearsay until such time as accusations can be formally confirmed or denied.

This is not the first time that Michael O'Donoghue has attracted attention. In 1992 he was cleared of charges of performing abortions which are illegal in the Republic. And in 1994 his name was linked to research into DNA selection which was condemned by the Catholic Church. A spokesman for Mr O'Donoghue said that the doctor was unperturbed by the allegations as they were completely unfounded, and he would be vindicated by the results of any investigation into his practices. He also said that it was clear that elements within the wider community were attempting to block his researches and besmirch his name through a malicious misunderstanding of his work and its value.

The paper followed the story up with transcripts from a speech Michael O'Donoghue had made to medical students at Trinity College. They pushed his views that life was marketable, if genetic traits were isolated and patented. This, he maintained, could lead to cures for cancer and other diseases, and on a cosmetic level to eradication of baldness or choice of eye colour, for instance. He extrapolated that mortality itself might become a consumer choice, which had sent religious groups into a complete spin. It read like science fiction, yet he assured the students that within a decade this would all be available to us. And he was the one to deliver, it seemed.

Of course, the newspaper had also chosen the most demonic photograph of him they could find. Here was a glaring face with flared nostrils and unruly hair. His dark eyes burned out from the page and into some soft area of entrail protected by the reader's rib cage. Here was the bogey man.

I re-entered Château Street with my mind whirling yet none the wiser as to where this case was headed. Now that Michael O'Donoghue was pursued by half of Dublin, he was unlikely to notice me, even though we had met informally the night before. I could not have foreseen this, but I felt outwitted all the same. Did the unfolding news mean that he would change his routine in any way? Or would he keep his head down, maintain normality and wait for the brouhaha to blow over, on the grounds that the public has a notoriously short attention span? I was antsy about what else fate might throw at me, because I was clearly not in charge of what was happening here. And then war broke out between me and the animal kingdom.

All I did was try to move Smokey Joe off the table,

because (a) he shouldn't have been up there, and (b) it was unhygienic for him to be in the middle of our lunch. I looked at the butter and was convinced that I could see the marks of a scaly tongue on one side. My mind summoned up a vision of him cleaning his hairy bum as I was arriving earlier, and I put two and two together. Elementary really, my dear Catson. So I made a shooing noise and flapped my hands close to his rump to shift him. Quick as a flash he nipped me on one wrist and swiped me across the back of the other. I often wonder if Smokey Joe has ever read his job description, which specifies that he is a house pet, not a hairy devil. I gave a gobsmacked 'Huh!' and looked for human support. No one had seen the incident. I could have sworn he was laughing at me now so I gave him a light smack on the bottom, at which he yowled in agony, and that got the attention of all. I might as well have been a vivisectionist at a vegetarian barbecue. Lucy rushed to the poor injured animal's side, cooing and petting him till he stopped his pitiful wailing. Barry could have taken acting lessons from this cat. Master Classes. He was fed some tidbits of smoked salmon as a reward for being so brave and went on his way, shoulders shaking with feline mirth. So, humiliating a human being is enough to make a cat laugh, in case you were wondering about the answer to that one.

No one mentioned the incident, probably because they couldn't find words to express the barbarity of it. My shoulder blades were joined up again, and my neck clicked into a rigor. I thought of famous people in history with a dread of cats, among them Napoleon, Shakespeare, Julius Caesar and Mussolini, and it seemed clear to me why: they knew what some of them were up to.

I suppose I was trying to make some sort of atonement when I offered to do the school run for Angela: a desperate attempt to come good after my transgression on to the dark side. (Anything to do with Smokey Joe Street is probably the Dark Side, whether he's with you or agin you.) I was also having an attack of that old favourite of mine, guilt; possibly the most powerful weapon for use on yourself, or others. My gran may have a finely tuned bullshit detector, my mum a gossip/intrigue one, mine is a highly trained guilt collector. A lot of people carry chips of regret around on their shoulders each day. I have a rock across my back made of sterner stuff: it's part conscience, part guilt and part regret, with a measure of mild self-loathing thrown in. But, hey, it ain't heavy, it's my boulder.

The job in hand was simple enough. I would collect Dominick and Mary, and two friends who were coming to tea, Dylan and Kylie. That way Angela got a bit more of a rest at home, and didn't have to deal with the pressures of after-school traffic, and hauling five kids around. I would only have to deal with four and a dog, because Rose would stay with her mum. At the back of my head rattled an idea that you should never work with animals or kids, but I suppose I thought that didn't apply to me, somehow.

On my way out, I paused to admire my mother's latest painting, and to re-ingratiate myself. It was a swirling mush of greens, brown and a dash of red. It was attractive, actually, and, as far as I could tell, abstract in the extreme. Or at least I couldn't make out any recognisable elements. I asked the stupid question 'What is it about?' and was told that it was whatever I wanted it to be. Duh.

'For me,' my mother said, loftily, 'it's about chaos and being a woman.'

'It's chaos all right,' my grandmother confirmed.

I could see my mother dart her a look, and decided that it was the perfect time to leave, while the heat was transferred to someone else. When aliens arrive from outer space, as they must, I believe the first skill my mother will learn is the ability actually to shoot with a glance of the eye. If they spare her. Which they will. She's a formidable weapon already, and is at least halfway to success on the look-shoot trick.

I often feel a pang of loneliness leaving a happy home, an urge to stay put and seek love and safety, away from the maelstrom of life and the hazards of earning a living. Not today. I hardly gave home a backward glance. I had been grilled, flipped and picked over. There was no point in hanging around for more. What else could they do anyway? Boil the bones and make some stock? Yes, was the answer, so I quickened my pace.

I gave Angela my injured banger to go home in and I took her four-door estate, which is like saying that I went from driving a moped to steering a tank. And why was the number four following me around? It wasn't even one of my Lotto choices. Maybe it should be. I consulted my own No. 4 as we stopped at a junction and he agreed wholeheartedly. So now I could look forward to an early retirement on a million or more pounds. All I had to do was identify the other five lucky numbers and Robert was my uncle. Actually I do have an Uncle Bob, but that's another day's work.

The Model School was relatively new and situated on a corner of Mountjoy Square, just to the north of the city centre. It's an imposing Georgian area that's seen better days. Merrion Square, where Michael O'Donoghue had his practice, would be a sister, but as it's on the southside, it houses the Arts Council of Ireland, the National Gallery, the National Maternity Hospital, several film production companies, and the headquarters of the Red Cross. Mountjoy Square, being northside, is that bit seedier, and boasts two large electrical outlets, a few derelict spaces, lots of rackrented flats and a hostel for young people. And if it were on the southside, the greenery in the middle would have more dazzling floral arrangements.

The school shared its playground, which also acted as a pick-up and set-down point for parents and children, with a small crêche where a lot of the primary school candidates started off their education. In their day Mary and Dom had attended, then moved up the ranks and out next door at the age of four or five. I decided that the number five was stalking me a bit too so I added it to my list of lucky numbers.

The yard was packed with mums and the odd dad waiting for the end-of-day bell to go. I recognised a few faces from my own school days, women who were now married and bringing up families. I fixed upon two who'd been in my class, Lisa Farrelly and Colette O'Brien. They both had the look of people who don't get quite enough sleep: a vague frazzling about the edges of the soul, an absence of sparkle in the eyes (though a glass of plonk could usually restore this) and a certain looseness of detail. Lisa, for instance, had hastily plaited her blonde hair at the back, but the strands were working their way free from their anchor, and the hairgrips shoved in at the sides were about to surrender their flimsy purchase. She had a small blob of ketchup on her chin, or maybe it was a particularly proud pimple but I thought not, and a dribble of soft egg yolk was pointing southwards from the lapel of her jacket. She was there to collect her son Josh. She had a three year old by the hand and in a harness. I was reminded momentarily of my grandmother and her dogs.

'This is Beth,' she told me. 'Beth goes to the crêche normally, don't you? But she's had a nasty cold for a few days, so she's been at home with Mummy, haven't you?'

The little girl sent her ringlets dancing up and down in agreement.

'And will you be going to the big school when you get older?' I asked.

More dancing hair.

Colette O'Brien lit a cigarette, and gave a deep sigh. 'This is my favourite time of the day, the calm before the storm. Have you fallen foul of procreation yet yourself?' she asked me.

'No. But Angela had a baby girl a few weeks back, so I'm mucking in with whatever help I can.'

'Babies,' said Colette, 'so close to human, aren't they?' We all gave a giggle. 'I've fallen three times myself, like you know who and his cross. They're all here, between the school and the crêche.'

'Well, as long as you don't go for making up twelve apostles, you should be fine,' I said.

'Oh, no chance of that. I found out what was causing it and I cut that out. The husband has a lovely singing voice now.'

Colette was the wag of the old days, the school prankster, the house demon, and the street one too. Her family had arrived in Clontarf after her father lost the fortune he had made in home heating and their circumstances were reduced. Today, the direction of the move would probably be reversed. Now the nouveau riche are moving into the area, rather than the nouveau broke.

Colette had a talent for seeking out mischief. She could also invent it when required, and when not. She led expeditions into the local parish church trying to find the way into the vault, when she heard that Mickey Freeney had found an open coffin there containing two eyeballs and a wooden spike. It was many years before we realised that Mickey Freeney had been born special and was very unlikely to have had that adventure. At Secondary School, she once locked all of the teachers into the staff room at coffee-break time and demanded money for charity before she would release them. We sat in blazing sunshine chanting for the donation until she judged that they'd given enough; this took two hours, during which time she took up smoking. And she delighted in fooling the relief teachers and student trainees into believing that she had a lisp.

Now she was married to a guy called Ray Leonard. He'd been a bit of a Jimmy Dean in his teenage years, but he charmlessly outgrew his biker's jacket when he started to drink too much, six months after his wedding, at which time he began to mislay his hair and acquire a belly. Rumour was that he still hit the sauce too much to hold down a job, which probably suited him in its way as he'd always been as lazy as sin but great fun with it.

Colette's hair was a shocked explosion of tinder-dry straw, the shape and attitude accentuated by a short cut. She ran a hand through it with some difficulty, scratching her scalp as she went. She caught my eye and confirmed, 'It's homage to Phyllis Diller.' Then she wiggled her nose, to chase off an itch. 'That's supposed to mean I'll have a fight with someone, isn't it? Give us a puck there, Leo, and I'll pinch you, and we'll be done with it.'

I did as I was told, though she pinched me harder than I'd hit her.

'Bitch,' I acknowledged. We weren't a million miles away from the old days now, right down to Colette smoking while we hung around a school yard.

'I suppose you heard about Mel,' she said.

'Yeah. I didn't even know she was ill.'

'She had a hole in her heart. Last week she decided enough was enough and stopped taking the medication. Then she just faded away. I saw her only a few hours before she died. She was genuinely happy. I'll miss the old bag. She was about the only good thing in that school.'

Her and you, I thought to myself.

'We despatched her earlier today.'

'Full metal jacket,' Lisa added. 'Nine priests concelebrating on the altar, and all the ancient nuns rolled out in their wheelchairs.'

'That probably confused them,' I said. 'They're normally only brought out to vote in elections, or against whatever referendum is on the go.'

'I really hope she was hovering around somewhere,' Colette said, 'because it was a hoot. Do you remember Mickey Freeney?'

'God, yes. That's freaky, I was just thinking about him.'

'Well, he's still going strong, I can tell you. He helps out at all the funerals and Masses in the local church. So today he was walking in front of the hearse and someone asked him who'd died, and he roared back, "Nun in box, nun in box." Mel would've loved that.'

We were chuckling merrily, when I noticed both of my

companions stiffen. I followed their line of vision to the gate, where a tall, pale woman in a designer coat had arrived. A hush descended on the playground. The woman tried to hide by a pillar, but all eyes were on her. She rummaged self-consciously in her bag, looking for something that she didn't need. In the false silence, I studied her. At first glance she seemed expensively turned out. And though she was, she was also three seasons out of date. Perhaps she was careful with her clothes, the sort of woman who can get real value from good things. She had some rings on her fingers, and possibly some bells on her toes, and a gold charm bracelet tinkled at her wrist. Her shoes had been costly when bought, but were now showing the wrinkles of age. Her make-up was natural and beautifully applied, but I was sure that the smudge on her right temple was a carefully disguised bruise. And there was one last fascinating detail: she was wearing a neck brace.

'Not a very popular person,' I said, indicating our latest arrival.

'You can say that again,' Lisa nodded. 'That's Carmel Lally.'

'I wouldn't piss on her if she was on fire,' Colette spat.

Before I could get embroiled in the ins and outs of the Lally intrigue, a bell rang and the double doors of the school opened and poured forth an army of little people. I located the two bobbing heads of the Street children, and pushed my way over to them.

'Hello there,' I said. 'I'm your chauffeur for today, so let's load up the car. Do we have a Dylan and a Kylie anywhere?'

Two kids close by nodded and I bundled them all off to the tank. There was a bit of commotion at the car, with neither of the visitors willing to get in, but I insisted and we hit the road for home. We also had an argument about who would get the front seat. In the end, No. 4 stayed where he was, paws on the dashboard, and the children sat along the back seat. I looked in the rearview mirror at the row of little heads and tuned loosely into their conversation. Dominick was doing his level best to annoy his sister.

'Mary, I'll be six soon. I'll be big then. You're not six, you're only four. You're a baby.'

'I am not a baby,' she wailed. 'Rose is a baby. I'm nearly five. I'm big.'

'Cut it out, you two,' I warned. 'I'm not having any of this fighting in my car.'

'It's not your car,' Dominick pointed out. 'It's our car.'

I had forgotten how logical kids can be. And he was right. But I couldn't let them see the whites of my eyes, otherwise I'd be overrun with bad behaviour.

'Well, I'm in charge, one way or the other, and I'm not going to put up with any of this carry-on from you lot. Especially in front of our visitors.'

The guests were very silent, so I tried to engage them.

'What would you like for tea, Dylan?'

'I want pasta,' he replied.

'We're not having pasta,' Mary said. 'We're having spaghetti.'

'Spaghetti is pasta,' Kylie chirped up.

'Yes, it is,' I agreed.

'Not spaghetti hoops,' Mary argued. The debate went into a bit of a loop then, with various philosophical pronouncements on pasta and its many guises.

'I don't want spaghetti hoops,' Kylie announced, finally. 'I want to go home.'

'Me too,' Dylan agreed.

'You will be going home later,' I explained. 'Your mummy will collect you from Dominick and Mary's house.'

'No, she won't,' Kylie said, tears welling. 'She doesn't know where we are.'

'I'm sure Dominick's mum has arranged it all with your mum,' I said. 'No need to cry.'

'We can have eggy bread, Kylie,' Mary said.

'I don't want eggy bread, I want pasta,' Kylie sobbed.

By any standards, this was excessive. I couldn't understand why she was so upset about what they were going to have for tea. But then again, I didn't have children, so I wasn't sure if this was commonplace. I was relieved when we hit the outskirts of Clontarf, where Angela and my brother Stephen lived. Now I could hand my cargo over to an expert.

Angela opened the door just as we drove in, and approached the car with Rose in her arms. I decanted the kids. She looked mildly puzzled.

'And who do we have here?' she asked.

I thought she was playing some sort of mock formal game, so I introduced the gang.

'Angela, I'd like you to meet Mary and Dominick, and Dylan and Kylie.'

She spluttered a little, looking from one visitor to the other, and said, 'I don't know how to put this to you, Leo, but you've got the wrong Dylan and Kylie.'

I looked at the impostors and felt my bowels loosen. I cursed Smokey Joe Street, and all of his seed and breed. This was the last time I would ever do a good turn. It was the last time I would be let for many years. Kidnapping. I was facing fifteen to life. And Mary Poppins could rest easy in her bed.

NINE

Strictly speaking, I should have been embracing the epitome of suburban life at that moment, rather than wondering how many pairs of socks to bring with me to prison. I had all the elements of standard happiness at my disposal here: comfortable home, noisy children frolicking, hopes and aspirations aplenty. There is still great pressure on anyone of my age to get settled and raise a family, to pass on genes, tradition, race memory (if you buy into that one), to strengthen blood lines, and sink into perpetuity. And some days, that all makes sense. But right now my shite magnet was pointed to top notch. The ley lines were clear. Any random crap could get to me without hindrance. Is this what having kids is all about? Especially if those kids are not your own, or even related? I didn't know. All I did know was that I would be lucky to walk the mean streets of Dublin ever again, cast as I was as the Child Catcher.

Back at the school, the lack of certain Dylans and Kylies

had been spotted. By their mother, as it happens. And when a similar set of Dylans and Kylies was located, in the playground, asking where they could hitch a lift to their tea appointment on the northside, someone had the nous to call Angela and give some Librium to the distressed and dispossessed mum. I was spared a trip to the cop shop. And a long spell indoors at the Republic's pleasure.

The real Dylan emerged from a car fifteen minutes later asking Angela, 'Have you sexified every man you know?'

'He's a bit of a card,' she explained.

As the impostors were readied for return to their rightful place, a row broke out, with complaints from the kidnapped about having been promised eggy bread and spaghetti hoops for tea. The first Dylan bitterly renamed me 'Mrs Liar Woman'. If I was possessed of a biological clock, it had stopped.

'Never a dull moment,' I said to Angela.

'No, but sometimes they sleep, and that can be nice,' she said. 'Of course, they never go away. You can marry them off and so on, but they'll always come back. Just multiplied, that's all.'

'I don't think I'm ready.'

'No one ever is,' she laughed. 'They really are worth it though. I highly recommend the whole experience.'

'I can't believe you're back in the denial club so soon after having a bloody Caesarean, for godssakes.'

'I have to admit that it wasn't the most pleasant. And poor old Stephen had to wait outside because it was a bit of an emergency in the end. They came out with Rose in some tinfoil and plopped her on a radiator, and didn't tell him whether I was alive or dead. Apparently there was another chap pacing the corridor, smoking, waiting for news of his other half. When Stephen said how awful it was, yer man agreed and said, "Two years ago they would have allowed you to smoke *in* there." '

She was then approached by a hairy mountain of a woman, representing the Vaginal Birth Action Group, who was most anxious to sign her up for a 'natural' birth next time. Angela left her in no doubt about whether there would be a 'next time', and assured her that she would perform the vasectomy herself if she had to.

'I wouldn't mention that to my mother if I were you,' I said. 'She'll go all Irish Mammy, and accuse you of cruel and unusual practices. And she'll take to calling Stephen "Poor Stephen". Your life would be a misery. What she doesn't know won't bother her.'

The small folk tucked into their grub on a low table in front of the television. A cartoon alien was shooting all and sundry with a laser, and that seemed acceptable to them. In the relative calm, I made some tea for myself and Angela. A minor skirmish occurred amongst the children, with complaints about people 'looking' at other people. It didn't last long, due to a tremendously loud explosion from the thermo-nuclear anti-hero on the box.

'There was a bit of aggro at the school today,' I said, reminded of earlier. 'Or rather, silent malice,' I added.

'Ah, that'll have been the Carmel Lally situation.'

'What's the story?'

'Well, there's a lot of bad feeling around, because Carmel slipped in the crèche a few weeks back, and she's looking for compensation. And if the crèche has to pay, it'll go bust and there'll be a lot of inconvenienced parents. Finding decent childcare is a nightmare.'

'But surely the crêche is insured?'

'Oh, yes, but as far as I know the premiums will go sky high, and it won't be worthwhile on a business level. It's a terrible situation. Some of the mums are very angry with Carmel. She's getting a lot of hassle.'

Once upon a time insurance companies had titles with Fidelity, Mutual and Providence in them. Now the closest you'd get is an Alliance, an altogether colder arrangement and one to be watched in a climate of suspicion; a 'who'll do who first?' world. The big buzzword now is Compensation, and there can be no 'Mutual' gain there.

My antennae started to twitch, shifting about for information. 'I might keep an eye on things,' I said.

'You just can't resist, can you?'

'No, I'm a very, very nosy person,' I admitted. 'I have to be, it's my job. I am a professional snoop, though that's not the greatest job description to be filling in on the census. So, I suppose I'll be on duty again tomorrow, if that's all right with you?'

'Absolutely. But do try to avoid any more criminal behaviour.'

Sound advice.

Angela seemed fidgety as we made for the door. I suspected an observation out of left field and braced myself accordingly.

'Leo, do you mind if I say something?'

'I don't know. You haven't said the something yet. Give it a whirl and then we'll see.'

'It's just that, mmm, how to put this . . .'

'Take a deep breath and let it out.'

'Right. You see, the thing is, it's not easy to stay with

someone indefinitely. Me and Stephen have formality here, a system: you know, marriage, kids. It's one way. But if you don't *have* to abide by the rules that we've taken on, why apply strictures to yourself that you don't need?' She halted, briefly. 'I don't think I expressed that very well, but I hope you get the gist of what I mean. Go out and have a good time, you don't owe anyone half as much as you think.'

'Thanks, Angela. And now that you've let it out, no, I didn't mind the something.'

Outside, the day was waning, and the suburb was bathed in a misty, milky light. It was also deceptive. As I walked to my car, the wind whipped up and bit me, the height of bad manners. And I couldn't retaliate, which was maddening. Even an attempt at hitting the wind back might have resulted in being locked up as a lunatic. I settled for bearing it a grudge. As I crossed the road to my car, a woman with a shaved head and a 'Free Tibet' sticker tried to run me down in her Mini. Car, that is. I didn't feel I deserved it. Perhaps she hadn't seen me, she was wearing sunglasses. Maybe I didn't interest her. Unfairly, I began to feel sour about Tibet. No. 4 barked at the empty road where the Mini had been.

'That's told her,' I said to him. 'Good for you.'

Then he cocked his leg against a small tree and piddled on it, and beyond, on to my shoe. As I watched the steam gently rise from my black suede pumps, I thought about going home to bed.

I glanced at my watch and realised that I could not justify taking to the duvet because a set of flimsy circumstances had got up my long nose. A sprinkling of adversity can usually be worked off with activity, mental or physical. And all the better if money can be a by-product. It was time to skirt by the Fledgling.

Even if I'd had only a vague notion of the whereabouts of the private hospital, I would have had no trouble locating it that day. As I approached, I could hear the noises of a gathered crowd from a street away. The entrance to the building was swamped by newspaper hacks and a television crew. Photographers snapped anyone coming or going, and a small Garda presence tried to shield transient patients and visitors. I picked No. 4 up in my arms and we inched our way through. I positioned us behind a number of journalists and eavesdropped shamelessly. For all the use that was. They were talking sport. I quickly tired of the argument as to whether or not a major English football club would relocate to Dublin (it seemed a daft idea to me) and asked one of them what was going on.

'Did you not see the *Herald* tonight?' came the incredulous counter reply.

I took this to be a hint that he worked for the paper.

'Eh, no, I've only just come out,' I tried.

'There's a story brewing about shifty practices in this place.'

'Who are you waiting for?'

'Anyone we can get,' he said. 'Preferably the main man.'

'That's whatshisname, O'Donnell or O'Donoghue or something, isn't it?'

'O'Donoghue, yeah. And he's up to his neck in it this time.'

'How do you mean?'

'Read the papers and you'll find out,' he snapped, effectively ending our dialogue. Thanks for nothing, pal, I thought.

★ ★ ★

I looked around at the gathered public. Some were curious bystanders, some were protesting. One woman held up a placard which carried only one word: 'Disgrace'. Suddenly there was a surge forward from the reporters. Microphones were thrust into the face of a woman who had just left the Fledgling, others barked questions. The camera crew jockeyed with the rest for position. She held up both hands for silence, which she got, then began to read from a prepared statement.

'The Fledgling Hospital and Trust has provided excellent medical care for over a decade. We are proud of our service. We are also renowned for our research into fertility and childbirth, for which we have been commended many times at national and international levels. Our staff is of the highest calibre. Recently, unfounded stories and allegations have been given unjustified prominence in the country's media. It is not our intention to join in this circus. We have nothing to hide, and we are certain that any investigation into our affairs will prove this. Until we are vindicated, we will make no further statements.'

She surveyed the crowd for a reaction, then added, 'Ladies and gentlemen, we have patients inside who are distressed by this commotion. Please go home. There is no story here.' She gave a saccharine contortion of the face and retreated. I bet Michael O'Donoghue felt a shiver run riot on his spine as the management hung him out to dry.

The protesters began to jeer. It was then that I saw a familiar figure, half hidden in a nearby doorway. She was leaning against the doorjamb and sobbing openly. I edged closer. Some jostling in the crowd knocked me and No. 4 into a metal barrier, and when we extricated ourselves the woman was gone. I searched right and left along the avenues of exit and entrance available, but she had disappeared. I recognised her, though; she was Mrs Bernadette Flood, and she had been inconsolable.

TEN

'Barry,' I said, 'be very certain that I *will* kill you if you so much as look at these loaves. They're on order, they're not for us, and most particularly they are not for Coleman Pearse, whom I have every suspicion I'll encounter in this very house later on.'

For no good reason, Mick Nolan chose that moment to butt in and stick up for Barry. 'You should have baked two of everything,' he said. 'Preparation, Street. Look ahead.' I remembered he'd always loved his food. 'Grub first, then ethics,' I muttered, quoting some writer or other.

There was no reason for Barry to complain. I had been making my own brown bread for a few weeks now, and modifying the recipe with each attempt. It was disgustingly healthy stuff and was keeping our jaws exercised and our innards clear, laced as it was with all manner of roughage. We called it the 'Dublin Brick' and at that time, it was the most regular thing about our lives.

111

As Barry and No. 4 curled up on the couch to enjoy guests thumping the heads off one another on Ricki Lake, I sat at the kitchen table for a coffee and a think. Snubby jumped on to my lap, and began to knead my thighs with her front paws. I hadn't the heart to stop her piercing my fatty deposits; with any luck the prickly massage might help shift some of the cellulite decorating those legs. I realised that the cats were feeling neglected because of the palaver of settling the dog into the household. I gave The Snub an extra special hug and kiss and was rewarded with loud purring. She also stopped hurting me for a moment. Noel sat on the chair next to me and Bridie boldly roamed the table. I let her, mindful of my run-in with Smokey Joe earlier. For all I knew, he'd been in touch on the feline bush telegraph and my name was muck here too.

I wondered at the dynamic between the three. Generally, they ignored one another, and we had peace. Now they had a tacit agreement to band together against the common foe. Bridie was a rinky-tinky-tinky cat, dancing like a kitten in a cartoon. Snubby was a toothless wonder with a placid nature and a strangely pungent bottom. Noel was the closest to macho, but even he had a wimpy habit: he sucked my hair, having been weaned too early from his mother. I looked at him now with his lovely black and white markings and a dark bandit mask about his eyes, and for no particular reason, I was reminded of Andy Raynor. He had never sucked my hair, but there were other areas of me that he had applied himself to, and I almost came in my pants as I savoured those memories.

I was squirming happily from buttock to buttock when the telephone rang. God must have been watching me because Father Con Considine was on the line, in town and on the loose for the night. 'Let's hook up,' he said. I heard Barry laugh in the next room and had a brainwave.

'Con, how do you fancy an evening of enlightenment and pints? Barry is working on the Literary Pub Crawl and I haven't been yet. It's an evening of literary drinking.'

'Or literally drinking.'

'That's the one. Are you in?'

'Done. We should hunt out Ciara junior and bring her along.'

'Actually, she's doing some work for me tonight. I'll explain later.'

I hung up with happy feeling in my heart. Second time today that a man had set me a-flutter, though in very different ways. Barry gave another chortle, and I reddened slightly. What was I up to, making dates with rogues and priests, when I had my own lad here at home? I did a Scarlett O'Hara, and promised myself that I'd think about it tomorrow.

'Barry,' I shouted, 'you've just sold two for tonight.' Then I had another thought. 'Make that three,' I added, dialling my dad to ask him along too.

'A what?'

'A pub crawl, Dad.'

'Yeah, yeah, I know that bit. But what was the rest?'

'Well, the two actors do bits from books by writers that hung around Dublin back whenever.'

'Sure what's the point of that? Walking around the town like gobshites, or worse tourists, instead of gettin' settled into a grand snug somewhere for a feed of pints. Hah?'

'It's supposed to be great fun,' I protested.

'Fun? Ah, no, I don't think so.'

'Right, well, I just thought you might enjoy it, that's all. Fair enough if you don't want to come.'

'Hold your horses there now. I didn't say I wasn't coming, I said it was a gobshite idea. Different thing altogether. And sure, I suppose I might as well have a look anyway. It'll make a change to see that other fella actually doin' somethin' with himself.'

I looked guiltily at Barry, who was oblivious to the trial ahead. He was laughing merrily as two of the television guests threw punches and slung insults. 'No way,' I could hear him say. Way, Barry.

'I saw that Brendan Behan once, you know,' John Street was saying. 'He was roarin' in at some poor barman that had probably thrown him out. He was as drunk as a lord. Terrible, the state of him.'

'Great, Daddy, you can tell me all about it later,' I said, and arranged to meet him at the set-off point.

If I had a pound for every person in Dublin who claimed to have known or seen or had a drink with Brendan Behan, Patrick Kavanagh or Myles na gCopaleen, I'd be a rich woman. Not to mention the people James Joyce owed money to.

I had barely replaced the phone in its cradle when it rang again. Maeve had something taped from earlier.

'It's nothing unusual, I'm afraid. Just some breathing, with a background of chat and music.'

'I'll drop by and have a listen before you leave for the theatre,' I said. 'Then I'm off into town for a little armchair drama. I'm going on the Crawl with a priest friend of mine and my dad.'

'What I wouldn't give to be a barfly for that one,' Maeve

said. 'Barry will earn his money tonight.'

I was uneasy that I had not heard from Ciara, nor seen her at the Fledgling earlier. I tried her mobile but it went straight to voicemail, so I did what any normal person would do and left an urgent and worried message asking her to phone me with any news, or indeed views, on life, the universe, anything, but mostly the O'Donoghue case. She later played it back for me, and I sounded not only needy but incoherent. She had the best of times whipping me with that recording for weeks afterwards.

I had time to spare so I made for the bedroom I shared with Barry to check out an outfit for the following night. It seemed, absurdly, to be a small act of betrayal, so I headed back down the stairs to explain the situation to my boyfriend.

'Sure. Whatever.'

'You don't mind then?'

'Why would I mind? I'll be working, so I couldn't have gone with him.'

I laughed uneasily at his joke.

'Well, as long as it's no bother, I'll tell him I can go along,' I said.

Why the petty lie here? I had already agreed to accompany Andy, so why shroud it in fake approval from Barry? I didn't exactly need his permission anyway. I was a big girl and could decide where to go, and who with, all by myself. I was acting like a woman with a guilty secret. But I didn't have one, so why the subterfuge? Why the need for some sort of cloudy justification?

And, in my perfidy and double standards, I couldn't decide whether I was flattered that Barry was not in the least jealous, or if I meant so little to him that he couldn't even drum that up.

I beat a retreat before my mouth took charge and made a pig's arse of the now mountainous molehill.

My office is neat, of necessity. It's where I first meet most of my clients, and their impressions of the place have to be good. I like it to look reliable, approachable, well run, and not a tip which suggests that it belongs to some nutty professor. To keep it like that is my own business, of course, as Mrs Mack is *un*reliable, *un*approachable, *badly* run and wouldn't recognise a tip if it came up and bit her on the bum. Scotch that, the only sort of tip she knows is of the money variety, and even then she's fussy about what she'll accept.

Home is a different world, not least because it harbours so much wildlife. And most of the time, I'm afraid to open the wardrobe door in case I'm crushed beneath the accoutrements of my life which have no business being in there, or stored anywhere else for that matter. Much of the stuff involved was rescued from my parents' when room was being made for Peter, Anne and Lucy who now share their house. It was a peculiar time, to see my childhood dismantled, ready for the chucking. In a fit of sentimentality, I grabbed the lot and moved it to the painfully inadequate storage space of 11, The Villas. It never did get tagged and bagged, just shoved into this and that cupboard, amongst clothes and shoes and old coats past their best, ready for the never never of nostalgia whenever it would strike.

In today's case, the past took things into its own hands and struck me: as I rummaged for a decent pair of shoes, which were a distant memory in their own right, a naked

Barbie doll spilled out at my feet, followed by some ancient magazines with pictures of long-forgotten pop stars with dodgy hairdos, and veiled references to sex; things are a lot more graphic these days. I grimaced at the fact that my body had not once achieved Barbie shape, and never would; but on a happier note, hair flicks were unlikely to return. A jewellery casket in the shape of a wooden heart opened to reveal a lack of treasures. And then came some school yearbooks. I opened up the pictures page of 1984, and there we were: Lisa Farrelly, Colette O'Brien and Leo Street, with three identical, atrocious perms, and the wide happy smiles of the hopeful, who don't yet have to worry about earning a living or finding someone for reciprocal love and cherishment. I sighed with resignation as I stacked the items of a past that could never be relived, and went in search of a cardboard box to put some order into the makings of a private investigator who was formally the proud owner of that truly awful hairstyle.

I began to wonder why I was not still friends with the girls I went to school with? Why had I not kept in touch? The answer was in my work. The world of a PI is a solitary one for the most part. You keep to the shadows, you skulk about, you don't strut, you never draw undue attention to yourself. You keep your clothes plain and your hair and make-up unremarkable. You blend. You never expose yourself unnecessarily. People talk, and soon everyone knows who you are and what you do. And if we are all separated by only a few degrees from any random person we meet during a day, no amount of disguise will allow the space needed for a detective to function.

Downstairs erupted into commotion. Barry had opened the door, with loud delight, to a roaring Coleman Pearse.

After spurious chatter, intermingled with various 'you talkin' to me?'s, 'get up, you hump', and dodgy impressions of Al Pacino and Marlon Brando, they began to sing 'There's No Business like Show Business' with impressive lung power. No. 4 added his one and tuppence worth, and was surprisingly musical, I thought. When I looked out of the bedroom window into the back garden, I could see the cats taking to the hills in disgust. Then a low hum began, joined eventually by the thuds of two grown men jumping up and down. A chant of 'me, me, me, I, I, I, ego, ego, ego' resounded through the house: the thesps were doing their warm-up for tonight's show. Self-regarding sounds, apparently, work the mouth best. When the air cleared and uneasy calm descended once more, I chanced down the stairs.

Coleman was fashioning another crude rhyme on the fridge door with the magnets. How this would prepare him for sharing the works of some of our finest Irish writers with a bunch of strangers, I had no idea. Certainly, if the verse in question was anything to go by, their influence on him had been minimal. 'Harass is just one word,' I told him as I passed by. He swore a little under his breath, and rearranged some letters to form the words 'bad' and 'ass', but the magic was lost and he abandoned his project.

'So, Coleman, you're in charge tonight. I hope we'll be a good audience.'

'Every audience is a good one,' he said, sententiously. 'And although this will undoubtedly be more special, because of your own lustrous presence, I'd like to think that we always give of our best. We are such stuff as dreams are made on.'

Well, that sorted me out. You had to hand it to him, he talked the talk.

'I heard your warm up. I suppose it's important to do all that and keep in shape?' I said.

'Oh, yes, my body is an instrument,' he acknowledged.

'Yes, it *is* a tool,' I continued, childishly.

Barry could see that we were going nowhere in a hurry with this line of banter, so he butted in. 'I thought you had to go by Maeve's before hitting town?'

'Yeah, yeah, I'm outta here.'

Coleman suddenly clapped his hands and made for the sideboard with the words, 'Ah, supper.'

'Oh, no, you don't,' I yelped, flinging myself on him. 'Those loaves are for a customer, and if you so much as look at them, I'll rip your arms off and post them to China.'

'Get away from me, she-thing,' he shrieked melodramatically, raising his hands to protect his face (his livelihood).

Barry wedged himself between us, prying us apart in the process. I flailed about a bit, trying to make contact with some soft bit of Coleman's flesh. I snarled, for effect, hoping for a suggestion of lioness protecting her cubs. Elegant it was not. Dignified it was not. I did feel it was necessary, however, because Coleman can and will eat his own body-weight at any meal, though his physique does not reflect this; another unfairness on the part of men. He was taken aback enough to ask, 'Are you having your period Leo? Because this is irrational behaviour, even for you.'

Even for me? The cheek!

'Let me at him,' I said to Barry. 'It's time he was taken out.'

Barry laughed and banished his acting partner to the sofa.

'I'll put these out of harm's way,' he said, moving the loaves to one of the kitchen presses. Then he turned to me and asked, 'Are you, anyway?'

119

'Am I what?'

'Having your period?'

I really couldn't tell if he was joking or not, so I gave him a sharpish kick to the shin and headed off. As I passed Coleman, he shook his head and pronounced that I was 'one feisty lady'. So I booted him too; no point in assaulting the head area, as there was little or nothing in there. I felt infantile and fulfilled all at once. And who says that violence is not the answer?

At the door I stopped. 'Oh, nearly forgot,' I said, sweetly. 'Break a leg.'

ELEVEN

Maeve was right, there wasn't much of note on the tape. And even more disappointing was that no number was displayed for the caller.

'Don't be too despondent,' she said. 'I feel a lot better now that something is being done about the problem. It's a relief to know that you're on the case.'

'I'm supposed to be the one reassuring you,' I pointed out, ruefully. 'At least I've heard it for myself now. Whoever it is seems to be watching television or listening to the radio, so that narrows it down to some three to four million people. I'll check on everyone who's got a TV licence first, and if that doesn't turn something up, we'll go back to the drawing board.'

Maeve looked suitably shocked, so I added, 'Joke.'

She smacked her palm to her forehead and said, 'Twit! Leo, please don't tell anybody I was thick enough to fall for that. I'd never live it down.'

'It'll cost you, but your deadly secret is safe with me.'

'How about I make it up to you in some way by leaving you in to town? I've got a cab ordered, with Peter's lot.'

My brother, Peter Street, is a rascally coachman with Northways Taxi Company. They are now much patronised, in all senses, by ourselves and our friends.

Something about this was trying to push to the fore in my brain. An ill-fashioned thought battled to be heard. And then I had it.

'Maeve, do they have your home number?'

'Yes. They'll ring if there's a delay or whatever.'

We both paused, weighing this information up.

'Before we lose the run of ourselves,' I said, 'I'm not, for one moment, suggesting that it's someone at the base. And then again it could be, so I'm not ruling it out either. What I am suggesting, though, is that lots of companies would have this number, even though you're ex-directory. Think about it. Do you get takeaways delivered?'

She nodded.

'Did you fill in your number on the forms for electricity and gas and the telephone?'

She nodded some more.

'So, you see, your number's no secret to anyone with access to any of the above. We'll keep listening for the moment, and I'd like you to make a list of any of the companies you think might have got your number in this way. You can stop nodding now.'

She gave two more and that was that.

We were about to leave when the phone rang again. The recorder clicked into life, and Maeve answered. Through the speakers came the sounds of distant, tinny music and heavy, laboured breathing. I didn't dare inhale myself, as if that might break the eerie spell in the room.

'Who is this?' my friend asked.

The breathing became agitated, then a long hissing of the word 'Bitch!' seeped around us. It was impossible to tell whether a man or a woman had spoken. Suddenly, a cackle of laughter burst through and the line went dead. Maeve put the receiver back in its cradle and burst into tears.

I ran to the machine, but there was no caller number displayed, not that I really expected a break like that. I put my arms around Maeve and tried to comfort her. The situation had escalated and I began to feel angry. And when I'm angry, I like to think that I get things done.

'You know, now it's time to call in the cops,' I said.

'No, no. I don't think there's any need for that. Yet. Let's see how you do, okay?'

'Are you sure? This seems like a crazy to me. Whoever it is might be ill or dangerous, we don't know. I don't want you taking risks.'

'No, I'll be fine. I'm sorry about the tears, it's just a release of tension. I want you to continue.'

'Promise that you'll call the police if it gets in any way worse than this?'

'Right. As long as you promise not to tell Mum what's going on.'

'You got it.'

We travelled into town in silence, which was hardly surprising. I left Maeve at the stage door with assurances that everything was under control. I told myself to make sure that it was. She agreed to ask Mark Rolands to stay for the foreseeable, and that raised a smile.

'It's not exactly a hardship, is it?' she said.

I kissed her on both cheeks and waited until she was safely signed in. Then I proceeded to worry a lot as I set off for my night on the tiles.

Grafton Street is the main shopping drag just south of the River Liffey. It is a hive of activity at all hours, and tonight was no exception. I was slightly early and considered going into Bewley's Café to be ignored by the waitresses. Instead I did some window shopping and listened to the city's buskers; two young lads were murdering a compilation of the latest U2 songs, and close by a girl in an evening gown was lashing out a bad version of 'Annie's Song' on a flute, which is not to suggest that there can ever be a good version. In a doorway, a mime artist was noiselessly trying to escape from a very ungeometric cube.

I wondered at the fact that I now had a friend who was a Catholic priest. I am in no way religious, in spite or because of being moulded by the nuns. Gun to my head, I would probably confess to thinking religion a lot of mumbo-jumbo invented to make money and assuage mankind's vanity all in one fell swoop. That's the cynical me with the weapon of destruction held against my temple. Somewhere inside there's another woman who wants to give every philosophy and notion a chance. The cynical one says the other one is a wimp and is hedging her bets. I stay out of the argument because it can get pretty nasty between those two.

It so happens that Con's job is being a Catholic priest; he doesn't foist this unnecessarily on anyone. In the same way, I don't normally draw the public's attention to the fact that I'm a private eye. As a person, he is kind and funny, with a maddening line in puns and the quiet decency of a man

124

who knows right from wrong and is prepared to act on it. I hope he hooks up with Sister Mel when he gets to heaven, and that they have a mighty laugh. I'll undoubtedly be roasting somewhere else, unable to join them.

I stopped outside the 'Dog and Divil' which was the kick off point for the Crawl. I was mindful that I hadn't heard from Ciara, so I texted her a message; the last thing she needed was her phone ringing if she was close to Michael O'Donoghue. I tapped in 'r u ok?' – 'yes' – 'n e news?' – 'no' – 'u sure?' – 'GO AWAY'. She seemed to be managing fine.

My father, John Street, was happily planted in front of his drink when I entered the pub. My heart warmed to the sight of his faded brown hair, speckled with the salt and pepper of age, style unchanged since the fifties, though not too bouffant now. His face bore the rosy glow of a man who enjoys a game of golf, a good dinner and a brace of pints thereafter. His familiar shape perched as if to the barstool born. He leaned the worn elbows of a green tweed jacket familiarly on the counter of the bar; you've leaned on one, you've leaned on 'em all. He had already made friends with the barman, vital for anyone who takes their drinking seriously. They were now on first-name terms.

'A pint of plain is your only man,' he declared as I approached, quoting Flann O'Brien, an accomplished drinker himself in his day. Then he raised his glass in a salute and downed the first half in one swallow. 'A grand pint, Joe,' he assured the publican. 'A darlin' pint,' he continued, more for my benefit this time. So he's brushed up on his O'Casey too, I thought. Or rather, dredged up the bits and pieces he could remember. I was dying to find out if he had any Joyce stowed away.

'Joe, this is my daughter, Leo. To tell you the truth, I'm afraid to order for her. I don't know what the young ones are drinkin' these days.'

'I'll have the same as yourself,' I said.

'A grand choice now,' my father said. 'But it's a terrible price here in town. That same pint in Kilbride's is tenpence cheaper. Would you credit that, hah? Two bob in the difference. Sure it's daylight robbery.'

I was waiting on a rant about how it's not right for women to drink pints at all anyway, but he resisted. My dad likes to wind me up on that and the issue of 'women drivers'; he takes great pleasure in remaining militantly unreconstructed.

We were nicely settled when the doorway darkened, filled as it was by the vast bulk of Father Con Considine. In keeping with our evening, he was stately and plump like the bauld Buck Mulligan himself. He was thus at any time of the day, in fact.

'You have disgraced yourselves,' he said, echoing William Butler Yeats in a famous address to a rioting Abbey audience.

'Again,' we chorused.

Con was in the disguise of civilian clothing, and did not match his pint of stout as priests and nuns normally do. He was looking well, all the same. I introduced the men, and it was clear that they approved of one another. Then he got to his news.

'I seem to be in for a transfer,' he said. 'They need someone to head up a parish near the canal with a lot of drug and prostitution problems.' He laughed a moment, then said, 'Apparently that's me.'

'Do you get any say in where you're sent?' I asked.

'Oh, no,' he replied. 'I go where I'm told. I wouldn't mind

this post though. I've grown a bit weary of the local carping where I am now. I feel a bit bogged down.' He laughed again, shrugging his shoulders and shaking his head. 'There are times when I have to remind myself of my Christian beliefs instead of descending into small-town bitchery.' He finished his drink quickly, slaking a long day's thirst, and we squeezed in another while the tour group expanded.

'Hearing confessions must be a hoot,' my father said.

The priest smiled. 'It can be a little too interesting at times.'

'Didn't one of our neighbours get excommunicated or something for hearing confessions once in the local church?' I asked my dad.

'That can happen,' Con acknowledged. 'You have to leave all of that to us professionals.'

'It was Maurice O'Leary,' Dad said, remembering.

'Yes,' I agreed. 'He was eleven years old at the time.'

'Rodents,' my father said.

'Pardon?'

'Rodents at three o'clock.'

I was puzzled. Then I noticed a small knot of college types in a corner to our right. The Daddy has a thing about students, and believes that if you see one crossing the road, it's as well to run them down, thereby putting them, and society, out of considerable misery. He has also been known to expound the theory that they are God's way of telling us there are too many people in the world.

'He hates students,' I explained to Con.

'Ah,' said the priest, unwilling or unable to go further.

We were saved a scene by the arrival of Barry and Coleman, and quick as 'get out' the show had begun.

127

The actors debated the merits of going or staying until Godot arrived. Although the tramps in the play stay put, again and again and again, we headed out on to the mean streets of Dublin – or should that be that two mean Streets sallied forth, along with a handful of other culture seekers? Outside Davy Byrne's on Duke Street, we were exhorted to eat gizzards washed down with a fine burgundy, and I began to wonder if Hannibal Lecter was a fan of James Joyce. I decided that he probably was. As luck would have it, a drunk who had made a great deal of pissing in a nearby doorway, followed us shouting 'shite 'n onions' as his contribution to the tour; everyone in this town is a Joycean, it seems. He got fed up when we hit Grafton Street thirty seconds later and lurched off in the direction of St Stephen's Green where he lived happily ever after, as in all of the best stories. The last we heard of him was a distant shout of, 'Yez are only a shower of hoor's melts 'n anyway.'

The Dublin Pub and Literary Crawl was as camp as a row of Eurovision Song Contests. It afforded two performers the opportunity to show off vocal and physical skills to an excess that bordered on over-the-top; or perhaps it was just this pair. They blossomed in our attention, and that of the many passers-by who stopped to stare. We were halted outside McDaid's, listening to a piece by Patrick Kavanagh, when I spotted a woman I thought I knew moving towards the swish Westbury Hotel. It could have been Colette O'Brien, if Colette was blonde, wore glasses and short-skirted business suits over high heels. Before I had a chance to check out this döppelganger, she disappeared into the lobby and out of sight. I was back to Irish Literature and the promise of another glass of porter.

There is nothing more attractive than to see someone you love do their job well. I had been to a few plays in which Barry had starred and I knew he was talented. But he had been through a lean patch of work recently and I had almost forgotten how good he was. Outside Trinity College, he was telling me of Oscar Wilde's trials and tribulations, and warming the cockles of many of my tender body parts. Every so often he shot a beatific smile my way, and I lit up like a candle.

We chattered happily, as a group and in our little sub-sections. My father was anxious to tell us about the various barstool poets he knew in his local. One of them wrote poems that actually rhymed, which my dad pointed out was where modern verse had gone so horribly wrong, in his opinion. Con said that parts of the Bible were as poetic as anything by Keats or Shelley, and the *Song of Solomon* was positively racy, with breasts likened to two goats in the moonlight and suchlike. I told him that I'd look up some of the aforementioned, as part of my spiritual education. My father said to let him know if they were 'any good'.

We made for the Palace Bar on Fleet Street where both actors treated us to Flann O'Brien's tale of a man becoming a bicycle, the various frictions between man and bike swapping ions and atoms from one to the other. I looked at my dad and surmised that he would, in time, become a pint of Guinness, if this theory were to hold true. As for Con, he would be an angel; but then again, he was one already, so no change there. I linked them both in happiness, with a little help from the brewery.

My own literary background consisted of a steady diet of Enid Blyton in my early years, followed by Nancy Drew and Cherry Ames, Student Nurse. In all of these, sleuthing was to the fore. Though there was an argument which said that what I really wanted was Nancy's perfectly coiffed red hair, and the yellow silk clothes which set her looks off so well. Nancy did more for the Ginger Brigade than she has ever been given credit for. I moved on to Harold Robbins as a teenager, which meant lots of steamy sex – perhaps it was time to return to him. We were force fed obscure Gaelic writers at school, and Mr William Shakespeare who, as every street scholar knows, was an Irishman in reality. There are still some counties in Ireland which speak his English. I pondered suggesting his inclusion in the Crawl to the lads.

As we crossed O'Connell Bridge, a sub-human howl announced Coleman's rendition of 'The Auld Triangle', *à la* Brendan Behan. The herd stopped in its tracks to savour the spectacle. As he strangled the jingles and the jangles of that triangle, my brain begged for mercy in my skull. Top marks for effort, close to zero points for artistic endeavour. When he was done we moved on, as did the curious throng of onlookers we had acquired. I looked into the murky waters of the Anna Livia Plurabelle for response, but she gave none, which was probably for the best.

There was something about our inexorable march north-wards which was bugging me. I hadn't thought that the Crawl followed this route. We stopped outside the Abbey Theatre, where Barry gave us Yeats, telling us to tread softly for we trod on his dreams, then announcing that our last port of call was the handily situated pub across the road. Well, of course it was; the two actors were now right beside their bus stop for home, and only steps away from a handy taxi rank, and all it had taken was a song and two extra poems to get in there. Coleman warned us of the perils of

130

drink. 'It is both a carrot and a stick,' he said, and, laughing, we all trooped to an upstairs lounge devoid of other customers. More pints and chat filled the agenda, life stories were swapped, jokes told and travel anecdotes related.

In a lull, Mary Lou Pheiffer, of Pennsylvania, Illinois, stood up to share a moment with us. We hushed to silence, awaiting her gem. She cleared her throat, gave a short hum, then began reciting aloud:

> My wound will not heal
> Now.
> Though it must,
> In time.
> I am woman.
>
> Heal me, Moon.
> Heal me, Life.
> Heed me.
>
> A wound.
> I am wounded.
> A woman wounded.
> The wound unhealing,
> Until middle age.

She nodded and sat down. The silence was palpable, painful, as we weighed up our responses as individuals and as a group. I am sure Mary Lou thought it profound, and so it was, in a way.

Then my father's voice rang out, 'Now for you, hah? Mighty altogether. Good woman yourself.' The crowd gave an almost animal cry of relief. We clapped our hands rapturously, the applause as much for my dad and his rescue as Mary Lou and her art. She held her hand up in self-deprecation. 'I am a mere wordsmith,' she said. 'A drone.'

'And that is what this night is all about,' declared Coleman. 'On behalf of myself and my partner, Barry Agnew, I would like to thank you all for coming along, and do tell your friends all about us.'

He grabbed his drink and sat beside the two prettiest girls he could find. I watched with curiosity over the next twenty minutes as he tried, valiantly but in vain, to get off with either of them. He was clearly puzzled.

'What do you think the problem is there?' I asked Barry.

He began to laugh. 'We live in politically correct times, Leo. I don't think Coleman has copped to it yet, but when he called me his partner, the girls automatically assumed he meant it in a gay way. He won't do that again in a hurry.'

Of course Coleman without a lady friend meant Coleman en route to 11, The Villas, but I let it pass and savoured his increasingly desperate attempts to win the hearts of the young ladies. When those didn't work, he moved on to the other older models, to no avail, and eventually admitted defeat.

Con had to leave. 'I'm staying by the Pro Cathedral down the road with a worry wart who wouldn't give me a key to get in. I'd better set a good example and go.' He shrugged on his jacket and knocked back the last of his whiskey. 'Isn't it great to think that you can get spiritual sustenance in two such different public houses, and so close together?'

'When you put it that way,' agreed my dad. He lifted his glass in salutation for the umpteenth time that night. 'Con, we'll see you again soon, please God.'

'Please God,' said the priest. 'Leo, I'll phone you when I know about the transfer. Take care, and ease up on yourself the odd time. There are plenty of people who'll give you a hard time in life without any provocation, particularly Ciara if she's given her head.' We laughed at the truth of this. He smothered me in a bear hug, shook hands with Barry and Coleman, waved to the rest of the stragglers, and left.

'Time to go home time,' I announced.

'Better call the bollocks so,' my father said. This was a charming reference to his eldest son, my brother Peter, taxi man *extraordinaire*. On a deeper level it was a term of endearment on my father's part, but a stranger would be hard pressed to spot this. In exchange for a set fee, somewhat lower than the going rate, Peter would leave us home, and put up with a lot of old guff on the way. This makes him patron saint of the travelling Streets.

Although he was in the area, my dad still managed to squeeze in that last pint for the road before Peter arrived. There was nothing back-seat about my father's driving; he planted himself up front in order to be of maximum annoyance to my brother on the journey. With John Street issuing orders, I could be certain of shedding Coleman at his own house, so the trip was pure pleasure for me. I interrupted my father's flow only to make sure that he knew precisely where we were dropping Coleman. And so we had the villainy of city publicans and the price they were charging for a pint, how the country had gone to the bad and the state of the roads was a national disgrace, and how all of this was basically down to every living taxi driver, but mostly my brother. The last twist of reasoning required to make that point work was non-existent, but my dad was happy with the sound of his own voice, and so were we.

I am a city girl. I like the look of Dublin day or night, with the exception of the anonymous modern obstructions so beloved of town planners these days. But when push comes to shove, I have to express a preference for the night-time town. Perhaps it's a penchant for neon and flashing lights. Whatever the reason, it is the time most conducive to my movie-like dreams and imaginings. It can also lull a person into a feeling that these are gentler hours, whereas of course the opposite is true. The cloak of darkness has shielded many bad deeds. Happily, I was not following any of the night's skulduggerers or duggerees, so I snuggled into Barry instead. His arm wound around me and he gave my shoulder a squeeze. I looked up at him and he kissed me lightly on the nose. I had a warm feeling in my groin as I smiled and looked back out of the window.

We were stopped at a traffic lights in Fairview, and I was giving the other cars the once over; some habits are hard to break. 'Isn't that bizarre?' I said.

'What is?' Peter asked.

'You remember Colette O'Brien who I went to school with? Well, I haven't seen her in years, but today I met her at the Model School when I was collecting the kids, then I saw her double in town tonight, and now there she is herself in that car in the opposite lane.' She was putting on a jacket, as it happened.

'I see her quite a bit at nights,' Peter said. 'I think she must have a job somewhere.'

We gave a short beep on the horn, but either she didn't hear or didn't recognise us, because we got no return signal.

I tried really hard not to show my merriment as Coleman loped up his driveway. I congratulated him on the evening's entertainment, but it did little to lift his spirits. It must have been a long time since he'd got home to his own house from the Crawl without a companion for his bed. Whenever he had been unsuccessful before, he would end up at mine, where he could talk shite till the cows came home, or more pertinently this cow, Leo Street. He played his moment at the door beautifully, allowing us time to admire his wry and tired unhappiness, above which he would undoubtedly rise. Then we were treated to a plucky wave of the hand, a jaunty jut of the chin and he was gone.

'Is that fella a bit of a half-wit?' my dad wanted to know.

'Nah,' I said. 'Things didn't work out the way he'd hoped tonight, that's all'

'Mmm,' my father grunted, unconvinced.

Barry and I were next to be decanted. There was an uncivilised spat about the fare, which my father 'won', leaving Peter the biggest loser.

'Call me tomorrow and we'll sort something out,' I told my brother. 'And try not to kill him before you get home.'

'Or after,' Barry added.

'Jesus, Mary and Joseph, am I ever goin' to get to me bed?' the Daddy barked. 'I swear to God I'd be quicker walkin'. Would you ever rev up and fuck off or they'll have search parties out for us.'

Peter threw his eyes to heaven and drove away.

'I really enjoyed tonight,' I said to Barry as we climbed the six wide steps to the house. I thought I might add those to the lottery list I'd been compiling. So far I had four, five, six, and why not eleven as it was now staring at me from the front door? Two more numbers to go and I was sorted and would never have to work again.

'Your dad was in great form,' Barry said, as much in wonderment as anything else. 'He didn't even have a go at me. He was way too busy paying attention or chatting with your friend Con.'

'You don't think he's finally accepted you?'

'No. Can't happen. Not possible. It's completely against all the rules of Fathers and How They Treat Their Daughters' Live-in Boyfriends.'

I had to concede this point.

'Those legs are doing something evil to me,' he said, running his hand along the outside of my thigh. As he pressed the evil something against my buttocks I opened the door and let us into the small hallway.

'Lucy says they're hose beast carry-on,' I told him.

'She's not wrong,' he murmured, as he kissed me, running his tongue along my teeth. We both tasted of beer and desire.

I came up for air. 'Hold that thought,' I said. 'I'll deal with any calls, then you'll have my undivided attention.'

He sped up the stairs, warning me that he wouldn't wait forever.

I checked on the animals, who were all present and correct. There was some evidence of a light contretemps, but they were settled into an accord now, so I didn't make a fuss; I had other more urgent matters to attend to. I had just one phone message, from Ciara.

'Secret Agent Number One reporting to management. Boring night, in spite of the press coverage. Nothing that won't wait till tomorrow morning. Talk to you then.'

There didn't seem much in there to suggest that I lose sleep over work that night so I rushed to the bathroom and performed some quick ablutions, checking for spots in the mirror and giving all of my relevant pits a wipe of a fragrant cloth. Then it was my turn to take the stairs at a leap. I presented my breathless self at the bedroom door. Barry gave a lazy smile from the bed. I undressed slowly, keeping as many of the sticking-out parts of my body as possible out of sight. I climbed under the duvet, enjoying the warmth he had created. Then I moulded myself to his familiar shape and we enjoyed a lingering caress before he moved his kisses along my throat and downwards. I writhed in delicious agony. After two or three minutes his movements seemed to get slower and his breathing more regular, so I stopped a moment. It was then that I realised he had fallen asleep on my chest. I was pinned on my back, like a bug in a rug.

TWELVE

I could not believe that the workmen were back on the road. They had spent so many weeks building the speed ramps, we thought we'd had our lifetime's share of grandi-fication and would never see them again. Two jackhammers drilled incessantly and though I tried my best to ignore them, I finally gave in and opened my eyes to the realisa-tion that the Kango hammers involved were myself and the still sleeping body pinning me to the mattress. My throat was raw from snoring. My sinuses were dry as the Sahara. It was 7.42 a.m. and my life was on pause, so I stared at the ceiling awhile. A stain in the shape of Australia was spread-ing from one corner to the rhythmic housetrack of Barry Agnew. What the hell were we doing together if our arrangement was clearly a matter of companionship now rather than romance?

Australia began to distort before my exhausted eyes, so I abandoned it for the sanctuary of the kitchen. I spent the journey down the stairs repeatedly reaching for the cord to tie my dressing gown, but it was nowhere to be found. I gave up and wafted about like a tragic Victorian heroine, though the eggy yellowness of the robe undercut the image somewhat.

The kitchen was a chorus of complaint. Top of the list was that No. 4 had decided Noel's basket was better than his own. Well, of course he had. I mean, where's the fun in sleeping in your own bed when you can do over a cat by stealing his? The radio told me that one hundred and eighty people had died in a train crash in India, Northern Ireland was in a fragile state, and two gay celebrities had been married in a ceremony in California to which I had not been invited. Michael O'Donoghue did not get a mention, nor did his clinic. Could media interest have died so soon? Perhaps. We live in a disposable world.

I nursed a cup of instant as I thought about the evening ahead. I had not been entirely honest with myself about my motives for going to Bridgecross. For instance, although there was a possibility that Michael O'Donoghue would attend, a much simpler way of finding out would be to phone his wife and ask her. Mick Nolan was revving up a head of steam over that, so I explained that I would have to go now, one way or another, as I had made a commitment to Andy.

'I don't give a shite what you do in your private life,' he told me. 'Though you'd want to sort yourself out there, if you ask me.'

'Which I don't,' I replied, tartly.

'Oh, grow up,' was all he had to say to that.

I've never liked the word 'proactive'. I suppose it conjures up images of life as a magazine article for me, with pumpy-jumpy phrases like 'strategy not stress'. But for all that, I thought I'd give it a go. And so I quickly fed the brood, showered and dressed, told Barry to go take a running jump when he asked for a cup of tea, and abandoned the car at 8.53 a.m. outside Mullaney Motors, with a note on the windscreen saying 'Fix this or else', and the keys in the letter box. Then I walked the rest of the way into town with my jolly canine companion, the inimitable No. 4.

We played a little game on the way. I tried to give him a new name, and he let me know which ones he liked, without committing himself to a choice. Top of the list were Englebert, Abelard and Tootsie, but the clear winner as we crossed the Ha'penny Bridge into Temple Bar was still No. 4. I was delighted to pass through various empty streets and small squares; I have an irrational irritation with people who insist on having their double-latte-espresso-hatchback-over-easy outdoors in the freezing cold, or the sort of light drizzle that drenches a person to the bone within forty seconds. We don't have the weather for a café culture, so let's just give in on that one, shall we?

I knew immediately that something was wrong at the Indigent Sweeps' place. It was in the air. I sniffed again and again to be sure. Normally, I would have been assaulted by the intermingled aromas of brewing coffee from the other offices, Piss Lite from the drunks who urinate against the outside wall when they can't make it to the next pub or club along the route, and the vague suggestion of Domestos courtesy of Mrs Mack. Yesterday I had spotted a brown streak on one of the walls, the origin of which I was loath to identify, but now it was gone. And the air was filled with a tangy, citrus odour which was downright pleasant. Some-one had obviously broken in during the night and cleaned the building. What kind of conscientious, positive, breaking-and-entering was this? What splendid rehabilita-tion would lead a criminal to leave only good behind? Or, the most unlikely of scenarios, had Mrs Mack finally lost it and done her job? Her voice summoned me from on high; today it was a strange, happy falsetto. I was very afraid.

Kevin Mack was the reason for the glories manifest in our world. He was a small ball of a man, with a gleaming pate unadorned by more than the lightest burr of fuzz, and three actual hairs carefully plastered from one side of his head, over the top, to the other. He had an easy smile and happy brown eyes with which he delighted me as he handed over a mug of scalding tar and a digestive biscuit. It was enough to make a girl fall in love.

'I won't be a patch on herself, but she's put me on duty while she's away so I'll do my best,' he said, as he turned his adoring orbs on his wife. She was enthroned on a tall stool by the door of her tearoom, from whence she could check on her empire without any hindrance. 'It's a bit like learning to drive,' he went on. 'She believes in putting you in the hot seat from day one, so you can learn the proper way.'

'I'll bet,' I managed.

'And I keep reminding her that she'll have to tell all her sins, because it's a pilgrimage she's goin' on.'

'Stop it, Kevin, you have me all mortified in front of Miss Street. He's an awful man altogether.'

Oh, to be a fly on the wall of that confessional. Most of Mrs Mack's sins were those of omission, I guessed. Like omitting to do her job. Which in its way led to a charge of theft, or at least taking money under false pretences, i.e. her wages. But who was I to pass judgement? False pretence was second nature to me, and I often dealt a half truth if I thought it would net me some information or release off a pointy hook. And while I was at it, hadn't I sent Ciara straight out into the field on her first day? Were we so different, Mrs Mack and I? I didn't want to answer that question, it was enough that it existed at all, so I gave myself a metaphorical shake by the scruff of the neck and cleared it away.

'There's a problem with the loo on your floor,' Mrs Mack told me. It was clear that I was to blame, in her books, for whatever aberration had caused this. 'The smell is only dreadful, isn't it, Kevin?' Again she looked the look which told me she knew what I was up to, and I would be dealt with accordingly.

'I'll have a butcher's later,' her husband said.

If it was left to the female of the Mack species, I would be found stultified by poisonous gases at my desk long before remedial action was taken by her fair beige hands.

'Thank you,' I said, meaning it.

Mrs Mack looked at her watch in an extravagant gesture. 'I'll take myself off to the Bureau de Change,' she announced pointedly.

'I'm glad you mentioned that,' I said, fiddling in my bag. I handed her an envelope. 'Get yourself something nice.' Inside was a twenty-pound note, which I hoped was enough of a tribute.

'Ah now, Miss Street, you *shouldn't* have,' she protested, putting one hand on her sternum to show how touched she was, while the other claw whipped the offering from me in double-quick time.

'Do you know, it's amazing how many people have been in to do the same thing this morning already,' her husband said. 'They all know what a treasure you are,' he told her.

Not for the first time I regretted shelving my first plan, which was to put a tea bag in the envelope, seal it and write on the outside, 'Have a drink on me'. Hindsight, you know? As always, it was about as useful as a pain in the eyeball. Ah, well, next time. In my dreams.

The stairwell did indeed fill with pungent air the higher I climbed. By the time I reached my office I had almost become accustomed to the overwhelming smell of fart. Almost. I unlocked the door, reached for an aerosol I keep for such emergencies, gave five generous sprays of 'Spring Meadow' and spent the next fifteen minutes sneezing.

When my sinuses clogged up and my breathing became less emphysematic, I dialled the O'Donoghue household and was answered on the third ring.

'Yes, we'll both be attending the Bridgecross function this evening,' Miranda told me, in a tone that suggested I was a complete cretin not to know that.

'Sorry to have bothered you,' I said, in my own pissed off tone, which wasn't half bad, if I may say so.

There was a minuscule pause, then she returned, 'I apologise for snapping. Michael did not come home until 12.30 last night, and we spent twenty minutes bickering before I went to the spare room for a sleepless night. But of course you'll probably know that already.'

Caught red-handed, Leo? Time for evasive action.

'You did promise to forward me his mobile phone bills, but I haven't yet received them.' Ball back in your court, Miranda.

'That is proving a little more difficult than I first anticipated,' she said, coolly. 'I am working on the situation.'

I've heard as many lies as truths in my time as a PI. My
gut feeling here was that Miranda had just told a porky, or
at least exaggerated the 'situation', as she so economically
put it. Two could play at that game, and, believe me, when
it comes to lies I can tell as good as I hear. It is not
something that I am proud of.

'I'll be presenting an update shortly,' I glossed. 'And then
we can assess what's best to do.' This was just meaningless
jargon, but I felt I had to improvise, be seen to be doing
something and so on. 'Now, if you'll excuse me, I have a
call to take.'

Another casual juggling of the truth, and why? Because I
did not want her to lose confidence in me. I needed the
money and I needed to finish this job. I calmed my racing
heart and looked around for something to do with myself. I
ran my fingers along the desk and realised that it was
dust-free. My office had been cleaned. I took this to be a
majorly good omen.

Maeve had faxed through a list of companies which might
have her home number. My initial thought was that this
phone stalker was someone who knew her or had met her.
I discounted the staff at the electricity and gas supply
boards, because there are a lot of people with the name
Maeve Kelly in Ireland, and when you see it on a bland
form, there is no reason to believe that it is one of our finest
actresses. If I had to I would return to them as suspects, but
something told me to look elsewhere first. That left a list
including her local Chinese and Indian takeaways, a hair-
dresser, a video store, a dentist, a doctor and two taxi firms,

one of which my brother worked for. She had also jotted down the following: 'I've only just switched to Northways Taxis, because the previous lot had become so unreliable. I can't be certain, but I think the calls started before the switch, so I doubt it's anyone there (Northways). I've been with all the others, doctor, takeaways, etc. for years.'

Perhaps, perhaps, perhaps, I thought.

My plan, such as it was, was to frighten the life out of some, or all, of the companies on my short list to see if that produced any change in the pattern.

The office telephone rang with a soft electronic burr. I grabbed the receiver and chimed, 'Leo Street's office. What can I do for you?'

You really can't buy that sort of training.

A whispering voice said, 'My name is Tara O'Donoghue.' There was a pause, and if it was for effect, it worked. I sat up smartly in my seat and gave encouragement to Miranda and Michael's eldest child.

'Yes?' I ventured.

'I know you're involved in, like, *things*.'

'Yes?' I repeated, for good measure. '*Things*' were still a little vague for me to commit myself or break client privilege.

Throat clearing on the line suggested a mild fluster. Then she continued, 'Ehm, I might be able to shed some light on, well, *things*. But I can't talk now, so I'd like to come in to the office tomorrow afternoon.'

'Of course, Tara,' I said. 'Can you tell me a little more about what it is you want to discuss?'

She made an indiscriminate noise which sounded like 'feckit', then added, 'Look, I think I know who's been threatening my dad.'

I was hooked, complete with line and sinker. I gave her a

time and a place to be the following day.

It's not good to wish your life away, according to my gran. I was now torn between a desire for tomorrow's meeting with Tara O'Donoghue and her intriguing information, and the expectation of a night out with Andy Raynor. And stuck there in the middle of the two was a need to get to work on tracking down Maeve's caller, which required a lot more time than I had available today. I felt helpless and inactive. I could not hurry events along, which left me feeling incapacitated and plain useless, to be honest.

I was scratching my head and feeling sorry for myself when I realised that I had no transport to deliver my bread order to Maeve's mum or to collect the kids after school. Mick Nolan began to laugh behind me; he is such a wise ass. I kept my poise, no way was I going to display weakness in front of him. 'Not a problem,' I said aloud. No. 4 looked up from his activities. I had made him a special ball to play with earlier on. Now it resembled a paper recycling kit, with shreds of the newspaper I'd used strewn across the length of the floor. No wonder he had been so quiet and content. I allowed myself one shallow sigh before scooping up as much of the mess as I could with my hands; I'm no vacuum cleaner, but it made some difference to the geography of the linoleum. Not a lot, but some. The dog found the exercise a real whizz, chasing between my legs, and even once climbing on to my back with a happy bark as I bent over his morning's work. I sat back at my desk, rubbed a furrowed brow and called Angela to arrange to pick up her tank for the afternoon's delights. Nearly back on track, I thought.

'Your face is covered in black streaks,' said the girl in the doorway.

'Jesus, Ciara, did you leave the house like that?'

'Don't be ridiculous. Mum was out, so I was safe enough. Ronan saw me, but he wouldn't dare squeal; I took some of his lecture notes hostage, and he knows I'll burn them if he says a word. What's with the camouflage?'

'It's a by product of a perfect morning,' I explained.

Ciara was dressed as every parent's dream. She wore a pale pink shirt, buttoned to the top, faded but respectable blue jeans, and a navy jacket. Her hair was freshly washed and swept off her impish face where her jolly freckles sparkled. You might almost have thought her harmless.

'I need to type up my report,' she said, throwing the case file on the desk. 'Not that it's scintillating.'

'We're saving the world next week,' I said. 'That should liven things up a bit.'

'Yeah, I'll be looking forward to that. What have you been up to, now that you're one of the bourgeois leisured class?'

'Well, since I saw you last, I kidnapped two children, then went on a pub crawl with my father, my boyfriend and a priest.'

'You are such a pervert, do you know that? Saw you at the Fledgling, by the way. Pity there wasn't a riot, it could really have done with one. A few of the journos tried to give chase to Michael O'Donoghue when he was leaving, but it was all a bit half-hearted. I was the only one who stuck with him – lazy bunch of fecks.'

'So, tell me in a nutshell what I'll be reading in this report of yours?'

Ciara flopped into the old armchair and propped her feet up on the desk.

'The most interesting thing about yesterday is that I think I'm being followed,' she said.

Even No. 4's ears perked up.

THIRTEEN

Most people do not expect to be shadowed, unless they are a politician or a movie star with a shady past, present and possibly future, in which case a hounding Press Pack is *de rigueur*. It's one of the reasons a PI is ahead from the start. We have the advantage because we're not generally considered to exist by the public at large. And unless your subject is suspicious and trained, or very, very perceptive, you should go unnoticed. So maybe Ciara was just being paranoid. I said as much, but she was steadfast.

'No, I tried a few evasions, but the car stuck.'

'Car?'

'Yeah. I couldn't get it to come close enough to read the registration or get a make, but it's grey, a metallic grey. Nice saloon shape, for all the good that is to us. If it's around after me today, I'll try again to get it to come nearer.'

'But who would want to follow you?'

'I've been thinking about that. And I wonder if it's me or

Michael O'Donoghue who's being followed.'

'Good point,' I conceded. I liked the way she was operating here, nice lateral thinking.

'For instance, I wasn't followed from home to here this morning. So maybe it's him who's got the fan and not me.' Solid, logical analysis.

'Are you good at cryptic crosswords?' I asked.

'Yeah.'

'Thought so.'

'Why?'

'No reason, just testing a theory.'

'Anyhow, he had what I gathered from you was a normal enough day, apart from making the national news. He had his surgery, did his rounds in the hospital, and for all I know delivered a few babies. He's so boring he probably plans when his patients have them. When he dodged the journalists, he doubled back to his office for a few hours, though he wouldn't have had any patients then. Perhaps he was catching up on paperwork.'

'Or reading a novel,' I offered, warning lightly against making assumptions.

'Or having a wank. Who knows?'

I lifted a hand to indicate that we would go no further down that road.

She laughed. 'A pervert *and* stuffy all at once.'

'Meaning?'

'I'm not the one who was out with a priest last night.'

'It wasn't a priest,' I said nonsensically. 'It was Con.'

'Bitch! Why didn't you tell me? I'd have loved to have seen him. How is the big fatty anyway?' She took her feet off the desk in agitation, and leaned forward for more information.

'He's fine, possibly relocating to Dublin, I'll tell you later when you've finished your oral and written reports.'

'Jeez, hang on to your knickers. You can be really uptight sometimes.'

'There is a woman out there paying for our time, not our gossip.'

Even I knew I was being unbearably prim, but a little discipline in Ciara's life would not go amiss. 'Or in your own,' said sly old Mick Nolan.

Kevin Mack appeared at the door, prepared for battle. He held a giant plunger in hands decked out in black, industrial-strength rubber gloves. The rest of his body was encased in white overalls, not unlike a forensics suit.

'I'm just off to see to that toilet,' he said. 'If I'm not back by next Tuesday, send in the cavalry.'

Ciara looked quizzically in my direction. 'The new cleaner,' I revealed. 'And now a member of the Cisterncian Order.'

Ciara groaned, and who could blame her? 'You can tell you've been out with Father Punmeister Considine,' she said, shaking her head sadly. She swung her legs up on to my desk again. With ease. She had long limbs, and with that the height to go legit, should she choose to accept it.

I was too short to be a cop. Butty, weenchy, vertically challenged, squat; whatever description you like. So I fell into the world of the PI courtesy of Mick Nolan, ex-the Force. He took me apart and reassembled me as the Private Detective Leo Street. Eventually, he threw me out. On the occasion of his death, as it happens. And on my bad days I long for a badge, or even a uniform, and the official length and breadth to go after the baddies and make the world a better place. In essence, I sometimes want the Force to be with me, because on top of everything else, when they're against you, you're in deep shit.

Ciara flicked through a notebook with a spiral wire through the top, looking for all the world like a cub journalist.

'I'll type all this up for you,' she said. 'But the pertinent points are: he headed out to his fitness club at 7 p.m. then at 8.30, looking all squeaky clean and shiny, he set off for Bernie Flood's house in Raheny, on Dublin's less fashionable north side.' She checked me with cheeky eyes over the top of her notes. I gave the tiniest of smiles and she continued. 'They were arguing any of the time I could hear them. I caught phrases like 'stay away from me' and 'you won't rest till you've destroyed us all' from Bernie. Oh, and one 'stay away from her', too, but I'm not sure who that referred to. He did a bit of the 'you're an unreasonable woman' and at one point burst out with 'of course I know what's bloody well best', but they moved off again to a back room and I couldn't hear the rest. She didn't see him to the door at 9.30 p.m., which was in keeping with the tone of things between them. He drove home via the Bridgecross Sport and Social Club, where I observed him have a quiet drink with some of his mates. Then he went home, without passing go or collecting any money, and was safely ensconced in Sea View, Booterstown, by 10.45.'

'How did he get in?'

Ciara was clearly puzzled by my line of questioning. 'The lady of the house heard his car and had the door open by the time he'd parked. In he went, home sweet home.'

'It would be,' I said, 'except that's not where he lives. Michael O'Donoghue lives at Sea Point, Blackrock, ten minutes further down the road.'

'Shite!'

We all have to make that first mistake. Ciara's was an understandable one: two similar addresses only moments apart by road. She was also not as familiar with the case as I was, and could not be expected to grasp every little detail on day one. My job here, however, was to give her a good bollocking to teach her a lesson. Or so the gospel according to Mick Nolan went. I remember that he used the words 'shoddy', 'incompetent', 'unreliable', 'amateur' and 'waste of space' on the occasion of my first tongue lashing from him. Well, those were the words from his opening sentence, others followed, one borrowing another, until I was on the verge of tears. I would not cry in front of him, not because of pride, though I wish it had been: I knew he'd fire me on the spot if I cracked. It was one of my first tests, and even Hercules did not have to endure as many as I did. Mick added to his tirade on each subsequent roasting, and it was a formidable oration to behold or endure. Oh, and I didn't need to fuck up to deserve it, any old occasion would serve, one size fitted all.

'What do you intend to do about this little turn of events?' I asked Ciara, who, it must be admitted, was pink with rage at herself. Or at least I can't believe that it was embarrassment, she doesn't hold truck with that.

'I'm going back out there to find out who the hell he went to see.'

'Correct,' I acknowledged. 'I know I shouldn't do this, but I'll tell you that he did get to his proper home. At 12.30.'

How do you know that?'

'Never mind. I do, that's all. I am a detective, you know.'

We let that hang in the air for a moment. Ciara digested it and prepared to bounce back.

'Given journey times, he would have spent just over an hour and a half in this house,' I said. Ciara nodded. 'Unless . . .' I continued.

'Unless he went somewhere else.' She put her head in her hands momentarily. 'I was so sure I had put him to bed,' she said.

'And perhaps you did. But whose bed was it?'

Ciara had a way with words. 'Fuck, fuck, fuck,' she said.

I was no angel in all of this, so I came clean on the details I'd omitted to mention when I hired her.

'Death threats?' Ciara repeated.

'Yes, and the weird thing is that his wife doesn't seem to think this is unusual, or even relevant to what we're working on. She was positively dismissive about them. There is something decidedly strange about the whole set-up. I wonder if there are other details she's not sharing with us. And I don't want to put either of us in danger. We're not being paid enough for that.'

I could have added a 'certainly' to the last statement because we were, in effect, sharing one wage then.

'Don't worry about me,' Ciara said. 'I thrive on the edge.'

'Ciara, I'm serious.'

'So am I,' she said.

I made a resigned noise. 'Just be extra careful. Now that the Fledgling is under scrutiny, things could get very mucky. If you feel, at any time, that you're not in control, back off. It's not worth getting hurt over.'

'Yes, boss.'

'For what it's worth, I'll be attending the same function as Michael O'Donoghue and his wife tonight,' I said. 'It would be best if you watched from outside in case he tries to sneak away. I'll keep an eye on him inside.'

'Why do I feel that I've got the rum end of this deal?' she asked.

'Because, as you've so rightly pointed out, I am the boss, and what I say goes. And as of now that's you. Clear up your mess. Find out who he went to see last night. I don't want to hear from you until it's sorted. Goodbye.'

I got up and opened the door to show her out. 'Vamoose, scram, skedaddle, go.'

She left.

The hallway resounded to the flushing of a toilet. As one echo died, another flush took its place, and then another. The air smelled high, but I thought I detected an improvement. I secretly prayed for Mrs Mack to stay on her pilgrimage as long as the Knights Templar had on the Crusades. Perhaps I should have given her more money.

It was lucky that I turned back to my office at that moment, because I encountered a happy creature leaving with a package which I recognised as one of the loaves I had baked for Maeve's mum. I gave chase. This was dog heaven for No. 4 as he dodged in and out of the legs of the furniture. I ducked one way then the other, trying to trap him on open ground, but he was too wily. Eventually I got down on all fours and tried approaching him on his level. He still had the advantage. But ego was his downfall. Cockily, he came closer and closer on each of his forays, and eventually I got a hand to his collar. He let the package fall. By now I had manoeuvered myself into a coil around the front of my desk with my arse pointing towards the door. Kevin Mack reappeared. I could see him through my legs, in an upside-down way. I could not move. If I let go of No. 4 he would escape with the loaf again. If I stayed as I was, every story Mrs Mack had no doubt told him of my eccentricities would be borne out. I had a vision of her as Beelzebub on one side of me, and the deep blue sea on the other. I stayed put.

'I see you're busy,' he said. 'I just wanted to let you know that I've freed up the system. This was the culprit.' The red knitted glove was all too familiar. I didn't think it would help my standing in his eyes if I admitted ownership, particularly as we were conducting this conversation in less than ideal circumstances for me. 'Good for you,' I squeezed out. 'And thanks again.'

He loitered a little. 'Can I help at all?' he asked.

'No, no, everything under control,' I said. ''Bye now.'

As he closed the door behind him, I let go of the dog's collar and lunged for the bread. I won, but No. 4 was a close second, and had a piece of wrapping paper stuck to his upper lip to prove it. As I struggled from the floor he slurped a wet lick across my face, and left the torn shred flapping on my cheek.

Closer inspection revealed that the dog had not drooled too heavily on the merchandise, and the wrapping had performed beautifully as a barrier. Neither were there any teeth marks. 'You were *this* close to visiting the vet,' I warned him, holding my thumb and forefinger together. He jumped up and down at the news. There are times when I think that no one is listening to a word I say.

I re-wrapped the loaves and packed them into a basket with a few other sundries from my life. Then I tethered the

dog, locked up for the day and made my bid for freedom.
Mr Mack had nailed the red glove to a notice board on the
ground floor. It was looking very sorry for itself, as any
object removed from a blocked loo would. He had rinsed it,
which was a small mercy. I wondered again about how it
had made its unscheduled journey. I was not in the habit of
wearing gloves, knitted or otherwise, for my visits to the
bathroom, although the building can get very parky in bad
weather. Toilet finger wear is not one of my fashion fetishes,
though I'm not condemning it in any way; we all need our
crutches to deal with life. Now, as the sorry red item hung
exhausted from the board, I knew that I would have to
remove its partner from the office under cover of darkness
and dispose of it in a humane way. If Mrs Mack could pin
the sewage crime on me, my life would go down the toilet
in the very same manner as the ill-fated glove.

You have to wonder about taxi drivers, don't you? Are they
really a microcosm of society? Are they a representative
barometer of the way a country is feeling? And where do
they get off with the idea that because you are captive in
their car, a privilege you are paying for, they have every
right to force their opinions on you? Eh, sorry, I'll pass on
the special offer of free advice with every journey, thanks
all the same.

I am usually careful not to complain too much as I am
genetically tied to a taxi driver, my brother Peter. Through
him, I know not to ask stupid questions like 'Are you busy?'
or 'What time are you on until?' Unless I deliberately want
to annoy the driver, in which case great sport can be had.
My hired hackney today was of the opinion that young
people had gone to Hades in a handcart, and that too much

159

zinc in the water was probably what had tipped them over the edge. And how were we to know what the government or other brigands were putting into the water supply anyhow? Fluoride was a villain, but zinc was just the worst of all bad things. And as for recycled effluent, that was worse than heroin. Without any warning, he started in on women. 'And as for the feminists,' he began. My annoyance meter was pointing way off the scale now. 'The feminazis, that's what I call them. Feckin' feminazis.' He gave a throaty chuckle, which only exacerbated how pissed off I had become. In retaliation, I found out that business was quiet and his shift finished at eight that evening, but he'd prefer to be working nights, because there was more money going around then. And that the cab was not his, he was cosying, because the price of a taxi plate had gone to hell in the same handcart as every young person in Ireland. I wanted to torture him more with talk of how brilliant it was that the government were issuing loads of new taxi licences, and that we would be awash with choice, but he had worn me down to a frazzle of my former self. I definitely preferred the quiet type who, by his very silence, had the ability to make you feel that you were worthless crud on the backside of humanity; that, I could relate to.

He started up a new whine about the evils of television. His voice had a strange frequency, annoying to all mammals, I guessed, and possibly injurious after prolonged exposure. 'It's all murders now,' he was saying. 'Of course in my day we only had the one channel.'

'That was murder enough,' I acknowledged.

By the time we reached Angela's even the dog was fed up with the incessant, nasal drone. In fact, he had started to bark any time the man opened his mouth in order to drown out the useless information spewing forth. If my dad wanted a taxi driver to call a bollocks, he should meet this guy and lay off Peter. I paid our fare and was treated to a homily on canine behavioural problems. There was a moment of danger when I thought I might burst, so I said, 'Shut *up*,' a little too loudly, and they both did. I was smiling by the time we got to the front door.

Angela stood, bleary-eyed, in the middle of chaos.

'The kids re-enacted the bombing of Dresden this morning before school,' she said. 'They won, of course. I fell asleep in the middle of clearing the mess up. Just nodded off on the floor. I sometimes feel that I'll never know a proper rest again.' Her hand reached up and scratched her scalp, distractedly. 'The big question is, where did I leave the car keys?'

For no logical reason, we found them in the fridge.

FOURTEEN

Maeve's family lived in Howth, a chichi peninsula further along the northern coastline of Dublin. It was, and still is, richly populated by the rich. Harvey, Maeve's dad, had made his money in packaging, and her mother, Sandra, was a retired nurse. They had a large, detached house with rambling gardens on the hill, overlooking the harbour. The view was a tranquil picture of two promenades embracing moored boats in the safety of their curved arms, and beyond, the Irish Sea. When they first viewed the property, Sandra had remarked she felt like she'd been there before. After the purchase was complete, a sign with the house name was hung on the front wall. It read 'Déjà View'.

Howth was sparkling in the gentle glow of the April sun, which is to say that the weather was mild. I recalled a summer's day I had spent here with Andy Raynor many years before. It was unremarkable by way or event, but it was one of the happiest of my teenage years. We walked and argued and ate ice creams, and laughed at the antics of various landlubbers as they struggled with their rudders and masts, and lay out on the hill looking at the clouds and enjoying the oneness of being together. Later, he put his arm around me and saw me to my door. Then he played havoc with my hormones and my underwear, and I was so happy that I nearly burst into tears. I did far too much crying then, and do far too much of it now. Things must change, I said to myself.

I crunched the tank to a halt on the gravel to the back of the house. A lurcher and a cocker spaniel came to investigate. There was much bum-sniffing before they decided that No. 4 was a jolly good type. Then I turned him loose to play with them. At this juncture he had more friends in Dublin than I did.

Sandra Kelly appeared, a vision in Ghost and Bruno Magli, enveloped by Chanel No. 19, and wearing the beatific smile of a contented woman. I felt another lottery number coming on: now I had 4, 5, 6, 11, 19, with just one more to find to win that jackpot. Then I too would dress beautifully and be calm in the bestowing of my largesse. She was carrying a Campari and freshly squeezed orange juice.

'Leo, you're very good to take on this latest task. And to deliver in person.'

'Not at all,' I told her. 'I'm always glad of a pleasant job and a nice drive.' I popped my basket on to the huge pine table that was the centrepiece of the kitchen. 'I've done you three loaves: a dark stout bread, which is delicious with some butter and cheese, a tomato with a crisp crust of fennel and sea salt, and an orange brioche for those ladies with a sweet tooth.' I felt unbearably proud of my work as I unwrapped it and enjoyed her obvious pleasure. I desperately wanted someone to take my picture as she paid me, but I affected an air of nonchalance, as if this were an everyday occurrence. Inside, I was churning.

Sandra Kelly did not smoke, and from a quick perusal of her wine selection, she drank only the best. Her face was remarkably unlined, a combination of quality skincare products and an optimistic attitude to life. She was lean, but in a way that suggested good genes were responsible rather than constant dieting. Her elegance was a manifestation of pure class. If Sandra was an older version of her daughter, Maeve Kelly had a lot to look forward to.

'Is today a special occasion?' I asked.

'Yes and no,' she replied. 'It's a sort of reunion of some of the girls I used to work with.'

I wondered what the collective for nurses was, retired or active. On this occasion I thought it might be 'a feast'.

'Maybe you know someone I'm interested in,' I said, an idea forming in my head. It was a long shot, but I asked, 'Did you ever come across Michael O'Donoghue, the obstetrician?'

'Oh, yes,' she replied. 'He seems to be in a bit of a pickle, doesn't he? I can't say that I'm too surprised. He's had a fine reputation, I suppose, until now, but none of us ever liked having to deal with him. He was arrogant, a bit of a bully. Liked to rule the roost. Of course, that was years ago, when he was new on the scene and thought he knew everything. If the newspaper reports are anything to go by, his years in practice haven't chastened him. To be honest, I always thought him a little dangerous. He never heeded anyone's advice but his own. Had what we would call a God Complex.'

Ciara had overheard the phrase 'of course I know what's bloody well best' at the Flood house. And newspaper coverage of his writings and speeches made it clear that O'Donoghue felt he was a Saviour of Medicine and Mankind. Was this why his wife did not find it unusual that he would receive hate mail?

'I never did see the attraction in him,' Sandra Kelly continued. 'He dated quite a few of our batch; not me, I'm happy to say. Some of the others were completely smitten, though, and fell badly for him. He was a heartbreaker. A lab technician called Miranda, I think it was, got him in the end, and she was welcome to him.'

I felt I couldn't pump Mrs Kelly anymore than I had without raising her suspicions, so I pocketed my money and my information, and felt absurdly successful. Driving back to the main road with No. 4, I pondered the notion of Michael O'Donoghue as manipulator, and wondered how that sat with a wife who was all edge. As I did, a metallic grey saloon passed the tank, and edged into the Kelly driveway. 'This town is only just big enough for the lot of us,' I told the dog, happily, as I jotted down the registration number. The car was driven by Mrs Bernadette Flood. I continued my journey back into the city centre with a satisfied hum in my craw. The building blocks were mounting one on the other.

Mick Nolan had had no room for passengers, or so the official line had gone. He did, however, have two sons, Jimmy and Jack, both of whom were vicariously blessed with their father's looks and their mother's brains – meaning they looked like cops but acted like airheads. Along with myself, they were trained by Mick to be Dublin's brightest and best. In the trade they were known as Dumb and Dumber. When Mick had died suddenly, of a bad bunker shot on the back nine of a golf course, I was surplus to company requirements and shed forthwith. I believe that Mick had it all planned, principally because he needed a change of scenery and could not bear to be in that office any longer. It was drastic action, undoubtedly, but once he made his mind up, that was it. He moved with me.

His son Jimmy was now standing in the yard of the Model School, casually posing with his hands in the pockets of his khaki raincoat. His thick, black hair was neatly parted to the side and slicked down with gel. His rosy cheeks matched the full red of his overblown, moist lips. He had overly long eyelashes for a man. If Central Casting had sent out their choice for the part of Paedophile No. 1 in the last television thriller, Jimmy would have been it. The sense of a lynch mob gathering amongst the waiting mothers and fathers was even greater than yesterday. I went to his side.

'Jimmy,' I acknowledged.

'Leo,' he said, without looking at me or moving his bow-lipped mouth.

'So you're on the Carmel Lally case?' I commented.

Now I had his undivided attention.

'How did you know that?' he gasped, forgetting to close his mouth when he finished the question.

I reached over and reattached his chin to the rest of his face. 'I'm a detective, remember?'

'You're not on the case too, are you?' he asked, his eyes narrowing suspiciously.

'That would be telling,' I said. 'Let's just say that I have a healthy interest in this one.'

He coughed into his hand and glanced around the

167

playground, looking shiftier by the minute.

'I don't mean to be rude,' he whispered, 'but you're ruining my cover here. You're, you know, kinda drawing attention to me.'

'Jimmy, you fucking pillock,' I explained, 'I'm drawing attention *away* from you.'

'Leo, now is no time to get jealous. I'm just doing my job, you know?'

'Jimmy,' I said, summoning up imaginary reserves of patience, 'you are a strange man, alone in a children's play area, wearing a dirty mac and looking like you just got out of prison. How much more attention do you think you could draw to yourself?'

'Leo, everyone here thinks I'm just another dad waiting for his kids,' he explained, just as patiently.

'Right,' I said. 'You're on your own.'

I've always found close encounters with the Nolan boys unsettling. They look like their father, even speak like him, but they are fundamentally different from him. It's as if they are a shell of him. They are as close to proof as you'll get that *Invasion of the Body Snatchers* is not a work of the imagination.

Funnily enough, Mick had nothing to say about any of this.

'Do you know that weirdo?' Colette O'Brien asked as I joined her and Lisa Farrelly on what I now assumed to be their regular spot.

'He's nothing to worry about,' I said, wondering if this was the truth.

When the kids emerged on to the concrete heaven they had a letter addressed to each household. It said that a formal insurance claim had been lodged against the crêche, and that the nursery was now in danger of closing. With her strings pulled by the malignant Gods and all the Fates, Carmel Lally chose that moment to appear at the gates. Suddenly shouts of 'Bitch!' and worse, filled the air, along with adjectives to elaborate the general mood of the crowd. I turned to my friends and saw that their faces were as twisted in anger as any of the others. Suddenly the Model School was a very nasty place. I grabbed Mary and Dominick and made for the exit.

'Who's the little blonde you were talking to?' Jimmy Nolan asked as I passed. 'The one with the mean eyes.'

'Lisa Farrelly,' I replied. 'Why do you ask?'

'She let the air out of Carmel Lally's tyres earlier,' he replied. 'And what about the other one?'

'That's Colette O'Brien. Why?'

'Oh, no reason,' he said. 'Just keeping an eye. You know.'

If he was trying to bug me, he had succeeded. And not for the first time. I had experience of Jimmy being enigmatic, as he saw it, and it never involved enigma. Other times he might blab away, parting with all sorts of information without realising it. Which was not to call him a *naif savant*, or indeed an *idiot savant*; lose the *savant* and you get the general idea.

Jimmy tried to move off, but had difficulty with the manoeuvre. He gave a puzzled tug, and pulled his foot away, revealing a large gob of Wrigley's on the tarmac. 'Gum shoe,' I said, with some satisfaction, and much accuracy.

A problem shared is supposed to be a problem halved. In the case of Jimmy and Jack, it was a double trouble. They worked together, which meant that Jack was probably on nights, shambling about after Carmel Lally. Even if she didn't spot them, the Nolans had a way of making their subjects feel oddly wary; must have been an electrical charge they left in the air. Well, now they were back in my life, like it or not. I bundled the children into the car and took off.

'Leo,' Dominick was saying, 'you know we are all an animal?'

'Mmn, yeah,' I agreed. You never knew where this might go.

'Dominick, just because we eat bananas doesn't mean we're monkeys,' his sister pointed out, with nice deductive reasoning.

'No,' he conceded. 'But when a monkey does eat a banana he does do a poo. And so do we.'

They both shrieked with laughter, then repeated the word 'poo' a dozen times. I found myself admiring their abstract subjunctive, or whatever it was, and lamenting the day that they would shed it, in the interests of grammar, of which there is none anymore if you believed arts programmes on the radio, or read any of the tabloids. I was experiencing a short-lived regret, as it happened.

'Leo, you are a poo head,' Dom told me.

Then we had a chorus of 'poo head'. No. 4 looked at me as if he thought I'd lost the plot altogether. When I analysed what they were saying, I realised why. Basically, the kids were calling me a shit head. Lovely. And grammar or no grammar this was not a joke. Which is not to dispute the truth or fiction of the statement.

I put a halt to the insults. Mary tried to make friends again.

'Leo,' she said. 'I did have a dream last night. I was up in the clouds and then I did reach into one of them and I was very happy.'

'Good for you,' I said, softening. 'How about you, Dominick?'

'I was a monkey and I did eat a banana and . . .'

'Right, right,' I said cutting him off. 'I think we can see where that story is going.'

'Your mother wants to know if you've got something nice to wear tonight,' Angela told me, as we nursed a coffee. She had given the children banana sandwiches for tea, and I found it a little disconcerting to watch them eat. They, in turn, rained angelic smiles upon me.

'I rooted out a decentish frock,' I replied as coolly as was possible under the circumstances.

'Thought so,' she said. 'It's one of the two you keep festering in your wardrobe, isn't it? Wait there.'

Angela was gone for two and a half minutes, which was precisely enough time for Rose to sick up on my black jumper. She was beaming at the acidic curdle when I looked, and Rose seemed pleased too.

'This used to fit me a century ago before that little vomit comet came along. One day, hopefully in my lifetime, I will fit back into it. In the meantime you may wear it for Prince Charming.'

The 'it' was a fifties-style, straight, raw silk dress, cherry red. I stopped short of dribbling, just.

'Lovely, Angela, but I don't have shoes to go with it.'

'Yes, you do,' she said, producing a pair of matching court shoes. 'And here are some hold-up stockings which I never got a chance to wear. They should do nicely with all the rest.'

'I can't wear those,' I protested. 'If anyone were to see, they'd think I was on the make.'

Angela gave me a teasing grin. 'You wear them to feel good for yourself,' she said, with mock-haughty emphasis, and more than a nod at the politically correct. The feminist cells in my head were cheering. They should get out more. 'Now, wipe that sick off your jumper, go home and spruce yourself up for a great night out.'

'It's just a favour for Andy,' I protested. 'He's hanging around with some leggy bimbo anyhow.'

'But not tonight. Have fun. Let your hair down. On second thoughts, put your hair up for that frock.'

'I presume my mother knows which dress you chose?'

'What do you think?'

'And does Andy's mother know?'

'As far as I know it was printed in this week's local newsletter.'

I sighed. 'As long as it's only the entire northside and its immediate environs that's in on the secret, I guess I can live with it.'

'She's very excited about this date,' Angela went on.

'Great. Better get cracking then. I don't want to let The Mammy down, along with tens of thousands of her closest friends. Not to mention Breda Raynor.' I turned at the door. 'And it's not a date,' I said.

'Of course not.'

People get the weirdest ideas; it's always best to keep things straight. This was only a pay-back, after all. Andy just wanted someone along as arm candy.

I decided to walk home. It was that or risk another cab, and I'd had enough lecturing from shiny, happy taxi people that day. If I called my brother out, I might run into more family interference, because the Street men are just as nosy as the

172

Street women. There are times when it makes perfect sense to me that I became a detective, considering how curious my family are. So far we reckon that we're safer than cats are with it. I dialled my little helper.

Ciara had been busy, and was justifiably proud of her information.

'Her name is Maria Flood, she's twenty years old and she works as a laboratory assistant for, of all people, Michael O'Donoghue at the Fledgling Clinic.'

'You don't say. And Flood? Interesting coincidence or real-life relation?'

'Real-life relation: Bernadette's daughter.'

'And I have another interesting coincidence for you. Bernie Flood drives a metallic grey car. It's probably in Howth even as we speak.' I read out the registration number for her.

'Nice one.'

'Ciara, I know all of this information seems to point a certain way, but we should resist that. We want facts, not our own opinions.'

'Boss, I have no opinions. I'm paid not to have them, you made that perfectly clear. I think you're the one with the fertile imagination at the moment, not me. I haven't reached any conclusion at all about this.'

'You are one cool cookie, Ciara.'

'Believe it. You'll also be impressed to hear that I have captured Maria's lovely visage on film and you can feast your eyes on that shortly.'

I gave her the name of the photographic studio I use for this sort of work and told her to collect my latest film while she was delivering hers.

'Right, I have no more time to waste on you,' she told me. 'It's much more fun watching journalists try to doorstep Michael O'Donoghue, even though there's feck all of that today. See you later, though hopefully you won't see me.'

'Roger. Over and out.'

'What you do in your own spare time is none of my business,' she said, and hung up before I could retaliate. I found myself laughing.

I liked working alone, always had. And so Ciara's presence should have made me feel uncomfortable or crowded. But this was not the case. I enjoyed having her along. It was fun, actually. I think one of the reasons was that Ciara was fresh to me, as well as to the job. Come to think of it, she was fresh with me as well; she was lippy with everyone. We had no history, we were making it now, as we went along. And I needed her. Work was getting done, and the company marched ever onwards towards world domination. But I felt uneasy that my enforced leisure time was turning out to be busier than I could ever have predicted. I had miscalculated and didn't have enough of it left to be a proper back up to Ciara.

Part of me has always been a guilt-ridden purist. Now, the big 'G' tried to gain a foothold, and I needed to justify my existence. This was not something Barry ever seemed to worry about. Perhaps being an actor, or an artist, brought with it a different set of values. Barry relaxed when he was out of work, and got on with the strenuous business of dissing everyone in showbiz, as well as hours of old-fashioned bitching. Often he refused to work if it was 'not right' for him. And of course he had an agent, who held his hand at these times and looked after him; in loco parentis. Me, I fretted. I worried. I borrowed money to pay the bills. I looked around for ways to make ends meet.

I couldn't relax about the fact that I was going to have a bath and prepare myself for a night out. I was a good quarter of a mile from home, walking purposefully along with my red dress over one arm and a fearsome guard dog straining on a leash from the other, but I could still do business. I rang Maeve for an update.

'I had another call, but it wasn't like the others. It came in while I was out doing some voiceovers. Why don't I play it for you and you'll see what I mean?'

She was right. This message had a soundtrack: it was the shower scene from *Psycho*.

'That does it,' I said. 'This has officially gone too far. It's time to put serious frighteners on the companies we know have your number, see what that turns up. Is there any way it could be a friend or a work acquaintance?'

'I really don't think so, Leo. I'm not fighting with anyone or in the bad books anywhere that I know of.'

'I have to say again that I think we should tell the police about this.'

'I know, I know, so does Mark. But I don't want all that attention. And I'm worried that the press will get hold of it, and you know what they're like when they get the whiff of a story. I'd have no life.'

'Okay, we'll give my plan a go, but if that doesn't work and the calls continue, we go to the cops.'

'Agreed. Leo, I really am grateful for this. Also, I think it's time we discussed money.'

'No,' I said, firmly. 'I wouldn't hear of it.'

'Leo, you're running a business. Get sense.'

'We'll talk about it if I get a result. How about that?'

'Done. Incidentally, don't you have a date tonight?'

'Maeve, it's not a date. I am doing a favour for a friend.'

'Why don't you do *yourself* a favour? Go home and have a good time getting ready.'

'Just for you then,' I agreed cheerily, as I rang off.

A butterfly stretched its wings in my tummy. I relished the sensation, the expectation.

I let myself and the dog into the house. Although I had preparations to make for an evening's socialising, I was first to be an intermediary in a trans-species war. No. 4 barked thrice to alert the cat population of his presence. Bridie was the only resident feline at the time. She arched her back and puffed her fur out to twice its size, then hissed something of a symphony and gave a yeowl of encore. No. 4, in perfect harmony, lunged forward with a bass growl, while Bridie swiped a claw across his nose, before disappearing at graceful but high speed through the cat flap. All round, a beautifully judged performance.

It might normally have worried me, or at the very least been jotted down for future reference, but all I could think of now was Andy Raynor. I kissed No. 4's injured snout and soothed his pride. Then I turned my attention to myself. I really can be a selfish cow sometimes.

FIFTEEN

I masturbated in the bath. It was the only way I could think of to reduce the mounting tension in my body, and I thought it might leave me less vulnerable to the charms of one Andrew Raynor, handsome man and knicker beast. I poured some drool into the water from an ancient Christmas present languishing on the shelf – a bit like myself, I thought at the time. It smelt plausible enough. By the time I finished, the bathroom was awash with suds; I hadn't realised that it was bubble bath, and I had been energetic. I searched for a wise message on the label, from Ovid or one of his cronies, but message found I none. Didn't really matter, I'd had a great time. I even stumbled a little blindly as I got out of the tub, so maybe there is a smidgen of truth in the old saying about wanking harming your vision. Then again I am notoriously clumsy, so . . .

No. 4 gave me 'a look' as I re-entered my domain.

'Don't you dare,' I told him. 'If humans could look after

their arses like you can, they would. It's a wonder you don't have to walk with a white stick, now that I think of it.'

I had the house to myself barring the cats, who had returned en masse, and the dog who decided on a snooze. It was bliss. I stood in front of the full-length mirror in the bedroom and posed a bit. Normally, Barry has exclusive use of this for preening purposes. My work calls for mono-chrome anonymity, so I don't have much call to fluff up the feathers. I did seem to be glowing, but the bath had been hot, and that could have resulted in this healthy flush I saw before me. I laid the dress and its accompaniments on the bed, putting the previous party choices to shame, and was reaching for the hairdryer when my mobile rang. This time the tune seemed to be a badly programmed version of the James Bond theme. I felt vaguely glad that Barry was going to so much trouble to follow up his ruse; I took it to be a sign of affection. But if he continued this for more than a week I would have to kill him.

'Good evening, Ms Street, this is your escort speaking.'

'Mr Raynor, how nice of you to call.' Andy had a fabulously rich voice, I decided. Pity he'd won Womaniser of the Year for a decade and half running.

'I just wanted to make sure that you had not forgotten our arrangement?'

'Andy, that would be difficult, seeing as how you've involved all of the women in my family, and yours too, probably.'

'I can't help it if your mother loves me. Can't blame her either. How is it I don't seem to have that effect on her only daughter?'

'Andy, leave it out. Tease someone else for a change.'

'Rightio. Now, to business. Do you have something wonderful to wear?'

'Of course.'

'Good. And are you dressed yet?'

'No, sir. I've just had my bath, and after I've dried my hair, I'll be climbing into full regalia.'

'Ah. So, a naked Leo Street, about to get into uniform. I have to confess that I am now thinking of touching myself in a rude way.'

I began to laugh. In the mirror I could see the reflection of a teenager from years past who had delighted in similar phonecalls from this same man. Be careful, said the older, wiser Leo, who was in my head somewhere. I shrugged her off, I was having fun.

'Are you naked?' he asked.

'Just about,' I replied, perhaps a little softly.

'Tell me more,' he purred.

'Well, I've had a bubble bath, and I smell of peach and orange, with just a hint of ylang-ylang, and a suggestion of sandalwood.'

'I can practically taste you,' he said, simply, to the point.

There was a pause between us, and I realised that my pulse was racing. To hear him so clearly on the other end of the line was so tactile, I imagined I felt his breath in my ear. Did he feel the same way too? After a time I continued, 'On the bed I have a red outfit with matching everything.'

'Uh-hunh. Why don't you lie on the bed beside those clothes and I'll come over now and help you dress?' His voice sounded hoarse with desire, and I sat on the edge of the bed to steady myself.

Downstairs the front door banged shut. 'Leo, I'm home,' a voice called. My body jolted back to the present. 'Fucking hell,' I said, without meaning to. 'I'm upstairs, Barry,' I shouted. 'Eh, sorry, Andy, where were we?'

'I'll be over at eight,' he said, and hung up.

'Do I have any clean jeans?' Barry asked, as he invaded the bedroom. He paused briefly in front of the mirror to admire what he saw there. He was pleased with the reflected glory.

I crossed my still-shaking legs. 'If you've washed some, then yes,' I replied.

No one could accuse Barry of being handy around the house. Having said that, he was well able to do the laundry, and the washing up, and other sundry domestic chores, when the mood took him.

'Shite, shite, shite!' he said, punctuating the rifling of his chest of drawers, and the spilling of men's clothes all over the floor. 'I can't find my Butt t-shirt either,' he said. This was a frayed old grey thing with the words 'Bite my butt' emblazoned front and back. It had once been black, and reportedly magnificent; before my time. Like his favourite Y-fronts, he felt it was lucky for him.

'Can't help you with any of that,' I told him. 'If you didn't wash any jeans, you probably don't have a fresh pair. And I haven't seen Mr Butt in a long time.' I let the double-entendre hang in the air, but he didn't respond. Instead he spotted the party clothes.

'What's all that about?' he asked.

'I'm going out with my friend Andy, remember?'

'Oh, yeah, that, him. Well, have a good time.' He gestured to the dress. 'That's Angela's, isn't it?'

'Yes.'

I don't know how he did it, or if he had done anything at all, but I now felt completely second-hand. I was a sham. I began to feel angry with Barry, then calmed down; this was not his fault, I was mad with myself, surely, not him. I was the one feeling like a fake, his words were incidental catalysts. There was no point in taking any of this out on an innocent bystander.

But suddenly I wanted rid of the baggage in my life. I wanted to have the house to myself and my pets again. I wanted the freedom to allow a sexy man to come over and ravish me on my bed before we dressed ourselves in beautiful clothes and went out to enjoy ourselves some more about the town. I was fed up of having to pander to a heedless, selfish git – often more than one, given the open-door policy operated by Barry. What if I just threw him out, right now? I went downstairs to the bathroom and splashed cold water on my face. That brought me to my senses.

'Do you have work tonight?' I asked. 'Is that why you need fresh clothes?'

Barry had taken to the sofa with a forlorn look on his face. 'Yeah, what am I going to do?'

'Why don't you wear the trousers of your dress suit and your white collarless shirt? You'll look fantastic.'

'I will, won't I?' he said, perking up. 'Thanks, Leo, I don't know what I'd do without you.' He pecked my cheek and ran upstairs to change. I felt drained, and my high good humour for going out had faded. I hauled myself up to the bedroom to finish my own preparations.

I often put off decisions. Sometimes it's because I'm unsure of the rights and wrongs of a situation. At other times, it's because I'm being cowardly. But now, I decided to defer any rash action, because haste might ruin a lot more than it preserved. It would be very easy to break up with

Barry. But in the long run would that be a good thing? Was it right to smash up a relationship rather than work on it? Surely running away from our problems was the easy option; too easy. I was certain that my own parents had had hard times over the years of their marriage, but they hadn't packed it in. They had persevered. And so would I. And tomorrow, we would have a long talk and make a new beginning.

'We should spend some time together now that I'm freer during the day,' I said to Barry, as he grabbed his jacket to leave.

'Yeah, great idea,' he said. 'See you.'

And he was gone. I was exhausted.

I noticed that I had a message on my answering machine. It was Mull of Mullaney Motors. 'Leo, this is Mull,' he said, predictably enough. 'Your car should be ready late today, so I'll leave it over to your house then. Eh, I need a word with Barry anyway. On the vehicle front, I really do think you should get yourself something new, this one's in rag order. Oh, and it's dark blue now, I couldn't find a match for the green.'

Barry was the reason he was coming over. Mull and he had a stupid arrangement over dope. Barry maintained it was a favour between friends, but I hated it; it made him look like a dealer, and it was only a question of semantics whether he was or was not. I started to hyperventilate.

I needed something concrete to take my mind off my home life, and that was work, normally. I racked my brain, then remembered an unchased detail from earlier. I dialled Maeve Kelly's mum.

'Sandra, it's Leo Street here. Sorry to bother you again, but I wanted to ask you about someone I saw driving up to your house earlier on. It was Bernie Flood. Isn't she a friend of Michael O'Donoghue's?'

'Oh, was, Leo, *was*,' she said. 'It's interesting that you mentioned him to me earlier. I'd forgotten that she used to do a line with him, if that's not too old-fashioned a phrase to use nowadays. It ended badly, which was par for the course with him. He married Miranda shortly afterwards. Whether that was related or not, I've no idea. We don't talk about it generally, and anyway we don't see that much of one another as a group these days. I did mention his name today though, what with all the stuff in the papers, and she said something to the effect that he'd get his just deserts now, then clammed up. I get the feeling there's no love lost there.'

'Right,' I said.

'By the way, your breads were a great success. I took the liberty of giving your number to a few of the girls. I hope you don't mind? I think you can expect some orders soon.'

I was stunned. 'Er, thank you,' I squeezed out. 'Thank you very much.'

I stood rooted to the spot. My handiwork was a hit, and it had made me money. My, oh, my. And yet again, a simple question had yielded interesting information. Some things never change, and at the same time wonders never cease. Would that observation be any good on a bottle of balm? I wondered.

My landline rang. When I answered, my niece Lucy asked for Barry.

'He's gone, Luce. Anything I can do?'

'Eh, no, Leo, just he said that myself and a few friends could go on the Crawl tonight, and I wanted to check if that's still okay.'

I could feel an unreasonable, slow burn begin in the pit of my stomach.

'I'm sure if Barry said that, he meant it,' I told my fifteen-year-old niece. 'Actually, he seemed excited about tonight's show,' I continued. I neglected to mention the special effort with clothing, or costume, or whatever he wanted to pass it off as. 'Enjoy yourself,' I said, as I hung up.

I sat on the bed with legs shaking for the second time in an hour. No wonder Barry had taken so much care tonight; when a teenager had a crush, you had to dress to suit, to nurture it, and to burnish your own vanity. I was furious. I was beyond fury, I was jealous. I went to the bathroom, again, and splashed water on my face, again. I'm not sure if it worked a second time. What I do know is that I now took sensual pleasure in dressing my hair and my body, and scenting the whole package. When I looked in the mirror that last time, I found my hands stray to the tops of my stockings and linger as I revelled in the freedom they afforded me. And whoever was in that picture looked hot and ready for action.

When Andy Raynor rang my bell, I downed the last of a brandy I had been nursing and went to the door. He gave a low whistle and put his hands around my waist as I stood basking in his attention. A moment lengthened between us, delicious with tension and promise. Then he leaned in to kiss my cheek. It left an indelible burn on my senses. 'You look great,' he said.

I knew I was glowing, if only because a beautiful man had complimented me. And I didn't care a whit if it was the truth or not. I didn't feel second-hand anymore, and I did not rush to explain that the dress was borrowed, as I normally would have. Tonight I was free of my self-imposed restrictions and self-deprecation; they were neither needed nor welcome. Tonight I could do and say whatever I liked. I decided that my final lottery number would be 1, in honour of myself. I would buy my ticket tomorrow, win the jackpot and piss off to somewhere wonderful while I decided what to do with my millions.

'That is one hairy house,' Andy also said, as he led me down the garden path. I was not sure whether this was another compliment.

Marion Maloney just happened to be putting out her empty milk bottles at that very moment. She was wearing her night vision, which is even more accurate than her daytime sight. She could also smell interest in the post-dusk air. She dashed to my gate.

'Leo, I was just wondering how your poor car is?' she said, full of anxiety. I had a mental picture of the battered jalopy hooked up to a bleeping machine in intensive care.

'It's going to pull through, against all the odds,' I assured her, a little dramatically. I couldn't help it, her concern was catching. 'It'll be coming home tomorrow. And it has turned completely blue.'

'Blue?' she repeated, updating her data pool. 'Of course it must be costing you a fortune in taxi fares,' she said, pointedly referring to Andy's two-seater convertible Mercedes.

I let her off the hook. 'This is my friend, Andrew Raynor.'

'Pleased to meet you,' she said, extending her hand with a girly smile. Fair play to Marion, she knows a fine man when she sees one.

'Enchanted,' Andy said, flirting outrageously.

I laughed out loud. 'I didn't think anyone used that word anymore.'

'More people should,' Marion said, in admonition of me in particular, for my bad manners, and people in general, for their ignorance. 'I can see that you're on your way out, so I'll not keep you youngsters. We'll talk again. Have a good time.'

She waved as we drove off, and stayed in her doorway until we had turned the corner.

'Nice bumps,' Andy said. It was hard to believe that he meant the speed ramps. He was not a man to miss some handy smut.

'You really are incorrigible,' I told him. And I smiled some more. I was happy. 'By the way, she means that. She really will want to interview you at some future stage.'

'I must make sure I have something interesting to tell her then,' he said as we sped into the night.

I felt a shiver run down my spine.

SIXTEEN

When a woman marries in the country, each of her neighbours lights a fire for her on her route to and from the
church. With our mothers involved, I expected a conflagra-
tion on every corner, and at every set of traffic lights we
stopped at. Luckily enough, no one was allowed to play
with matches that night. Instead, the lights of the shore and
the bay twinkled merrily, blessing us on our journey southwards. Oranges mixed with umbers, burnt and unscorched,
speckled through with dots of white and cream from
thousands of bulbs decorating the city. The waters of the sea
and the river were still, as if holding their breath, and from
within them a parallel universe gently waved, impressionis-
tic in its undulations.

'A fiver for them,' said my companion.

'Oh, it'll cost you more than that, Andy Raynor.'

'It's a long time since I've seen that sort of smile on your
face. What do you know that I don't?'

187

'Not a lot, really. I'm just relaxed, I guess.'

'Or happy, maybe?'

'Maybe.'

We drove on, over the river at the toll bridge, along by Ringsend and on to the Strand Road, with its panoramic view of the coast, before turning into Sandymount.

'I hope you won't get a nose bleed being so far over into Injun territory,' he said.

'Nah. I spend a lot of my time poking around this end of town. I could probably pass as a native now.'

'I appreciate this, Leo. Thanks for coming.'

'Don't mention it, a friend in need and all that. I think my mother's a lot more excited about it than anyone else,' I said, keeping my voice as neutral as possible. It was crucial that I believed this too, and if I passed this off as the truth, the night would be easier to deal with and to get through. There is nothing so unseemly as a grown woman with a crush on an ex from so far back that he probably can't remember that they ever went out together in the first place. This man had a girlfriend who was serious enough to get brought on nights out with his mum, and I lived with a partner. Sorted. No conflict of interest. No room for misunderstandings.

'That smile is back,' he said.

'Enjoy it, I am.'

He laughed and said, 'I will.'

When Andy smiles, the world brightens. When he laughs, it sings. He's just one of those guys.

'You're a very nice man,' I said, before I could stop myself.

'Thank you. You're a very nice woman.'

'I wonder, am I, Andy? I tell a lot of fibs, you know.'

'We all do, Leo. It's human nature. And now I have to insist that we have that smile back in place because we are within thirty seconds of the club.'

'As Sir wishes.'

'That's what I like to hear.'

We swung into the forecourt of Bridgecross. In the distance I could see the old railway after which it was named.

'Does this car turn into a pumpkin at midnight, or anything like that?'

'No, Cinders, it does not. And even if your wonderful dress turns to slavish rags at that time, you'll still look great to me.'

'Thanks.'

He came around to the passenger side to let me out. I know a few women who would swoon at such an action, thinking it chivalrous, and others who would deem it smarmy. I think he carried it off on this occasion.

'That could have been so cheesy,' I said, as I alighted from my carriage.

'Is there no romance in your soul?' he asked, in mock horror.

'This is not romance, Andy, it's persistence.'

'Still top marks,' he pointed out. I could feel that I was smiling 'that smile' again. Time to rein in.

'If it were romance, we wouldn't be out in a crowd of two hundred people of your acquaintance,' I added tartly.

'If I had asked you out on your lonesome, you wouldn't have come,' he replied.

This was true. We allowed a truce.

Bridgecross is the largest sports club in Dublin city. It has its own cricket pitch, indoor and outdoor tennis courts, all-weather pitches for hockey and rugby, and a five-a-side facility for weekend sports people. This evening the club-house, newly refurbished at a cost of trillions, was lit up to welcome us all. The well-heeled of the capital parked their expensive cars and escorted their trophy partners up the steps to the main door. We fell in step and Andy ushered me along with just the suggestion of an arm about my waist. It felt good; we fitted each other. We sauntered with the ease of two people who had known one another forever. And, for once, the goddess of grace had regarded me with favour: I did not stumble or go over even once on my sister-in-law's heels. Hallelujah.

Before we went in the door, I stopped Andy to ask, 'Will this be a night of "Agadoo" and "The Birdie Song"?'

'If that's what you'd like, I can arrange it.'

I stood with my mouth hanging open at that awful notion. It can't have been an attractive sight, but he leaned over and kissed me nevertheless. I recoiled and hit the door jamb with a vicious 'thwack'. It was all too sudden. It had the effect of closing my gob though. Guiltily, I realised that I had thought 'too' rather than 'so' with the 'sudden'. This would have to stop.

'Jeez, Leo, I didn't know you were that allergic to me,' Andy said, as he helped straighten me.

'I'm not – I mean, I am – I wasn't expecting that,' I burbled, rubbing the worst hit elbow.

'I'll give fair warning next time,' he said.

'You will not. There can be none of that carry on. It's not right. And neither is interactive shite music.'

'If you say so.'

'I do.'

'Do you need me to kiss that elbow better?'

'No,' I shouted. He held both hands up in mock surrender.

We walked through the door and I was a teenager again, in a room full of people determined to have a good time. The smells were different: no more Brut or Lynx, no more Lenthéric fragrances, or Charlie. Instead the air was steeped in Issey Miyake, Calvin Klein, Chanel, some Poison, and a dash of Obsession. The complexions of the anxious faces searching for a part-time thrill were clearer than in the old days, but the intentions were the same, and the promise of the dry grind against a thigh during the slow set was still an option after all these years. Heads turned. I blossomed. They may have been admiring Andy, but I was happy to share the attention from the side. He put his arm around my waist again, firmly this time, and we walked on. 'I'll introduce you to some people,' he said.

'Where do you get them from?' asked a man in a navy jacket, with the embroidered club crest and gilt buttons. He was wearing *slax*. I immediately assumed that he called his wife 'the little lady', not particularly as an endearment, but because he couldn't be bothered to remember her name. My instant annoyance also suggested that he would hold his knife as if it were a pen, a habit I cannot abide. This, it turned out, was Bob Moran.

'I'll be with you both as soon as I've done my greeting duties,' he promised.

'Oh, no hurry,' we assured him, earnestly.

A woman in a pink confection fluttered up to see us. She was Mrs Bob Moran. She hung adoringly off Andy's free arm, cooing musically to him. Quite the coquette. But then he had a range of similar effects on most genders. I merited a nod. Meanly, I imagined her uttering phrases like 'heavens to Betsy' a lot. When Andy extricated himself, we headed for the sanctuary of the bar area and he explained that Mrs Bob was a relentlessly helpful woman who did a lot of good work for charity.

I scanned the room while Andy bought us a drink, but I did not see Michael and Miranda O'Donoghue. I checked my phone to make sure that it was working, in case Ciara wanted to call me. It was. I was as on duty as I could have been at that time. And the knowledge that I had a deputy in the field was a gift.

Mr Bob Moran turned out to be 'great gas', according to himself. He also thought that I had the funniest name he'd heard in a long time. 'The Streets,' he guffawed. 'Sure Dublin is full of them.' I should be paid for every time that I hear this; I could retire on the proceeds. 'And what class of a name is Leo for a gorgeous young lady like yourself?'

I creased my face into a pained grin, for Andy's sake. 'Oh, now,' I said, casting my eyes upwards, as if it would take an aeon to get through that one.

'Are you anything to that poofy lad, that ballerina, Wayne Street?'

'No, Mr *Moron*,' I replied, thinking that no 'oxy' need apply. 'I think you mean the dancer Wayne Sleep.'

'Do I? Well now, aren't you the clever one all the same? Oh, Andy is the boyo can pick them and no mistake.'

The 'them' stung; I was all too aware of how many women had accompanied Andy to similar functions over the years. Bob had reached a plateau of wit, as far as I was concerned, but before I raised my clenched hand to thump him, my phone rang and I excused myself.

'Yo, Management, it's the proletariat.'

'Ciara, you may have saved a man's life in here. I was about to punch a stupid fart's lights out when you called.'

'All in a day's work,' she said. 'Just to let you know that I saw you arrive with a most picturesque man: who is he? And the O'Donoghues have just pulled up, in a metallic grey car.'

'Curiouser and curiouser.'

'It might be, mightn't it? Don't worry, I'm not racing to any conclusions. I can't tell if it's the one that's been following me because I haven't got it to come close enough to check the reg when I've spotted the tail.'

'We'll put it in the mix and see what comes up.'

'So, who is he?'

'Pardon?'

'Ooh, *pardon*, la di da. Who is the hunk?'

'He's an old friend of the family, nothing more.'

'Sure, boss.' I could hear her chortling on the other end of the line.

'I've got to get back to this party,' I said.

'I'll bet you do.'

'Ciara,' I growled.

'Talk to you later, or tomorrow, whichever. Be a good girl now. Remember, I'll be keeping an eye on you.'

Someone was watching me: a taste of my own medicine.

Andy was in conversation with the O'Donoghues when I returned. I don't know why, but I felt a little shocked by that. I was now right on the coal face. Miranda could sense my unease and relished saying, 'Are you sure we haven't met somewhere before? You seem so familiar to me.' Her cold, grey eyes dared me to engage.

'I have one of those faces,' I murmured, eschewing the challenge.

Her husband was also giving me more than the once over. 'It's funny, but I feel the same way too,' he said, agreeing with his wife, which was probably a first in a while. 'Of course, I see a lot of women from day to day,' he continued. He just stopped short of remarking that we all look the same after a while, I thought. Or was I tarring him, unfairly, with the same brush as Bob Moran? And he had 'met' me before, on the night of my car bashing as I followed him home. All of a sudden I felt hot and moist, which is good in some situations, not so in others; this was one of the bad times. I excused myself to visit the loo, or the 'Little Ladies' as I'm sure Bob would have called it.

The washroom was full of regular-sized women talking about a member who was steadily spreading glandular fever amongst the club. I waited long enough to ascertain that it was not Andy, and to learn that someone called Serenity had had twins the day before but planned to be back on the hockey team by the end of the following week. She had chosen the names Oswald and Thierry for the babes, and I took from this that they were boy babies; an iffy assumption in this day and age?

Bob had rejoined the growing band of Andy's company when I returned. Miranda's look of disdain for him could have been cut with a knife. He was remarking that fair was fair and fowl was chicken as I came within earshot, and with that she rolled her eyes and abandoned the group. Her husband looked relieved, Bob didn't even notice she'd gone. Andy was wearing a lazy grin as he watched me try to deal with the nonsense that was Bob Moran, now confessing that he was 'a rugby kinda guy'. Michael O'Donoghue just seemed intent on getting drunk, and after the day he'd had, perhaps this was no surprise. Out of sheer politeness, or perhaps loyalty to Andy, he asked what I did for a living, which I brushed off with 'office work, you know'. He told me that he was a doctor, and he made babies. I was interested in his choice of words.

'Like, in a test tube?' I asked.

'Oh, that. And I deliver and so on. I have that power.' He was so utterly casual that I wondered if his megalomania was imagined by others, or if his supposed God Complex sat so easily with him now that he hardly noticed it.

'I saw your picture in the evening paper,' I admitted.

It was the truth, of course, though somewhat short of the whole truth, given that I had seen much more than that of him over the last few days. He grunted and finished his drink in one gulp, then turned to the bar to order another. I took that to mean that he had nothing more to say to me on the subject.

Bob returned his attention to me, and his monopoly meant that I missed being introduced to a fun-looking group of Andy's friends. What was it about me, apart from my hilarious name, that attracted Bob? I wondered. And why couldn't he control it anyhow? I had about as much interest in this guy as I did in Quasimodo's jock strap. On reflection, the jock strap option was infinitely preferable.

Apparently no one is more than six degrees of separation from any stranger they meet. Move along a list of people you know, and you'll come up with a connection. And at the heart of this, often, is a 'hub' person; someone who'll turn up on many lists. I looked across at Andy Raynor and decided that he was one of those central people. He moved in many circles; was as busy as any big London Under-ground station, and on more interconnecting lines than most. Given his profession, I also came to the conclusion that if we are normally separated from others by six degrees, none of us is further than two from a journalist at any given time. Which would be of no comfort to Michael O'Donoghue. He could take some solace from the fact that Andy was a political reporter, although like the doctor he was an expert on the female reproductive system. My warning bells tried a light tinkle at this point.

Bob was still invading my personal space, in spite of the fact that I was clearly not paying him any quality attention. I was rescued by a pan-fried man in an aloe vera sauce.

'I fell asleep on a sunbed,' he confessed.

The resultant blush on his cheeks gave him a perpetual air of embarrassment. The Moron wandered off, leaving Michael O'Donoghue sozzling away behind me and my new beacon friend.

'Don't mind Bob, he's not the worst. I'm Billy.'

'If he pats my ass once more, I'll break his arm,' I said.

Michael O'Donoghue let out an involuntary chuckle. Maybe he wasn't so bad after all.

The music had started and Andy was whisked on to the floor by a woman in her forties who writhed around him like a belly dancer. He had the knack of bringing out the eejit in all of us, it seemed. I looked at his tall, handsome form and was reminded of Barry. I know that comparisons are invidious, but I couldn't help but remember how inordinately proud Barry had been of a dump he'd taken recently. He'd weighed himself afterwards and discovered that he was eight pounds lighter. I could see him in my mind's eye, planted in front of Groundhog News, watching the same reports on the hour every hour, and smiling wistfully as he remembered his remarkable feat. Of course he wouldn't be there tonight, because he was too busy scrambling my niece's head and heart. It made sense in a way; he was really just an older teenager himself.

Andy came to take me away from my thoughts. His timing was flawless, as always. Just as we stepped on to the dance floor, the tempo slowed. He held one of my hands and used his other arm to encircle my waist. I put my spare mitt on his shoulder and tried to think pure thoughts. We swayed together in time to the music, and I was certain that he was edging closer with every beat. I tried in vain to stiffen, to send out a negative body signal, but the truth was that it was delicious. I could feel toned muscles under his shirt, and a very toned one in his pants.

Then, with even more impeccable timing than Andrew Raynor, real life interrupted.

At first I didn't notice the commotion over the noise of the music and the hum of my eager thoughts. But, little by little, events at the edge of the dance floor encroached on us. A woman was standing in front of Michael O'Donoghue, gesturing wildly and, it seemed, screaming at him. I craned my neck for a better view.

'You have to be the most curious woman I know,' Andy said.

'I hope you don't mean that as in odd,' I said. 'It's my job to be curious. I have an insatiable thirst for knowledge and information.'

He smiled indulgently. 'Here's the deal. I'll steer us closer, if you pay me full attention once the fracas is over.'

'Deal,' I said, drinking in those dark eyes of his.

As we approached, friends and acquaintances were trying to calm the situation. The woman yelled, 'You've ruined me! You promised me everything and you gave me nothing. You've destroyed me. I could kill you, you bastard.'

Miranda watched from the shadows, a smile flitting across her extraordinary face. When she caught my eye, she turned away and missed the rest of the action as a result. It was just then that the shouting woman shut up, and threw a pint of lager over Michael O'Donoghue.

A bouncer told everyone that the show was over, and escorted the assailant away. She went quietly, spent from her exertions. Michael O'Donoghue was aghast. He stood silently fuming at the incident, and quite unable to save face. He tried in vain to wipe away the drink drenching his suit and shirt, but gave up when he realised the futility of this and said his goodnights. I could see him ask his wife to leave, but obviously she refused. He took out a mobile, made a quick call and left. Ciara was back in business.

Something about the woman bothered me. She seemed familiar, but I couldn't put a name to her. The harder I tried the more buried the information became. There was nothing for it but to let my stubborn memory relax and choose its own sweet time to reveal all.

'Enough?' Andy asked.

'Sorry. You know I can't resist a scene.'

'Don't I just?'

By rights I should now have been following the unidentified woman while Ciara tailed Michael O'Donoghue, but these were not normal circumstances. And I am ashamed to say that reason was buckled to the floor as Andy swirled me gently to the middle of the throng of dancers, and we took up where we had previously left off.

It was exhilarating. We were back in the spotlight of our own emotions and the rest of the world was excluded. Work was forgotten. Bridgecross and its attendant function were forgotten. They receded further with each note of the music. We leaned together, slowly moving from foot to foot. He reached down to kiss the back of my neck and I was lost. Molten heat poured into every joint of my body and my ears filled with a ringing noise. His lips brushed lightly up and down, finding new erogenous zones, and I felt myself pushing against him with urgency.

'Come on,' he said, in a low voice laced with danger. 'We're leaving.'

We didn't bother with farewells, but grabbed our few possessions and rushed out into the night, and his car, and pleasure so long awaited.

SEVENTEEN

I had often dreamed of speeding through the dark in a flash motor with a good-looking man who was about to make outrageous love to me. The dream and, I can report, the reality are exciting and vital, at the time. On mature reflection, it's nice when the man is your own live-in lover, but life does not always deal that hand. Then, in the dull grey pallor of hindsight, excitement and vitality disappear through a suddenly glimpsed window. But, happily, hindsight is just that, and can be ignored until later, when it is cued to make an appearance, whether you want it to or not.

Andy was nothing if not stylish. He blipped open the electronic gates to his house as we pulled up, with a timing borne of habit and panache. He steered me through his front door and on to a couch with effortless ease. We could not wait for the intense white heat of our first coupling, and so we did not. He even said my name as he came, which was a nice touch, I thought. Then we really got down to business, this time in his vast bed. I'm not sure that there are names for some of the things he did to me, as he brought me again and again to where I wanted to be. It was heavenly. And amusing, as he made me feel at ease with our love-making. We laughed and touched and kissed and licked and sucked, and plenty more besides. My groin usually ached from desire, now it was throbbing from sheer frantic exertion. I was sure that I would not sit easily for days. Great!

As I lay in the circle of his arms, cuddled and sated, I asked, 'Well? Worth waiting for?'

'Oh, yes,' he said, kissing me on my forehead, tenderly. 'But now that I know what I've been missing all these years, I'm raging I didn't do this sooner.'

Me too, I thought. I laughed involuntarily as I remembered something.

'What is it?' he asked.

'Nothing. My grandmother was right about you, that's all.'

'Is that a good thing?'

'In this case, yes.'

'Tell me more.'

'Can't, I'm afraid, it's a bit personal.'

He climbed on top of me, pinning my arms to the bed. 'Tell me, or I'll be forced to torture you.'

I thrashed about trying to get out from under him, but he was immovable. Finally, I gave in. 'She compared your penis very favourably with a donkey's,' I told him.

He guffawed and said, 'I want to reassure you that it's conjecture on her part, even if she is correct.'

I cuffed him lightly for his arrogance and snuggled closer.

'You do realise that this is the second time you've ended up in bed with me in a very short space of time,' Andy murmured.

'Mmm. But last time I really just *slept* with you, and I don't remember a thing.'

'And do you think this might be a little more memorable?'

'I guess.'

'Witch.'

'Mmm.'

We nuzzled together some more and I began to nod off. Then with a jolt I was awake and in a cold sweat. What had I just done? I must have taken leave of my senses. Andy held me tight, kissing my face and neck. 'You're fine, Leo,' he assured me. 'There is nothing to worry about.' I wanted to believe him. I returned his kisses and felt tension ooze away. I fell asleep.

We were spooned together when I woke with another start at 3 a.m. The room was in darkness, and Andy softly said, 'I'm here. It's okay.' And it was, you know. I felt happy and good. He stiffened behind me, and we began again. I abandoned myself to him, to us, and enjoyed each carnal moment. At 4.15 I stirred from my glow, which I was sure had lit up the bedroom. 'I have to go,' I said. 'I can't stay the night.'

'Yes, you can.'

'I can, but I won't,' I said. 'I'd better have a shower.'

These were some of the hardest words I'd uttered in years. I didn't want to go. I wanted to stay with this man. I felt safe and cocooned with him. But I also knew that I could not hide here, and that sooner or later I had to face the world and my life, and sooner seemed the better part of valour just then.

'I'll make us some coffee,' he said.

Of course he didn't, he joined me in the shower. And when I kissed him goodbye on his doorstep, thirty minutes later, he gave a groan and pressed me against the door jamb. He raised my dress, and caressed my thighs, then my buttocks, moving inwards to my clitoris. I was saturated for him again. As he thrust himself into me he moaned, 'What are you doing to me?' I might well have asked the same question.

When I was finally ready to leave he stood back and said, 'You look beautiful.' And, at that moment, I believe I was.

My heart started its *Titanic* routine as I told the taximan to take me to 11, The Villas in Clontarf. I dreaded going home. And rightly so; I was now no better than any of the cheats I'd followed over the years. The playing field had suddenly become all too level. I had betrayed someone I'd declared I loved. But are you *in* love with him? asked a small voice. I was a mass of confused thoughts and emotions. On one level I felt elated, untouchable; on another I was scum. The only plus I had going for me was that the driver stayed quiet for the entire journey.

The moon was a spotlight in the clear night sky. It lit up The Villas, shining pure and pearl-like in the heavens. A soft, cold wind rustled the grass, making it whisper. I've heard in songs that this sort of grass is a gossip and likes nothing more than to pass on scandal and innuendo to the trees, who in turn broadcast it to the world. I followed my breath to the front door, quietly inserting my key in the lock, slipping in under a cloak of secrecy. The little house was at rest. No. 4 stirred, but was too immersed in his canine slumbers to announce that I was home. The cats weren't too put out by my arrival either. Barry's couch was empty, which was a relief. Silence bathed the house. I was grateful.

Stealthily, I washed myself in the bathroom, at once shivering to the memory of Andy and eager to remove evidence of my infidelity. I was deliciously sore, and my body felt joy at the remembered closeness of him. That old sack magic. It was my inner self which was having a hard time dealing with my night of passion. I felt exhausted and dragged myself up the stairs, where I saw that Barry was unconscious and wearing a t-shirt and boxers. I followed suit; it was April and nights were cold. I climbed into bed and fell into a deep sleep. If it was troubled I was not aware of it, I was literally too shagged to notice. Barry never stirred.

The next morning, or should I say later on, my body felt as if it had been put through a mangle. I was like an infirm woman of ninety as I tried to get out of bed. Barry was downstairs pottering around, and a glance at the clock told me that it was now 11 a.m. I was more alarmed than the alarm, horrified at the lateness, but unable to spring into action as many of my muscle groups appeared to be in spasm or actively locking. I lay for a few moments in the tranquillity of my duvet, which was warm and uncompli-cated. I decided to stay there forever more.

Forever isn't what it used to be. In my case it lasted all of eight minutes. Then Maeve rang and my early retirement from the human rat race was over. I didn't move far, mind, just reached a hand out from under the bedclothes, but it was enough to acknowledge the rest of the world and one of man's greatest technological achievements, the telephone.

'I'll *not* beat around the bush,' she announced. '*How was it?*'

'Maeve, you're getting excited about nothing. I've told you before and I'll obviously have to tell you again, it was just a favour for a friend.'

'*Right.* We can do this one of two ways: *either* you give me *full* details over the phone, *or* I come over in person *now.*'

I was grinning from ear to ear. Was this it then, the thrill of the forbidden? How could betrayal leave me with such an exultant rush of adrenalin? If this was infidelity, was I now an infidel? I wanted to tell her that Andy Raynor had short circuited my electrics several times, and that I longed for more. I wanted to tell her that some of my inner workings had fused from the thermo-nucleic activity of my illicit adventure, and I could hardly stand for sore muscles. I wanted to scream and shout and dance around the room with delight. Most of all I wanted to tart the whole thing up to sound acceptable, which in my gut I knew it was not. But I couldn't. Barry had arrived with a cup of coffee.

'I'll call you later,' I said. 'I have to get going properly on your nuisance calls today, one way or another. THANKS, BARRY.'

'I *knew* it, I just *knew* it!' she squealed, but in a hushed way. 'I can't *wait* for the gorys. Ciao.'

I shuffled to a sitting position, duvet tucked tightly around me. I could still smell Andy on me, feel him in me.

'I don't mean to sound ungrateful, but what's all this in aid of?'

Barry shrugged. 'I suppose I must like you.' He flashed me a full-toother. Suspicion kicked in, which was a bit rich on my part, really.

'Is this some sort of guilty peace offering? You haven't done something awful to my niece, have you?'

A psychiatrist might have had a field day here, or at least a good couch morning: I wanted Barry to have a horrid secret to share with me, so that I could let myself off the hook I'd stuck myself upon. However, as is often the case, reality triumphed over hope, and he had nothing sordid to rescue me with. I gave it one last go, with reason as straight as a drunk's meander home after a skinful.

'She has the most awful crush on you, Barry, and I don't think it's a good thing to lead her on too much.'

'I know that, Marm. She's a nice kid and we have a bit of fun. I was dying for some adult attention when I was her age, but everyone treated me like an overgrown child. I think it makes her feel grown up to be having a laugh with me.'

I gave a little snort. 'And you're not much more than a big baby yourself still.'

He gave me a sing-song 'Takes one to know one,' pulled an utterly childish face and ran down the stairs before I could retaliate. Then he released the hound, and I was faced with the choice of abandoning my bed, or death by affection, doggy-style.

No. 4 won and soon I was under a hot stream of shower water, washing that man right out of my hair. I became energised as I liberally applied the suds; I resolved to sort the Maeve situation, perhaps not for all but maybe for once, and allowed myself a frisson of anticipation at the prospect of Tara O'Donoghue's visit that afternoon. I emerged from the bathroom in a shroud of towelling, feeling great.

'That must have been some night out,' Barry said. 'You're glowing.'

I stopped in my tracks, did a guilty double take and lied. 'Nah, mixture of the shower and not drinking too much. I have a lot to do today, so I'm starting on a decidedly up note.'

For one awful, eternal moment, I thought he was going to ask me back to bed, but he was distracted by the news and I was saved by the world in general and Ireland in particular. The lead story was the ongoing investigation into the Fledgling Clinic. We heard a taped interview with a woman who preferred to remain nameless, telling a story of spending a fortune on in vitro fertilisation which hadn't worked. This in itself was nothing startling, the failure rate was high. But she went on to say that Michael O'Donoghue had promised further and even more expensive pioneering techniques, and after another year of failure she had begun to suspect that it was all a scam.

It seemed to me that this would be very hard to prove, if it were true, but it certainly meant that Mr O'Donoghue had a full plate with the Medical Council, the media and the Department all delving into his practices and ethics. Not to mention myself and Ciara. I did wonder, though, if the news people were just hyping a sad situation from which no one would emerge well. It was a depressing story of human desperation and manipulation and I felt the dark clouds of morality gathering over my head. I was firmly in their domain now, through work and play; rest would have to wait.

'Would I be right to suppose that we are without our full complement of actors today?' I asked Barry.

He raised his eyes at my continued pursuit of an old theme. 'Coleman changed his speech last night and scored,' he told me.

208

'Let's hope he has great luck every night from now on.'

'Relax, Leo,' Barry said. 'You'll live longer.'

Instead, I left the room which elongated Barry's life somewhat.

I was feeling a bit sniffly, so I put on my favourite woolly jumper in an effort to ape the comfort of a duvet. It must be admitted that it had the same shape as the bedclothes and was hardly flattering, but it did the trick. It was also nice to be back on the road in my own ratty old banger, now disguised as a blue car. I bumped out of The Villas with my trusty No. 4 at the dashboard, and headed for Maeve's old taxi firm. I might have stayed on for an argument with Barry about his part-time drug dealing, but I didn't feel I was on high enough ground after my evening of sin. A quick retreat for regrouping seemed a goodish plan. I gave my head a scratch, sneezed a few times and went on my way.

I don't think I have ever been in a taxi waiting room with a healthy atmosphere. This one was as musty as a marathon runner's underpants and had spots of mildewy damp in every corner, and all along the magnolia wall by the door. Some graffiti told me that Deano was a homo, and Lee luvs Candice, which was nice to know. The seats were a mixture of plastic chairs and some clapped out cottage-style arm-chairs, ejected from a smelly bedsit and worn shiny by too many tired and/or drunken arses.

The controller sat behind a reinforced glass partition, warming herself in front of a Super Ser with all three bars blazing; her legs were a patchwork of purple brackets, or 'abc's' as we used to call them when I was a kid. I was vaguely surprised that her tights didn't melt from the proximity of the fire; there's the wonder of nylon for you. She was an eighties throwback, complete with Charlie's Angels hair and lurid make-up. She was also big into shoulder pads.

I introduced myself and explained that I was here on behalf of Maeve Kelly, and why. I also told her that we had every reason to believe that the malicious calls were coming from this office, and that if they did not stop immediately, the cops would be called in. I trusted that she would pass this message on to the rest of the staff. She suggested that she might. I didn't feel I'd hit pay dirt, however. For one thing, there was no radio or television in the office, so the background noise was minimal, and certainly didn't match what we'd heard on the recordings. Still, it was a start. The elimination process had begun. We left in a hurry when I noticed a steaming pool on the lino, fresh from No. 4's bladder, I suspected.

My next stop was Maeve's doctor where I asked an ancient retainer if there was any chance that someone could have rifled Maeve's records for her phone number. I endured a lecture on patient-doctor confidentiality, gave my own about police intervention being the next step, and left with the impression that I had not yet located the culprit. A trip to the Chinese takeaway proved entirely fruitless as it only opened in the evenings, but the Indian equivalent was doing a roaring lunchtime trade. I bought a sag aloo, a chana dhal and two peshwari naan, dropped my bombshell and had an impromptu picnic in the car. No. 4 liked the naans best: 'lightly cooked cloud' he seemed to say.

I had hoped that the heat of the food might dispel my impending cold, but if anything my nose was streaming even more after the feast. Between that, an itchy scalp, a sore arse and a troubled conscience, the day began to pall. I allowed myself a vision of Andy bearing down on me wearing nothing but a smile. I had been very naughty indeed, but, dammit, you only live once, unless you're a Buddhist.

I wasn't sure how to proceed with the Andy thing. Of course there could be no 'proceeding' in my current situation, I reminded myself. But I wanted to see him again. In actual and horrible fact, I wanted to shag him as soon and as often as possible. In order to do that I would have to streamline my life somewhat, and in stark reality that meant getting shot of Barry. I didn't know if I had courage enough to do that. And I was by no means certain that my being available featured anywhere on Andy Raynor's list of desirables. A ladies' man, by definition, is hard to pin down. Andy was a serial dater, perhaps even a speed one, and now that he'd had me, he was probably done with me. That thought precipitated a panic and heralded depression, so I fired up the engine and headed out to collect the kids from school.

As I strolled from the car I spotted a shop which had a lottery machine, and decided to play my numbers in the next draw. I jotted down 1, 4, 5, 6, 11, and 19, and also allowed the computer to choose a random quickpick for me. If you're not in, you can't win.

EIGHTEEN

Jimmy Nolan sat in his car wearing shades and trying to look like a regular human being. I expected Mick to make some comment about what a gobshite his eldest son was, but he was strangely silent. I realised that he hadn't said anything at all for quite some time. Strange. I saluted Jimmy as I entered the school yard, and he pretended not to notice me. But rather than let him think that he had done a subtle thing, I returned and rapped on his window until he paid me attention and rolled it down.

'What?' he wanted to know.

'Just wondered how the case was going?'

'For starters, you're ruining it. That do you?'

I shrugged. ''Spose,' I said.

He relented then. 'If you really want to know what's going on, you could do worse than talk to your two buddies. They lead very interesting lives, after hours, if you know what I mean.' He rolled his window back up. Actually, I didn't know what he meant, but I nodded sagely at him and went to join Lisa and Colette. They began to look angry as I approached, which worried me. Then I saw that they were looking beyond and behind me, as were a lot of other parents. Carmel Lally, I guessed, correctly. But this time Carmel did not skulk in, she took centre stage and began to shout.

'I have had enough of you lot giving me a hard time! You have no idea what I'm going through, and if you did you still wouldn't understand the pain and pressure that I put up with every day. I don't know which of you is responsible for the harassment I'm experiencing, but when I find out, you'll be sorry you ever started with me. Leave me and my family and our home alone, do you hear?' Her voice had begun to crack with emotion. 'Leave us alone.' She rushed into the crêche, away from the crowd. I looked at Colette and Lisa and saw that they were smiling, slyly.

'What's going on there?' I asked, lightly.

Lisa replied, 'Oh, a spot of bother with her car, I heard, and her garden was dug up a bit, I think.'

'And someone daubed paint on her garage door,' Colette added.

Suddenly they didn't look like the people I had grown up with. There was a cruelty in their faces which frightened me, and I didn't want to be involved in their schemes. I made my excuses and put some distance between us. Were they responsible for the attacks on Carmel Lally's property? Did Jimmy know the score? I made a note to look into the matter later that evening, when I had some time to myself.

Mary showed me a beautifully illustrated book she'd made that day. It was called *The Queen Was Sick* and went along the single line of 'One day the queen was sick,

BETTER THAN A REST

because she ate too much'. It was a simple parable, with colourful graphics, not least the sick. Domnick was no less wise as he told me that 'water will always find a way'. I had no reason to doubt him. They both liked the new colour of my car, and wanted to know exactly why I had changed it. Then I remembered where I had met the woman who had thrown the pint over Michael O'Donoghue at Bridgecross. In fact, we had promised to keep in touch. I even had her name and address on a screwed up piece of paper in my handbag. But first things first.

My delivery of the children was swift and efficient. I was anxious to get to the office to deal with Tara O'Donoghue and whatever baggage she brought with her. The needles of potential began to click together in search of the correct tension and the right pattern. Would the result be a complex Fair Isle, or an Aran-style slipover? Might it be a plain but functional scarf, or a pair of gloves destined to end their day stuffed down an ancient toilet bowl?

I rang a sleepy Ciara, and reeled her in with the promise of a one-on-one with an O'Donoghue. She promised to hang by as soon as she was compos mentis and fit for human consumption, or whichever came first. And before I left Angela's, I got a general idea of where Carmel Lally lived. I could nail the address down easier if I had a notion of where to look. I had not thought about Andy or Barry in an hour and a half and that felt good. Keep busy, fill the day.

The Indigent Sweeps' Society was the very model of spick and span, and Kevin Mack was singing as he worked. My glove was still hanging on the main notice board like a little red badge of shame, and I felt guilty as I walked by, denying it. No. 4 gave it a glance, but was far more interested in getting off his lead and racing up the stairs. I figured this was good exercise, so I let him. It was not lost on me that the glove was the same colour as the dress I had committed my 'adultery' in. Or, to be more exact, the garment I had shed beforehand.

My office was ordered, gleaming and fragrant. I put on a pot of coffee to percolate and found myself humming. With any luck Mrs Mack would join a closed order of nuns while on her pilgrimage, or be kidnapped by an obscure religious cult and never returned. Then the rest of the world could live in perfect harmony without her. Kevin would eventually recover from the shock, losing himself in his work until then, and taking solace in it after his acceptance that she was gone. I was happily indulging in these thoughts and a good scratch of my head when Angela phoned to tell me that the kids had brought home another letter, this time telling all parents that the school was infested with nits.

'What're they?' I asked, like a big gobdaw.

'Headlice and their eggs,' she explained.

I stood bolt upright. 'LICE!'

'Yes, but don't worry, you can get rid of them easily enough, you just have to be diligent.'

I was totally freaked out by the news. My head now felt like it was on fire. Angela talked me through getting a nit comb in the local pharmacy, along with tea tree oil shampoo and conditioner. And she broke the news that it would take at least three weeks to deal with the outbreak. I was diseased, unclean. And I might have passed them on to anyone I had made head-to-head contact with over the last few days. I could now officially kiss goodbye to any notion I'd had of forging a romance with Andy Raynor; who would want to sleep with a woman who'd given them headlice?

My day began to crumble and fall apart.

'What do they look like?' I wailed.

'You'll know when you see them,' Angela replied, then hung up.

I sat back down in my chair and sneezed a bit, blew my nose and rubbed it vigorously; my nostrils were decidedly tender. I could feel my eyes tear up with irritation, and my sinuses began to ache. My head was host to the armies of insect hell. All I needed now was thrush to complete the package. Were these the wages of sin?

I was nursing strong caffeine and murderous thoughts when Ciara landed. I couldn't taste the steaming liquid because I was now totally bunged up and feeling very sorry for myself.

'Germ City, Arizona,' she said. 'You don't take proper care of yourself.' She was the picture of health, of course, just to rub it in. 'Did you get the ride at least?'

'Ciara, what kind of question is that to ask your boss?'

'A good, sensible one. Looking at you now, even though you're a fright with that lurgy, I'd say you did. You're sitting differently, that's always a sign.'

'Ciara, we're here to discuss business, not my love life.'

'Aha! *Love life*. You did get laid. Brilliant! You needed it. And he's a big gorge, for an aul' fella. What's his name?'

'Andy,' I replied, without thinking. Then I corrected her. 'He's not old, and he's just a friend. You've got the wrong end of the stick.'

She just grinned at me. I let it go.

'These are the photographs you wanted,' she said, throwing a large envelope on to the desk. I sifted through the black and whites.

'Oh wait,' Ciara said. 'They seem to be mine, but that

can't be. I only just gave the guy my film.' She frowned at the riddle.

'No, these are ones that I took,' I confirmed.

'Odd,' she said. 'Because that's Maria Flood.' Ciara pointed to a portrait of Michael O'Donoghue's colleague with the Egyptian bob hairstyle.

'That's the woman he gave a lift to while I was following him.'

'It's the woman he went to see very late the night before last,' she added. 'Daughter of another woman he's been known to call on in the wee small hours.'

'Do you think he's up to some pervy, shag all the family, thing?' I mused.

'Could be. It's up to us to find out.'

I put the photographs down and filled her in on the pint-throwing at the Bridgecross function.

'He did look a bit sodden when he left,' she remarked. 'I had to keep myself from screaming with frustration when he got home because he just stayed there like a lump. The wife arrived back an hour or so later, all the lights went out, and when there wasn't a move out of either of them within the next hour, I decided to grab some shut eye myself in my own bed. I'm getting really fed up of that car.'

'That's the glamour of the job.'

'Shite. I'll probably end up with varicose veins and all,' she moaned.

I knew what she was talking about. If you spend enough time sitting in the confined space of your driver's seat, you end up going numb from the waist down. But only after your body isolates each area in a ring of muscle, ligament and bone ache, before robbing it of all sensation. In this way, I am well aware of where my coccyx is, for instance, but not where it goes to, my lovely, when the paralysis sets in. I spend a lot of time flexing my legs and toes to silly songs and rhymes in my head, just to encourage the blood to keep flowing in my veins.

We both turned to the door after a few small taps alerted us to our visitor. No. 4 had given up all pretence of guard-dog duty, and was snoring in a box under the desk. The intruder was carrying neither axe nor gun, so he didn't get fired on the spot. I would issue a warning presently; for now he would be let lie, as sleeping dogs should.

Tara O'Donoghue was in the throes of teenage acne and puppy fat. As a result she saw more of the ground than her surroundings as she shyly hid her adolescent horror. She hulked awkwardly into the room, unsure of where to place herself. A brief 'hello' was marked by the sibilance that comes of brace-wearing, in her case a version nothing short of a crown of thorns nailed into her mouth. It's hard to lisp on a word without an 's' but she was cursed even on that. I welcomed her and indicated the armchair, where she sat self-consciously hugging a leather school bag to her chest. Her knuckles were white. She refused coffee, nodded at Ciara as I introduced her, then glued her eyes to the floor. I picked up the baton and ran with it.

'You seemed anxious to talk to me about something,' I began.

This didn't have much effect.

'What was it that you wanted to tell me, Tara?' Her knee twitched. 'Did you have something to show me?'

She raised her eyes to meet mine. They had something of her mother in them, but were a warmer colour and looked troubled. When she spoke, she was the voice of

219

upper-middle-class south county Dublin, a version of Valley Speak, Irish-style.

'I need to speak to Mr Street. Like, he's the one I'm here to see.'

Ah.

'Em, Tara, there's been a bit of a mix up, I think. You see, I'm Leo Street. And, eh, I'm not a man, as you can see.' At least I hoped she could make that out.

'Cool,' she said. 'So you'd be, like, Miss Marple or someone?'

'When she grows up,' Ciara interjected, mischievously.

Tara smiled at this.

'So now that you've found me, what did you have to tell me?' I asked, steering us back to our original point, and shooting the slightest of daggers at my lovely young assistant.

Tara looked from one to the other of us, and decided that we weren't the worst in the world. Then she took a deep breath and began.

'My dad has been, like, getting these letters, you know? I don't know how many, 'cos I'm away during the week, but I've, like, seen maybe three.'

'Could you tell me what they say, generally?' I prodded.

'Well, they're, like, all "you're gonna die" and "you're scum", you know?'

'Yes. And what do they look like, Tara? Could you describe them to me?'

'Oh, better than that,' she said, loosening her grip on the bag and beginning to undo the straps. Her nails were bitten to the quick, and the exposed skin showed red, raw and too young to be protecting anything. I marvelled at how she could get a grip on such thin slivers with the width of the hardware she had on her teeth. Jagged shavings of dead skin were still attached to the areas around the tips of her fingers, indicating that the gnawing continued long after the nail had succumbed. She ceased her rummaging and produced her booty. 'I've got one here,' she said, raising the item to show us. Good girl, Tara.

I suppose we all watch too much television these days. But there are times when you could run over to the set and give it a big, wet smacker on the screen. This was one of those times. Not only did Tara O'Donoghue have a threatening letter in her possession, she had wrapped it, and the envelope it came in, in clear plastic. I made a sound which expressed praise, and she rewarded me with a glimpse of a thousand pounds' worth of dental hardware.

'I wore latex gloves when I handled them,' she added. 'We've got lots of that shit around, what with Dad being a doctor and all, like.'

I could have kissed her.

The letter was all colour and malice. A plain white sheet of paper held various magazine and newspaper letters glued to it. The message was straightforward: 'You will die for your aberrations. You are the lowest of the low. You will burn in hell'. The culprit had neglected to sign a name or codeword. The envelope simply said 'Michael O'Donoghue', no address and no postage stamp. Hand delivered, then.

All three heads pored over the cellophaned evidence, then I remembered my 'condition' and jerked back. The others hardly noticed, busy as they were collecting impressions. A quick scan of their locks revealed nothing in the way of wildlife.

'What makes you think you know who did this?' I asked Tara.

She gave me a distrustful look. Oh, no, now was not the

time for her to go all Marcel Marceau.

'You did mention that you thought you knew who was responsible,' I added, as if she owed me.

Tears began to edge from the corners of her eyes. I reached for a tissue. 'There, there,' I cooed. What in hell is that supposed to mean or accomplish – there bloody there? There *what*? *There* where?

She blew her nose, and reached for the bag a second time. This next offering was a selection of magazines, also carefully wrapped. Some were up-market glossies of the sort that advise on how many orgasms you should be having per day, and what to read while you're waiting for them. And some were fashion rags full of designer labels and stick-thin women and men who probably didn't even exist but were digitally manufactured.

'I'm assuming that these have letters missing?' I said.

Tara sniffled and nodded.

'And where did you get them?'

'I found them in my mum's wastepaper basket,' she wailed.

This was strange. Even if Tara's mother were responsible, why was her daughter suspicious enough in the first place to be rooting around in her rubbish?

'Bummer,' Ciara was saying to her. 'I hate it when they get involved in this sorta shit.'

They both nodded wearily. A vista was opening up here that I probably wasn't ready for.

'Let's go through life at home for the last while, shall we?' I said quickly.

Two sets of young eyes turned to me. 'Tara,' I clarified.

'Well, I'm not there, like, all the time, you know? But they row a lot, I know that. And they don't really bother to hide that from me and Ben anymore. It kinda all came to a head with Mum's new car recently. She really wanted a new one, even though her old one wasn't that old or anything. And it just had to be a certain kind of grey. Just *had* to be, like.'

Both Ciara and I concentrated very hard on the desk top during this piece of information.

'Anything else?' I asked, casually.

'I've only heard bits of the arguments. Mum says she doesn't approve of Dad's work anymore. She's gone all holy on it, like. You know, kinda religious and stuff, quoting the Bible, or at least it sounds kinda biblical. And I wouldn't mind but she doesn't even go to Mass, like. I'm hoping to work in genetic research too when I've done college and all that. It's the way of the future, you know?'

'Does your mother know you have this letter or the magazines?'

'No way. I'd be, like, really dead meat. I mean, I'd probably get grounded and all.'

'Right. Tara, I think you should leave these here with us, and I'll go see your mum about all of this. Okay?'

She nodded.

'And you have my number if you need to talk to me or if you come across anything else you think might be relevant.'

'Hang in there,' Ciara said. 'You know parents, it's probably just a phase they're going through.'

'Tell me about it,' said a worldly Tara O'Donoghue, hoisting herself to her feet. Then she stopped dead in her tracks.

'Oh my God, you know about *her*,' she gasped, indicating the photograph of Maria Flood on the desk with a pudgy, gnawed finger. She was now visibly unsettled and her breath quickened, while Ciara and I held ours. As if sensing that the game was somehow up, Tara sank back into the chair and gave a pained sigh.

'Dad came to visit me during the week at St Columba's about a month ago. Sometimes he does that, you know, if he wants to talk, like. But this time he had *her* with him. Maria, that's her name. He was being all vague and mysterious about 'news' that he'd have for the family soon, and I think he thought I'd be all chummy, like, but no way. I didn't want anything to do with her. He kept saying that he knew me and her would be great friends in the fullness of time, or some other stupid grown-up phrase, like. I haven't seen her since, but I bet that's another reason why my parents are at each other's throats.'

'Thank you, Tara, for being so frank with us,' I said. 'We'll try to get to the bottom of things from here. There is just one thing that I'm still wondering about, and that's how you decided to come to me with this? How did you know to contact me?'

She gave a watery smile and said, 'Good detective work.' Then she shuffled off, leaving an imprint of her unhappiness behind.

'Jeez, that Mrs O'D must be properly pissed off at her hubby for seeing other women,' Ciara ventured.

'Yes. But does she even know about Maria? And don't forget that she doesn't seem to share any zeal for his researches either. Would she actually act on her threat, I wonder, or is this just meant to scare him? And why insist on a grey car? Is she aware that Bernadette Flood drives one too? *They* know one another from ages back, remember, though how friendly they are now, we don't know. And which car is on your tail and consequently his?'

'We're close to something, aren't we?' Ciara said.

'Yep,' I acknowledged. 'But I'm not sure what it is. You know, I think it mightn't be a bad thing to give old Miranda a bell.'

I reached for the phone and dialled the O'Donoghue number, putting the call on the speakers in the office so that Ciara could hear. As always, it was answered on the third ring. I did the preliminaries then got to the reason we were speaking. 'Miranda, some very interesting evidence has come into my possession and I think we should discuss it.'

'Oh, really?' was the disinterested reply.

Sod this for a game of cowboys, I thought. I crossed my eyes to Ciara, in a thoroughly adult and professional manner, immediately regretting it, as I didn't want her picking up my bad habits.

'Yes, really,' I said, getting briskly back on track. 'I have in my hand one of the death threats issued to your husband. And I know where it came from. When should we meet?'

Her pause was well-nigh imperceptible. 'Today is no good,' she told me. 'I'll call you when I've established a convenient time. I must say though, Miss Street, that I really don't see what this might have to do with my husband and his affair. I do hope you're not wasting my time and money on an unrelated goose chase.' And then she simply hung up on me. I disconnected from my end to stop the repetitive tone of an electronic 'fuck you'.

'And that is the woman who hired us,' I told Ciara.

'Niiice.'

'Now what has she got to hide?' I wondered aloud.

'And why did she tell you about the threats in the beginning? Was she trying to throw you off her scent?'

'She couldn't have known that I'd get my hands on one of them, that's for sure. What *is* she up to?'

Ciara and I sat thinking for a few moments, but the sound was not unlike two empty cans clattering along the road. I glanced at my watch and made a decision. 'I'm off. I've got to go see a woman about a car.' I caught her expression. 'No, not that woman and not that car. They might be related, though. I'll tell you after I've dug about a bit. You're in charge. Be careful and keep in touch. Things may hot up considerably now, and I want to know where you are and who you're with at all times. Savvy?'

She saluted, hand to head. 'Aye, aye, Captain.'

I left.

Then I went back.

'Forgot the dog.'

'He knows,' she said. 'I wouldn't like to be in your shoes.'

I thought mothers could lay on a guilt trip, but none that I've seen in action could hold a candle to No. 4. I had to carry him down the stairs. Kevin Mack met us at the foot and said, 'Ah, the poor wee thing, is he not well?'

'He's fine,' I said, a mite tersely. 'Just feeling massively sorry for himself.'

Mr Mack rubbed the dog's white and black and tan head, and gave him a piece of chocolate which he produced from his pocket. No. 4 brightened enough to wolf this down, then slumped back into my arms like a dead weight.

'He'll be better again before he's twice married,' Kevin said. I think this was meant to be a comfort to me. Imagine being lumbered with the cost of two weddings, which I would have to bankroll as a lone parent. Much as my own dad would love to see me live as an 'honest' woman, he knows he'll have to foot the bill for the accompanying revels, so he's not as eager as my mother to bring the subject up. He's really never been in any danger of paying out for his only daughter's honour, more's the pity.

'Give it a rest,' I said to the dog. 'The long face won't work with me.'

I still ended up carrying him to the car.

'Garlic, and plenty of it,' was Molly's advice for my cold, as he hoiked some more phlegm on to the gravel from the endless supply within his frail body.

'Thanks,' I said. 'I'll remember that. And it'll ward off vampires too.'

He bobbed his ancient head up and down. 'The cross is a handy tool as well, for getting rid of those lads.' I looked hard, but there was no trace of irony. More reasons to be afraid of the dark.

'The little fella needs a bit of sunshine,' was his verdict on the dog. Now it looked like I'd have to shell out for a Mediterranean holiday as well as two weddings. This was one expensive mutt.

He cheered up once he got into the car. As usual he took up position with front paws on the dash, back legs on the passenger seat; Iggy Pop, eat your heart out. I flicked on the heaters, and when we'd built up a head of speed, I could see the warm air blow over his face, flapping his ears back. His long pink tongue lolled out of the side of his mouth. All he was missing was a pair of goggles.

We stopped by a pharmacy to get an arsenal of supplies for my various ailments. I sprayed my head liberally with a leave-in tea tree oil conditioner, in a make-do measure till I could deal with the problem properly. All it did was drive the vile creatures mad and more active than ever. I gave myself a good, vigorous scratching, and with my scalp raw, headed out on my next mission. The song is correct: sometimes it's hard to be a woman . . .

NINETEEN

Kate Mulligan lived in a terraced house on a quiet street adjacent to the canal and town. I imagined it was the sort of area which had unofficial hanging basket competitions in the summer. In the cold April air, it seemed scoured and deserted. Her familiar red car looked forlorn on the road with its crumpled front bumper. In all likelihood there were flecks of my old paintwork still embedded in it. I parked a few doors away and dialled the number she'd given me. She answered on the eighth ring and I invited myself over for a little chat. I left No. 4 in the car because he couldn't be trusted, the mood he was in; this was a dog who'd been barred from at least one pub that I knew of, for activities I knew nothing of. Better to be safely clichéd than sorry.

Kate looked awful. No, worse than that. I reckoned she was normally a dress size twelve; now her clothes were hanging from her skeletal frame and I thought an eight would do. Her breath had the sweet, rank smell characteristic of hunger. Dark circles indicated her eyes, which were blood-shot from crying and lack of sleep. I didn't think she'd washed that day. She was in that bizarre mixture of agitation and torpor which epitomises severe depression. I felt it best to leave out any beating around bushes.

'I saw you in Bridgecross last night,' I began.

She gave a hollow gurgle, which I took to be a laugh. 'If I'd had a gun I would have killed him there and then,' she said.

'Were you following Michael O'Donoghue the night you ran into me?'

'Of course.'

'Why?'

'You know, I really don't know that. I suppose I was waiting for some plan to occur to me along the way. I've not been too rational this last while.' She twisted her cardigan as she spoke, moving on when one section was tightly bound up; it left a hedgehog pattern on one side.

'No,' I said. 'Why were you following him at all?'

'Ah. You might want to sit down. I'll make us some tea.'

I looked around the room, which had seen better times. The once cheery orange ragrolled walls now looked smeared with grime. Rings from long-forgotten cuppas and glasses of red wine were evident on all surfaces. Dust and despair lay heavy over the house, and didn't show much sign of lifting. I was afraid to drink what was eventually put in front of me. The mug had seen many other brews in its day. Brown circles marked the interior and dark dribbles of various lengths decorated the exterior. I thanked Kate, and nursed the mug in my hands; at least it kept them warm. I had begun to shiver from the chill, but she seemed oblivious. I thought she might at least have noticed the steam from her breath each time she spoke, but apparently she did not.

'Michael O'Donoghue has ruined my life,' she said. 'Death is too good for him. But before he goes, I need some answers.'

She began to rock gently, and salt tears wet her cheeks. After a time she resumed. 'This used to be a very happy house. Are you married, Leo?'

'No. I live with a guy.'

'Well, you'll have some idea then.'

Only if I was in a fulfilling relationship, I thought, but didn't interrupt her with this observation.

'My husband Mark and me were mad to have children. After a year and a half of trying, with no success, we thought it might be good to get everything checked out. Nothing to panic about, just a look at all of our respective bits to make sure that we were both working properly, or what have you. It turned out that I needed a little hormonal prodding on egg manufacture and Mark had a slightly low sperm count, but nothing to be concerned about. It's a mucky old business, but we were both up for it and we took all of our tablets and temperatures and so on. Still there was no sign of a baby. And that's when Michael O'Donoghue suggested we try some of the newer products available.

'He explained that some of them were still a little unconventional, but we didn't care. We weren't desperate at this stage, we just wanted to have a baby and be done with the whole process. I did get pregnant and we were delighted, of course. By then Michael O'Donoghue was practically a god in our eyes.'

There was that word again. It made me feel distinctly uncomfortable.

231

Kate had begun to cry again, softly. 'I lost the baby at four months. We were devastated, both of us. And there were complications, which meant it was going to be even more difficult to conceive again. But we regrouped ourselves and went on an *in vitro* programme. It was tough for Mark too. It's not the easiest thing to be sent into a room alone with a magazine to try to produce some sperm while an army of medics is waiting outside. Anyway, to cut a long story short, we ran out of money. It's a really, really expensive procedure. And the pressure was unbearable. We'd started to fight, and throw recriminations around. It was awful. Then Michael O'Donoghue suggested that we join a test project he was in charge of. It was highly experimental, he said, but he had high hopes for success.

'At that stage I would have done almost anything. I was a crazy woman. Mark went along with it because he loved me, but I knew he had his doubts. After eight more months of agony, and pain too – there were some surgeries involved – Michael O'Donoghue told us it was hopeless, and he just shed us. Just threw us off the programme, said we were of no more use to him. He was so cruel, so heartless. We were in bits. And there was nothing we could do about it. He'd made his mind up and that was that.'

I left my mug on the kitchen table, it had gone completely cold by now. I was glad of my leather jacket and woolly jumper, lumpy or not.

'Then something happened,' Kate said. She began to have difficulty getting full sentences out. She was struggling for control of her emotions. In bursts of two or three words, interspersed with laboured breathing, she told me, 'I went back to the clinic one day, to ask for my charts, and I met someone. She said she'd help me, that what was going on wasn't right. She told me some terrible things.' Now Kate was sobbing loudly. I didn't know whether to comfort her or to let her finish her story. Whatever she knew had broken part of her, and it was doubtful it could ever be fixed. Her speech was disjointed with weeping.

'She said that Michael O'Donoghue had kept bits of my baby, for tissue samples. And that he had samples from me and Mark. He had stolen bits of us, of our very selves, for his FUCKING EXPERIMENTS. How *could* he? How *dare* he? Who does he think he is? GOD?'

She was gasping for air now, struggling to keep herself conscious. Her panic and sorrow were palpable, pressing down on the house and everything in it. I knew, without being told, that Mark had left, and she was alone in her crusade for justice. I went to her and put my arms around her. When she was calm again, I said, 'That was you on the radio this morning, wasn't it?' She nodded. 'So what now?'

'We expose the bastard, and all of his evil.'

'Can you tell me who your source is?'

'No.' She shook her head slowly and blew her nose. 'No.' She held my eyes in a gaze of pure hurt and said, 'Do you know what the worst thing is? I have no idea what that bastard has done to me. He experimented with me, and I have no idea what he did. And I will kill him, given half a chance.' She looked away into a middle distance that only she could go to.

I left, shaking. What sort of person would prey on the desperation of a young couple and leave them torn apart and ruined? Their lives were rent asunder, their dreams betrayed and destroyed. I got into the car and hugged No. 4. In all of my visit, Kate Mulligan had not once mentioned our cars. She hadn't even wondered why I was asking those questions.

We spend most of our adult lives avoiding pregnancy; this is the thrust of birth-control education. No one tells us what to do when the opposite is the case: how to deal with not being able to conceive. Then the label of 'barren' is thrown about, an ancient stigma courtesy of the fruitful and ignorant. I felt anger rise in me for Kate and Mark and all those couples like them whose lives are used and ruined by unscrupulous bio-pirates and immoral scientists just out to make their mark in the cut-throat world of scientific competition. I waited a moment for Mick Nolan to put the boot in about excessive 'mawkishness' on my part. He didn't. Odd, that.

Lots of detectives that I know would have established all of this by telephone. They could make a visual at any time, and follow up with a call. All nice and neat and sterile. That's not my way. I believe in the one to one encounter, but it has its disadvantages. This was a prime example. I had got close, too close, and it can burn a body out. I was touched by the raw emotion of this woman's plight and that made things personal.

I dragged myself home for some sort of comfort, all the while saying a silent prayer that Barry would be out. He was. I boiled a kettle and made a hot lemon drink fortified by two extra Aspirin. Then I washed my hair and ran the nit comb through it. Angela was right, I did know the creepies when I saw them, and their vile grey eggs. I felt terrible, and for the first time in months, I crawled into bed at tea-time and fell into a deep and sweaty sleep. I really didn't care if I never woke up again.

I did, of course, life being inexorable. It was dark as pitch in the room, and I was totally disorientated and groggy. My nasal passages had solidified and my mouth, having done all of the breathing work, was the Gobi of oral areas. That didn't last long. When my brain let my sinuses know that I had rejoined the world, the waterworks started again. I stuffed two lumps of cotton wool up my nostrils, which were flaking and tender from the friction of too many tissues. I tried to move, but was trapped in a deep mattress crater; the power of gravity and pain held me prostrate. My muscles and bones ached, begging me to stay in the warm safe bed, but I had places to go, and people to see. By the time I had heaved my racked body downstairs, I was a little more alert, and rested, in an exhausted sort of way. I did not fall apart under the hot shower spray, which was a surprise of the pleasant variety. I bundled myself into several layers of clothing, told No. 4 that he would have to guard the castle and the cats, fed the lot of them and took to the night.

It's not often that business mixes with pleasure for me, so I was chuffed to be able to start the evening with a visit to the Chinese takeaway featured on Maeve's list. I ran through the usual dire warnings of a swoop by the cops if the nuisance calls did not stop. Then I treated myself to some spring rolls and chicken with cashew nuts and fried rice. Feed a cold, I told myself. The car was fragrant with the oils and spices of the east (Dublin) and I stopped just short of having the same again. A glance at my watch told me that it was eleven o'clock, which I felt was as good a time as any to wheel by Carmel Lally's in search of paint daubers and garden diggers.

The house was a detached dormer bungalow set off a tree-lined road which was itself off the main coastal road in

Clontarf, townside. Not cheap by any means. I drove up and down a few times, assessing where best to leave my car, and settling for an unobtrusive space a few doors along from Casa Lally. I scanned the area, my eye lighting on a familiar vehicle close by, within full view of the Lally drive. Inside, I saw the sleeping form of Jack Nolan. I couldn't even muster mild amazement. After all, we're dealing with a man here who once ordered a buffalo mozzarella sandwich and asked where the meat was when it arrived. I left him to his dreams. Again, I was surprised that Mick was schtum. Where had he got to?

I crossed the road to the Lally pad and began a surreptitious survey of the property. The generous driveway held a station wagon, essential for family transport as I now knew from the school runs. It was parked in front of a closed garage to the side of the house, newly painted to cover whatever graffiti had been added without the Lallys' consent. The front garden was about a hundred feet in length and thirty feet wide, and it also showed signs of recent attention, no doubt to repair the damage done by the unwanted visitor. A narrow pathway led to the back garden which was a considerable size, if neglected. In the broad moonlight, it looked like a jungle adventure waiting to happen. Kids' bikes and toys were strewn throughout, and I could make out a sand pit close to the kitchen door.

I went to the front again, and stood back for an overview. Something was puzzling me. Through the thin membrane of the curtains I could see the flickering of a fire. Nothing unusual here, it was a chilly night and lots of homes throughout the town were showing similar jolly lights. It was just that these seemed too jolly. Without warning I was attacked by a fit of sneezing, and when it subsided and I had blown my nose for the umpteenth time, I found that I could breathe freely again. Which meant I could also smell. And what I could smell was fire. Not domestic fire, a house *on* fire.

I banged loudly on the front door as I reached for my mobile to call the fire brigade. I barked the address to the 999 number and continued to call at the door for Carmel and her family. The commotion attracted a few neighbours, one of whom was a chunky man who obviously worked out. He began to throw himself at the door to break it down while I ran around the back of the house again. I tried the kitchen door. It was unlocked. As soon as I opened it, a huge fug of smoke enveloped me and drove me back. My eyes stung, wickedly. I put my jumper over my nose and mouth and tried to figure out the geography of the room, but the smoke was too dense. I could feel it burn my lungs and invade my hair and clothes. I called out to Carmel as loudly as I could, but the fumes were reducing any sound I could make. I heard sirens in the distance, and prayed that the fire department would get here in time to save whoever was trapped. If the back door was left undone, then it was reasonable to assume that someone was home.

The noise and flashing lights of the fire engines brought other neighbours out on to the street. It's hard to resist the fascination of a potential tragedy on your doorstep. For all that, there was a silence about this gathering, and the squawking of walkie-talkies and the hum of the fire truck were really the only distinguishable sounds in the air. Firemen surrounded the house and invaded it through both doors. The fire was concentrated to the front and they quickly doused it. I envied them their metal breathing apparatus; my biological equivalent was also manmade but

237

my innards were clogged and painful to use. They emerged
with two small bundles and a larger one. Tears stung my
eyes and rolled down my cheeks, creating rivulets through
the soot. I rushed to the ambulance with the men and their
human treasure. 'Are they alive?' I asked. 'I'm the one who
made the call.'

'Yes, they're alive. But they need attention. We'll send
them to the nearest hospital, you can follow on if you
want.'

I walked back to the front door and told the man in
charge who I was, more or less. I asked about the fire.

'Don't quote me, but it looks as if someone put something
like a lit firelighter in through the letter box. That fell on to
the carpet and it went from there. It's a good thing you
came along when you did. Any later and it would have
taken a greater hold and they might all have died. As it is
they'll be pretty sick with smoke inhalation for the next
while. Whoever did this should be locked up.'

I agreed.

I joined the neighbour who had helped me at the start. If
he was anything to go by, I must have looked a right sight.

'That poor woman,' he said. 'She has nothing but trouble.'

'Where is her husband?' I asked. 'We should probably call
him.'

'She chucked him out a fortnight ago, and I don't know
where he went to. He's been back a few times to see the
children, but I don't know where he's staying. He has a bit
of a drink problem, and one night it got out of hand and he
hit Carmel and she kicked him out. Can't blame her. It's not
something anyone should have to put up with.'

I recalled the suggestion of a bruise on Carmel's face the
first day I saw her. 'Was this regular, the beating?'

'Oh, no, I don't think so. He'd normally settle for breaking things and making a lot of noise. She called the Guards
on him a few times and that always calmed him down for a
while. He'd go on the wagon, and I have to say there was
no nicer man you'd meet in a day's walk when he was off
the sauce. Then he'd go back to his old ways and be a real
Mr Hyde.'

A horrible thought was forming in my head. I let it out.
'Do you think there's any chance he did this?'

'Oh, God, no. Oh, no, I wouldn't think so at all. No. He's
bad with the drink all right, but he'd never do anything to
harm those kids. He's plain crazy about them. Oh, no, no, I
can't see that at all.'

'You know someone's been messing up the garden and
that?' I said. 'Have you seen anything suspicious?'

'Oh, that, yeah. Carmel seemed to think it was to do with
her insurance claim. She slipped at the crêche, I think, and
she's been in a neck collar thing. Mmn, no, I haven't seen
anything odd, but then again I'm out at work most of the
day. My mother thought she saw a blonde woman lurking
around the place, but there are a lot of couples with kids
coming and going all the time, and the Mammy isn't as alert
as she used to be. Could be nothing.'

Or could be something, I thought. 'Do you think we
should ask her if she saw anything tonight?' I asked. I
hoped he realised that I meant this as a rhetorical question.

'No, no,' he said. 'She's in the hospice now. I can't do
anything more for her at home.' He looked away, so that I
wouldn't see him cry.

You drive along street after street, road after road every
day, and you look in at the houses where people are living
their lives. And you just don't know the half of what goes

on behind those doors. The daily living and dying of a nation. Behind one façade joy, behind another sorrow, with no distinguishing marks to help you know the human minutiae or magnitudes of this world.

I gave my details and a brief statement to a cop who'd just arrived, and agreed to come down to the station for a fuller report at a time convenient to the Force and myself.

'I believe you've been here before,' I said.

He looked at me through suspicious eyes. 'This house is known to us,' was all he would part with.

Jack Nolan was stirring as I walked by his car. If his father wouldn't say it, I would: 'Gobshite!' I turned around and called the policeman. 'Officer,' I said. 'This man was here for the evening, perhaps he saw something.' Yeah, and I'm winning gold in the unicycle marathon at the next Olympics, I could have added. Jack was infamous for sleeping on the job, his excuse being that he had a demanding wife and hyperactive kids. My own opinion was that he was the laziest man alive, and the public should be warned before parting with money for his services.

It took me a while to get motoring again. I was knocked for six by the gritty vapours in my lungs, mixing as they were with gallons of sticky mucus. I'd heard of smoking out wasps' nests, and wondered if the same was true of the nits from my thatch. It was an extreme measure, and not as fragrant as the antiseptic smell of tea tree oil. I would stick with the conventional approach from now on, I decided.

I was not certain that Carmel Lally's husband was innocent of any involvement in the night's events, but even so, I had an idea who two of the other prime suspects were in this scenario and the thought did little to cheer me. It was time to visit my old school chums. What did I expect when

I confronted them? A full and frank confession, complete with a statement to the police? Hardly. But I wanted to know if they were involved, even if it tarnished some childhood memories. Most of all I wanted to clear them of suspicion. But I'll admit that I wasn't expecting a good result. I tried not to assume that I knew anything of what was going on, but it was hard not to jump to a few conclusions. With a heavy heart, and heavier lungs, I pointed the car in the direction of Lisa's house. I needed some answers, though I wasn't sure yet what the questions were.

My breathing had settled into a worrying wheeze, as I tried to regain a regular pattern for delivery of oxygen to my body. It was true then, and is still true now, that if you don't breathe you die, and I was acutely aware of that. I coughed once or twice in the hope that this would loosen the blockage in my lungs.

I thought about Lisa Farrelly. To be truthful, we had never been the best of mates at school, but as is the way of these things, we saw a lot of one another. I remembered the day she had punctured every bicycle in the school yard with her compass because she hadn't got one for Christmas. It wasn't funny, even at the time. And a more uncomfortable thought was that she wouldn't have thought too hard about sticking that compass into a human being, though to my knowledge she never did. Would she be vicious in protecting her children's right to daycare? To be a mother was to protect, after all. But where might the line be drawn?

Call me suspicious, but the first thing I did was to feel the bonnet of the car parked in the driveway. It was warm. Someone had made a journey earlier that evening. I rang the bell, which did a Big Ben thing, and a few moments later I was looking at the lady of the house.

'Phew,' she said. 'Have you gone all crusty and started living the good life outdoors?'

'No.' A short answer, which probably wouldn't get us very far. 'I just saved Carmel Lally and her family from a fire. Another few minutes and they'd've been killed.'

Did she redden slightly, or was that my wishful thinking?

'Why call to tell me?' she asked.

'I just thought you might know something about the incident.' I was grasping at straws and added, 'A blonde woman was seen leaving the scene shortly before I arrived.'

We both let that sink in briefly.

'I've been here all night,' she said. 'The kids can vouch for me.'

'I'll bet,' I countered. 'Why is your car engine still warm then?'

She let the silence last just a touch too long before coming back with the information that her husband had gone out to the shop because they'd run out of milk and bread for the morning. A little too much detail, I thought, and why hadn't she mentioned that her husband as well as the children could vouch for her whereabouts that evening?

'Tell it to the cops when they call,' I said, bluffing still. Then I upped the ante a little by remarking that the neighbour who had seen the blonde woman acting suspiciously was hopeful of an identification.

I could tell she was rattled, but to be fair anyone would have been in the same circumstances, whether they were innocent or not. I let her stew.

Colette's house wasn't very far from Lisa's. I knew it was outrageously late to be calling, but hadn't my brother Peter seen her out and about late at night? I made a deal with myself that if the main lights of the house were on, I would knock, if they were not I would go home and return in the morning at a more suitable time. Luck was a lady that night and the lights were shining. I thank you.

'Jesus, you look like you've been dragged backwards through a very mucky place.' Colette stood in her doorway holding a glass of white wine. 'Come in and I'll make you a hot whiskey. I can practically smell the germs off you.'

I followed her into the house listening to a non-stop volley of words. 'Ray did Santa Claus one year in town and he had every walking infection in Dublin sit on his knee. We didn't know what to give him for all the diseases he caught. I think he was glad of the cold, though, because it stuffed him up and he couldn't smell the children's breath when they were talking to him. A mixture of cheese and onion crisps and chocolate and Coke is just awful, he says. We got a collection of soothers too . . . the state of some of them! Worn down to the nub. It was a great way for parents to get the kids to give them up. Jesus, what a year that was! I suppose you got the letter about the nits? They're a curse, and a bitch to get rid of. I hope you have your special comb and so on?'

By now, I was sitting in an armchair by the fire with a steaming hot toddy in my hands and an overwhelming desire to doze off.

'What brings you here at this hour?' she asked.

With a heart-weary sigh, I told her the story of Carmel Lally's fire.

'And you thought I might have something to do with that?' Colette looked visibly upset at the notion.

'Everyone has a lot to lose if the crêche closes down.'

'That's no reason to go around trying to kill people.'

'True.' I sipped my whiskey. We both studied the fire for a bit. Then I said, 'You've been seen out a lot at night-time recently. That might look suspicious.'

Colette smiled. 'I have a job with those sort of hours,' she said, and sized me up before continuing. 'Actually, I can't present an alibi for earlier, though I was working. What I do is technically outside the law, and the people I deal with would be reticent about coming forward to say the least.' Then she let off a laugh. 'Your face is an absolute picture, Leo! And it's not just the soot. Close your mouth at least.'

'I can't,' I said. 'I'm using it to breathe through.'

Colette wore a mischievous smile. She was toying with me, I could tell, in the way that used to drive our teachers nuts in the old days. Whatever went through her head, she decided to come clean.

'I'm a call girl,' she said. 'That's how I make my money. I work as a whore.'

My chin hit my chest.

TWENTY

Like I've said, you can't always guess what goes on in the privacy of a life. My job takes me into the specifics sometimes, but as far as people in general are concerned, I know as little as the next person. I looked around Colette's comfortable home and I saw that it all made sense. Ray was more unemployed than not, and wouldn't have been much help financially with the regular upkeep of a house and family. His wife now had a cash-based income, which was enviably tax-free, I assumed.

'Ray doesn't know, in case you're wondering,' Colette said. 'So I'd appreciate some discretion.'

'Of course,' I spluttered. 'What do you tell him, if you don't mind my asking?'

'Not at all. He thinks I do shift work in one of the hotels in town.' She snorted and added, 'Of course, in a way I suppose I do.'

I began to laugh. Huge guffaws seized the muscles in my

torso with that special ache somewhere between pleasure and pain that mankind will never be able to identify or isolate. 'Colette, you are unbelievable,' I said, with genuine awe. 'The things you get up to. You'll have to write a book about your adventures.'

'Oh, the things I could tell you about this country,' she said, letting the remark hang to tantalise me.

'Is it not dangerous?' I asked. I've seen the bleaker end of the sex industry in my excursions through the underworld. It's not a place I would voluntarily choose to be.

'Leo, I know this will seem hard to believe, but I'm lucky to be doing what I am. I don't have a habit to support – barring Ray and the kids,' she chortled. 'I work decent enough hours, I get well paid, and I'm not out on the streets desperate for a score. It doesn't knock a spot off me. I couldn't care less about the actual act itself. And, the clients I see most of often look after that end of things themselves, whacking off and whatnot. Sometimes they just want to talk to someone who won't argue back, or they might want to be chastised – I'm very good at that, thanks to living in this house. And other times I might just have to walk around a hotel room with or without my clothes on.'

I must have had some sort of 'oh, sure' expression on my face because she said, 'Really, Leo, it's a lot less hard work than serving in a bar or cleaning up after people. I have my own safety procedures in place, and I rarely take on an unknown quantity.'

'I think I saw you going into a hotel the night before last, early in the evening.'

She thought a moment. 'Ah, yes. I had to dress as a businesswoman. That was for a little Japanese man who visits three or four times a year. He likes to watch me lie about in a variety of submissive poses. It makes him feel powerful. Then I admire his penis, and he refuses me sex when I beg for it. I leave him the panties I've been wearing that day and he pays me generously. He never lays a finger on me. He doesn't want to: that would undermine his dominance.'

'What would the nuns make of it all?' I asked, as I finished the last of my hot whiskey and got up to leave.

'Well, you know, Mary Magdalene was no saint, but Jesus thought she was okay.'

'Yeah. She isn't a saint yet either, is she? I haven't been keeping up with the march of the martyrs over the last while.'

'Em, not as far as I know. I'd have asked Mel normally, but she's off schmoozing with all that lot now and not returning calls.'

'Isn't it weird that no one we know who's died has given any sign that there is something after we shuffle off the mortal coil?'

'Maybe it would be cheating if they did.'

'Yeah, I guess none of us would make any class of an effort then, just a bit of genuine repentance on the death bed and you're in.'

'I'm going to try that anyway, just in case.'

'How is Ray?' I asked.

'He's fine, fine. He's the one writing a book.' Her eyes met mine. We both smiled.

'Good old Ray.'

'Yeah. I know a lot of people think he's useless, but he's one of the best men I've ever met. And funny and sexy on top of that.'

'Hard combination to beat,' I acknowledged.

'So how *is* Andy Raynor these days?'

'The same.'

'Wow.'

'Yeah.'

We had reached the door. I turned to Colette and asked the question I'd been reluctant to put since I'd arrived. 'Do you think Lisa might have done something stupid tonight at Carmel Lally's?'

'Maybe,' she said, hedging. 'But even if she did, I don't think she would have meant to harm anyone. Just warn Carmel off, perhaps? You know yourself that she was never any good at thinking through consequences.'

I could only reply 'Mmm' to that.

'Leo, I know it's hard for you to understand this, but when a mother feels that someone is threatening her children or her life with them, there isn't much she wouldn't do to protect them or their way of living.'

'You're right, that *is* difficult for me to believe.'

We said our goodbyes and I headed out into the cold, hurrying to the car before it caught hold of me and froze my already aching bones. I sat in and honked up my blocked nose into a paper hanky. The contents of the handkerchief were an upsetting molten black. Why had I looked?

The early hours of that Dublin morning saw me battle to keep my eyes open. I drove with the care of a learner, window down to blast my face with icy wind. I yearned for my warm bed, with its flannelette sheets and all-encompassing duvet. I would have some Aspirin, climb into a pair of pyjamas and hide under the covers for as long as sleep would let me. I could practically taste the sensation. It would be a different night from my last, but that was a madness best forgotten. Or was it? Was it a sign that I could or should change life to accommodate another situation? Was this the time to make a big change? I found that with each block I passed I was wider and wider awake as I thought about Andy and the world he might offer. Of course, the fact was that he had offered nothing. He had shown me a good time, but promises had not featured. What it did underline was the staleness of my arrangement with Barry. If we were now, as we seemed to be, friends who loved one another but rarely made love to celebrate this, then surely we should have a different living arrangement?

At what stage in our lives do we take our courage in hand and change everything we are comfortable with and used to? Surely it shouldn't take a crisis to precipitate this. It often does, but from time to time can we not act according to our hopes and aspirations rather than a momentous incident? Steely resolve was gaining a hold on me.

I parked by my familiar curb for which there was, as yet, no municipal charge. Some day soon the inner city would reach out this far and claim taxes, but for now we were safe. There were lights alight, and I expected a few live specimens of the human animal to be dotted around the downstairs living area. What I found was a more furred variety. The lack of a distinctly human presence was a comfort: I am a total coward when it comes to confrontation, I've decided.

The apparition in my bathroom mirror was enough to frighten two continents. My face was a grey mixture of soot and sweat, with red areas of demarcation for my eyes and nostrils. I sniffed my clothes, to no avail; my nose was not functioning in the traditional manner. I reached for the luminous pink toilet roll which had been a birthday present

249

from my family and pulled off half a mile. Then I blew my hooter so hard my ears popped. The paper roll filled again with a glutinous gack reminiscent of green and black Playdo mixed in a bizarre marbled effect. I hurried under the shower and sluiced away the night.

There was a pain in my face where my sinuses should have been, and my head was threatening to burst so I dissolved some medication and downed it in one gulp. Eight eyes were watching my every move, so I lined up three bowls at one end of the kitchen and one at the other and began to fill them from the requisite tins. The hairy ones approved, and fighting was kept to a minimum. I could barely keep my eyes open as I slowly climbed the stairs, into my peejays and under bed clothes warmed by Barry Agnew. So much for resolve. Oh, what the hell. There was no point in waking half the neighbourhood with a row-stroke-discussion that could wait until my head stopped throbbing with a cold and nit bites, and I had enough sleep in me to bear the agony that it would generate.

It was a very dark 3.30 a.m. when my phone rang and Ciara said, 'Come get me. I'm in Donnybrook cop shop. Michael O'Donoghue is dead.'

Parking around Donnybrook Garda Station is a bugger at any time of the day or night. I wedged the car into a tight spot in a nearby laneway, where I thought it wouldn't block the path of too many ambulances. I crossed the deserted main road, led by the shining blue light above the door. Ciara was in reception, looking cold and lonely, and very young.

'Thank God for that,' she said. 'If I have another cup of the rat poison they call tea here, I might as well book a coffin for myself.'

The Desk Sergeant smiled. 'She's a character,' he said.

Ciara was done giving her report on events, so I bundled her off to the coffee dock of Jury's Hotel in nearby Ballsbridge. She didn't offer to drive there herself, and I didn't press her. She was drawn and shaken. We walked past the main desk where a young couple were drunkenly booking in for the night. They were fighting over whose credit card they should use. At the rate they were going they would be fit for nothing but sleep by the time they got to their room, I thought. Illicit sex takes energy, as I had come to know so recently myself, and I didn't fancy their chances that night. Life is gone in an instant, grab it while you can. I knew then that I was going to see Andy again as soon as possible. We had things to sort out, I hoped.

Ciara was very quiet. When we were settled in front of two mugs of frothing steam, I asked her what had happened.

'I've never seen anyone die before,' she said, studying her spoon intently. 'He must have died while I was looking. He's dead. He just . . . expired. He's dead.'

'Put some sugar in your coffee,' I told her. She didn't respond, so I heaped in two large ones and stirred.

She took a gulp, then gagged. 'Fuck, I've burned my tongue. Ah, shite, this is going from bad to worse.' But at least she was back with me in a slightly less distracted state. She panted like No. 4 for a few minutes then proceeded with her story.

Michael O'Donoghue had a humdrum day of private practice patients, then rounds at the Fledgling, where the only excitement appeared to be a slight argument with one of his staff.

251

'How do you know that?' I asked.

'I went in for a while. I was going stir crazy in the car so I sat in a waiting area near his office reading magazines. I was getting nicely stuck into an article about female circumcision when I heard raised voices, not loud, but enough. It didn't amount to much, just him asking where some files were, and saying that the system was a disgrace. I didn't get a good look at the woman involved, though she was probably young enough because she shifted down the corridor at a fair pace.'

He lunched with a male colleague in a sandwich bar on the edge of Merrion Square, where, according to Ciara, he went mad and had butter *and* mayonnaise on his ham salad ciabatta. 'He didn't need to worry about a heart attack,' she commented. A few journalists had doorstepped him that evening as he left the clinic, but they didn't seem interested in following him further than the corner. 'Lazy bunch of gits,' Ciara said. He drove to Sandymount Strand and sat watching the sea from his car before making some calls on his mobile, during which he was clearly agitated. Afterwards he walked along the beach, kicking up the sand, then sat behind his steering wheel for a while more. When he had bought as much time alone as he probably could, he returned to the family home. Ciara could see no evidence of his wife's grey car, either following her or in the driveway.

'Then there was nothing for hours. I thought I'd go mad.' She drained the last of her coffee. 'Little did I know he'd make up for it so spectacularly.'

I ordered us another shot of caffeine each; we were both so wired now, it would not make that much difference to our systems.

'We were headed along the coast road when it happened.

He was taking it at quite a lick, and on a corner he lost control. Odd, though, he didn't slow down at all, just ploughed into a skip full of odds and ends outside a house with a Sold sign attached to it. Nice housewarming present for someone.'

'I wonder what happens now,' I said aloud.

'Yeah, hardly much need to follow him anymore. He's unlikely to be making too many more journeys.'

'Ciara, I'm really sorry you had to go through this. It can't be easy for you.'

'It's different, I'll give it that,' she said. 'I guess we'll be needing another job, a.s.a.p.'

'Down but not out, eh?'

'Company policy, boss.'

It was about then that it dawned on me why Mick Nolan was no longer around. I had to sort things out with him, and soon. I owed him an apology.

'You should go home and get a good night's sleep,' I told Ciara.

'Yes, Mum.'

'Tomorrow we'll type up our report, such as it is, and calculate any money owed. Jesus, I hate grubbing around for that at a time like this. We'll play it by ear.'

I told Ciara about my own investigations that night, including an instructive story about Jack Nolan to lighten our mood.

'He was complaining about hangovers once upon a time,' I began, 'so I advised him to put three Rubex in a pint glass of water and leave it by his bed to drink during the night whenever he might waken. That way, he'd be getting re-hydrated by a tasty orange drink with some vitamins included in the bargain. He arrived to work the following day a pale shade of emerald. He swore he'd tried the cure but it didn't work. When I quizzed him, I discovered that he'd put three spoonfuls of *Radox* in the water and drunk it. I'm sure it made for a very fragrant vomit.'

Ciara smiled for the first time in ages. 'Relax with a Radox barf,' she said.

When I told her about my visit to Kate Mulligan she looked pensive again, mulling over some thoughts in her head before giving verbal shape to them. 'You know, Maria Flood works at the Fledgling, and obviously both she and her mother were involved with Michael O'Donoghue. What if she's the source who was going to help Kate?'

'But if she was having an affair with him, that would be an odd thing to do. It would be a massive betrayal.'

'True.'

'Might it have been her he was rowing with at the clinic earlier?'

'Could have been, I suppose. And of course he saw her later in the evening . . .'

'We should speak to her so.'

'Even though we're no longer needed on the case, with our main interest currently negotiating at the Pearly Gates?'

'I hate loose ends,' I said, fidgeting in my seat. 'Maybe just one last teeny-weeny dig about. I mean, what harm is there in a chat?'

'Easier said than done, I'm afraid. She's unconscious in the hospital.'

'Back up there a bit, Ciara. What happened?'

'Oh, didn't I mention it? Maria Flood was in the car with Michael O'Donoghue when it crashed.'

TWENTY-ONE

I am not overly fond of hospitals; I rarely go into one for a good reason. Mostly I'm there to check on broken people, or damaged ones. And occasionally I have to get fixed up myself, so the sight of one can trigger memories of pain that I would normally rather forget. I had not been in Dublin for Rose's birth some weeks earlier because of a case down the country so I missed the one happy event which might have put hospitals on a temporary reprieve list for me.

I pulled up outside Saint Benedict's and parked the car in the vast area designated for such things. Traffic was brisk, given the late hour, or early whichever way you wanted to look at it. Then again, I don't suppose illness and death follow a timetable convenient to regular office hours. Benedict's was built in the sixties, in the days when hospitals still got saints' names in good old Catholic Ireland. It was a boxy, pre-cast concrete structure that had not weathered well, and now sported tentacles of modernity that neither matched the main building nor attempted to. It didn't inspire confidence at first glance, but I was looking at it from the luxurious standpoint of good health. No doubt if I was rushed in by ambulance, Benny's would be the Grace Kelly of hospitals.

I passed the nurses' home, from which chatty young women and men poured forth to do a red-eye shift for far too little money. It's known as the 'Virgin Megastore' to the drinkers who sup in the cavernous pub across the road. My caffeine hit had begun to wane, and I wondered if I should have left this bit of business until the morning. Ciara had been despatched for some R 'n' R, after a spirited dog fight. I was feeling distinctly weary myself, but couldn't resist a quick shufti at the Flood situation. If things were too tense, I could come back another time.

My nose had begun to dribble again. I popped two tablets which I thought might be Aspirin; the label was too worn and old to read. Even if they were Smarties, I was willing to give them a try. Placebos are fine in my book.

I entered the building through the swing doors of the Accident and Emergency Department, past some smokers, pacing up and down furtively in the cold and an eerie backwash of second-hand light. Good for future business, I surmised. Inside was all disinfectant and mild panic. Fluorescent bulbs shone down, cruelly removing any trace of personality from worried faces. Apprehension bounced off every wall, endlessly revived and renewed with each admission.

Nurses and doctors moved swiftly from one area to another, all studiously avoiding a pool of blood on the floor. I followed suit. Crying, choking and groaning supplied a soundtrack in the curiously hushed air. Was this what's referred to as ambient music? I continued along the antiseptic blue corridor leading to the main reception desk where I found a middle-aged man in a uniform reading a pile of yesterday's tabloids. He didn't seem too interested in my presence but I persisted and was finally rewarded with the information that Maria Flood was in Intensive Care. As a relative (ahem) I was allowed to look through the large windows into her room, where she was hooked up to more technology than the main Microsoft computer system.

Maria looked even tinier in this environment. She lay silently on her back, arms resting on a crisp white sheet which seemed to pin her to the bed. Bandages swathed her head, letting only the merest wisp of dark hair escape. There were tubes in her nose and mouth and a drip fed liquid into a vein in the back of her alabaster hand. Monitors regulated life in a gentle ebb and flow, softly, fearful of disturbing their patient, yet hopeful that she would awaken. She was motionless, but for the gentle movements of her chest as a ventilator helped it bring oxygen into and throughout her body. I had the impression that if she moved she might somehow break. Her stark form shone against the dim background of her transparent cube. She looked safe.

I found her mother watching paint peel in another dingy corner of the medical sprawl. She looked as worn as the hospital itself, hunched into an almost foetal position in her chair. I had never been this close, but I could see that Bernadette Flood was taller than I had expected, perhaps 5' 7" or 8". Her hair was shoulder-length and dragged back into a loose plait, with strands of silver appearing at the sides. She brushed an invisible stray wisp away several times, unsure what to do with herself or her hands. She had a pale complexion, rendered even more ghostly by her present situation. And in all of this, two soft brown eyes struggled to make sense of her predicament. I kept my introduction short and to the point. She was distracted, obviously, but she was listening and that was a start.

'How is Maria doing?' I asked.

'She's stable, but we're not sure about the extent of her injuries. It's weird, I can't sit and watch her even though I spent years as a nurse. It's different when it's one of your own.'

I made a soothing noise.

'She's only young, you know. She's got her whole life ahead of her.' Her gaze had returned to the wall.

'Bernadette,' I said, recalling her. 'Would you mind if I asked a few questions? I'll understand if you're not up to it, but I'd really appreciate it if you could answer me. I just need to figure a few things out, and you're the only one who can help me.'

She shrugged, as if to suggest that it couldn't hurt. In fact, it might, but a window of opportunity was creaking open and I pushed it just a little wider.

'Bernadette, I need to know what your connection was with Michael O'Donoghue.'

'Right, all the easy ones first, then,' she said, drawing her lips into a smile that never reached her eyes. Nowhere near. 'It's odd to think of it as "was" now.' Her voice dropped. 'But not unpleasant.' She ran both hands along her thighs awhile before continuing. The action seemed both to calm and galvanise her. The navy gabardine of her trousers purred and fell back perfectly into place each time; quality is always worth paying for. When she spoke again, I saw that she was struggling to keep an even tone, but it was impossible not to hear venom somewhere beneath the surface. She kept her gaze on the floor, nervously raising her eyes from time to time to punctuate her story. Or was she just checking me out, analysing my reaction – or shaping it?

'I met Michael when I was just twenty. I was nursing at the Rotunda and he joined the staff hot out of medical school and determined to make his mark as an interim. That meant off the field as well as on, if you get my meaning. He was terribly charismatic then. Yes . . . that's the word . . . terribly . . . terrible. It was attractive in a handsome young blood. We all hoped to be chosen. Of course, he was horribly arrogant too. But again, this was put down to youthful exuberance. He was good at his job, very good, so there were never any complaints about that. He managed to catch the eye of the Master and of the money types around. In time he secured a small grant for some studies he wanted to make into DNA and what have you. He was clearly a man going places. Eventually, he got around to dating me. Looking back on it now, I see that it was most likely some kind of rota he had in his head; just knocking us down like bowling pins.

'He was as fierce when it came to romance as he was with his work. I really don't know where he got his energy from. He was able to survive on about three hours' sleep a night, which of course is handy for any doctor. Inevitably, rumours went about that he was taking drugs to stay awake. If he was, I never saw any evidence of it. He just had one of those metabolisms. I think he enjoyed going out with me because I'm a good listener. He took this for adoration, and maybe it was a bit of that too. Whatever the case, it suited him. I suited him. And it was handy that we worked in the same hospital, easier to see one another and so on. All part of the manipulation of circumstance and people that suited Michael. I didn't see it like that at the time, but that's what it was. I was useful for getting him the odd interesting sample as well. He didn't like to be seen to do too much grubby stuff; that wouldn't have looked good in a golden boy.'

An orderly came by with a refreshment trolley. 'Ah, Bernie, there you are. I'd say you could do with a cup of tea right now.'

'Thanks, Stan, that would be lovely.'

'And yourself?' he asked, turning to me.

'Tea would be great.'

'Tea for two and two for tea. I had a look in at Maria. No change. But at least she's comfortable. You're not to worry now,' he said, handing over the scalding disposable cups. 'She's in the best place. Amn't I right?'

I passed mine from one hand to the other in rapid succession, waving the empty one each time. I cannot get over the fact that thin plastic doesn't melt at these temperatures. I'd hate to think what that says about the manufacturing process. It's not natural.

We sat in our regulation chairs, juggling, listening to the rumble of Stan's cart as it faded into the distance, accompanied by the squeak of his crêpe soles on the polished hospital floor. All that was left in the air was the sound of women blowing on tea to cool it. Bernadette Flood looked over at me. 'It's ridiculous, isn't it? Here we are, removing the prints from our fingers with the heat, and when it's right to drink we'll have all of seven seconds to get it down before it goes completely cold.'

'How involved were you with Michael O'Donoghue's researches?' I gently prodded her back to her recollections.

'Oh, hardly at all. I was a nurse, not a scientist. I really couldn't follow a lot of what he talked about, let alone did. As long as he wasn't sewing body parts together and electrocuting them, it seemed fine to me. He was very involved with his test tubes while I was a bed pan woman.'

'I take it there was a parting of the ways at some stage?'

'Yes. He met a laboratory technician who was on the up and up, so he dumped me. I was devastated. Lost weight, couldn't stop crying. Eventually, I got a job in another hospital, and that was the saving of me. I met the most wonderful man and married him. People say there's a rebound time, and maybe there is. But when the right person comes along you just know, rebound or not. And that's what happened to me.'

Something about that last statement echoed deep inside of me, and it had nothing to do with this case.

'And Michael? Did you keep in contact?'

'No, no. Next thing I knew, he was getting married too, to the lab woman, Miranda. He's still married to her. Sorry, was.' She sipped her tea. 'Quick,' she said, 'it's just right now.'

We drained our cups and tossed them in a brown bin in the corner. Bernadette went to check on Maria. I made good my opportunity to visit the Ladies. All those diuretics flowing through my system had to exit sometime. It's disconcerting when urine smells similar to the last meal you had or the last round of drinks. Tonight, I was treated to the coffees and teas of the Orient, mixed so as to be pungent yet indistinguishable. It made me wonder about people who drink their own first thing each morning. I mean, what about that Tikka Masala you had the night before; could you face it again for breakfast in liquid form? My stomach growled with hunger at the prospect, which was worrisome. I looked at my watch and the bad news that it was now 5 a.m. I took up my place in the waiting area once more. A yawn welled up, but I refused to let it out; next thing I'd be hosting a festival.

Bernadette had not been so lucky. When she returned she was in the midst of a spree.

'I won't keep you up much longer,' I promised. 'You obviously need a nap.'

'Don't worry about me,' she said. 'This is what I grew up on, really. And I don't want to miss Maria waking up . . .' Her last statement trailed off, because no one was certain that Maria Flood would ever do that.

'Why were you seeing Michael O'Donoghue again?'

'Oh, that,' she said, disgusted. 'He could never leave things be. Especially if he wasn't the centre of attention.' She paced the worn linoleum. 'Maria started work at the Fledgling eight months ago. Of course, when he figured out who she was, he took a special interest. Took her under his wing, you might say. Then all I heard was "Michael this" and "Michael that". I didn't interfere, because she seemed to be enjoying the work, and it was a wonderful opportunity for her. Then things took a turn. She came to her Sunday dinner very upset one week, and when I eventually got through to her, she told me that she knew all about me and him. Well, what was there to know? A short-lived romance with no love lost. But I had underestimated that bastard. Do you know what he'd done?' Bernadette was struggling now, searching for ways to explain. She waved her hands in every direction, seeking the right words and attitude. 'He'd told her that he was her father, and that he had stopped me from having an abortion when I was pregnant with her.'

262

She shook her head violently. 'Jesus! Imagine that. How twisted can a man get?'

'I take it he was not Maria's dad?'

'NO. For one thing I would have had to have been pregnant for a year and a half if he was. I don't know what he thought he was up to with that particular yarn, or what he intended to achieve, but it backfired on him, I'm happy to say.' She allowed herself a pained smile. 'Whether he knew it or not, *that* was when his troubles really started.'

She looked around for something to do with herself as she spoke. 'Times like this, I'm sorry I gave up smoking.'

I worried that she had broken her concentration and would stop talking about Michael and Maria. She caught my eye and read my mind.

'Where was I?' She looked back to some middle distance in her mind, then continued.

'I've never seen Maria so angry. She felt betrayed and manipulated. Of course, those were Michael's specialities. Yet he still thought he could get her back on side. He started to visit her at home, then me. Wouldn't leave us alone. Do you know, I think he almost came to believe that somehow she *was* his daughter. I never understood what he thought he'd achieve with the charade. Perhaps he calculated that she'd be even more loyal to him if she believed they were related. Maybe he wanted her help with his illicit experiments. It doesn't make sense to me; he was so rational and ordered about everything else in his life, a control freak. He seemed a little unhinged in these last weeks. But Maria was adamant that she would expose him, so she started to delve into files from before her time. I don't think it made for pretty reading. From what she told me it seems he was making babies to his own design, if you like. Experimenting on early fertilised cells, then chucking them when he was done. Often he wouldn't tell the couples involved whether they'd actually succeeded in conceiving, which to me was the cruellest thing of all. He was a completely immoral man, Miss Street. He deserved to die.'

Somewhere in the sterile distance, a patient cried out in his sleep. It could have been the sound of Michael O'Donoghue reaching the portals of Hell. It seemed to spook Bernadette and she got up to go and check on her daughter. I followed and we both stood watching the machines by the bed draw their electronic chart of life in peaks and dips, the steady beeps beating out a reassurance.

'Why were you following him?' I asked her.

'Who?'

'Michael O'Donoghue.'

'What makes you think that I was?'

'A silver-grey saloon was seen tailing him over the last week.'

'That's a common enough colour and you know it.'

Interesting that she didn't deny the proposition. But she was clearly exhausted now and wanted shut of me. I could see her lips pressing closed into silence. I gave her one last push.

'Why do you think Maria was with him tonight?'

'They were on their way to my house,' Bernadette said. 'We were all going to sit down and have this out. She rang to tell me they were leaving. When the next call came, and they still hadn't arrived, I knew something was wrong.' She raised a hand to her mouth to stifle her anguish.

'It must have been a terrible shock to you,' I said, probably about the blandest words ever uttered.

'Yes. And no one was to know that Maria would be in the

car . . . Why didn't she take her own? Why did she travel with him?'

'It was an awful accident,' I conceded, still trying to gauge her last sentences. Bernadette gave off a sound which could have been classified as nervous laughter.

'The Guards were here earlier,' she said. 'They don't seem to think that it *was* an accident. They think there was foul play involved.'

'You mean, Michael O'Donoghue might have been murdered?' I was mistress of the obvious that night, but there are times when only that will do.

Bernadette turned to me and twisted her mouth into a parody of a smile. In the subdued light, her small, white teeth looked like fangs. 'Imagine that,' she said.

I don't know how I got myself out of the hospital, I just remember feeling that it was imperative that I left. I'm not sure if I said 'goodbye' or simply lurched away. The world was buzzing angrily about me and an unpleasant feeling of foreboding flexed its icy fingers around my heart. I sucked in the cold night air as I staggered back through the car park. A mist was trying to settle before dawn, but nature was playing hardball and negotiations were ongoing.

My head was thumping and my chest struggled against cement-like congestion. I had lights flickering in my peripheral vision, like an Aurora Borealis of pain and disorientation. I was torn between a desire to pass out or to vomit, both manifestations of exhaustion and a shattered mind. I laid my forehead on the steering wheel while I waited for the car to heat up. My skull was full of voices, all of them wishing Michael O'Donoghue harm. I had so much to do, but I would be useless until sleep had soothed me. In slow motion, I started the engine, put the car in gear and carefully headed for home. I don't remember much of the journey or of letting myself in and getting undressed. Just the wonderful sinking, sinking, sinking into oblivion.

I jerked back to consciousness at seven minutes past noon when the telephone finally got my brain's attention. With a groan, I lifted the receiver to my head and croaked a response.

'You sound like I feel,' Maeve said.

'Welcome to Hell,' I returned.

TWENTY-TWO

I chewed on some charcoaled toast, dreading the moment I swallowed when it would scrape my throat like a cheese grater. I looked at the line of pills which were to make up the rest of my brunch. Beside a steaming hot lemon drink, laced with Paracetamol, stood a line of vitamins, decongestants, Aspirin and a nasal spray. It was certainly a cure that could kill, and I was beyond caring which outcome prevailed. Then came the nit comb and tea-tree oil conditioner. Lovely. A perfect marriage of insult with injury.

Barry had left a note on the kitchen table telling me that his Chelsea socks were AWOL. I couldn't find a sympathetic fibre in my body with which to share his loss. I don't think I would have given even a half shrug of regret if the house had burned down around me right at that moment. It might have warmed me up. The heating was roaring at full blast, but I still shivered. I was also jittery about life, work and everything, in roughly that order, and in a way I usually associate with hangovers; that sort of unreasonable panic is impossible to deal with and I detest it. This morning, above many others, I had full reason to be anxious.

I hauled myself to my feet when I had ingested as much of my burnt breakfast and medication as I could. The room did a few revolutions, and when it stopped my head took over on the spinning. This was not auguring the finest day of my life. I desperately wanted to return to bed, and sleep until I was fixed again.

Angela called to check on how many ailments I had picked up from the kids. 'I'd say it was them who gave you pretty well all of those,' she said. 'They're walking around like the living dead themselves, and I nearly didn't have the heart to send them to school today.'

'Believe me, Angela, I think I may have deserved punishment anyway because I am a very bad person and payola time comes to all who sin.'

'Get down off that soapbox, would you? The bush telegraph is buzzing with news of your heroics last night. So you can't be that awful.'

'Don't bet on it,' I said, as I tried to expunge an image of my infidelity from my mind's eye. 'If I die, and that is my preferred choice right now, tell the world I did my best, even if it wasn't good enough.'

'Will do. Actually, I called to say that you don't have to collect the children today if you don't want to. I'd say you're wrecked from your adventures.'

'If it's all the same to you, Angela, I will. I'd like to follow up on the Carmel Lally incident.'

'The choice is yours. Good luck out there, it's a dangerous place.'

'Now you tell me.'

'By the way, the husky voice is great. Very sexy. You might want to keep that.'

'Sex causes nothing but trouble,' I growled, vowing to remember that forever. It did nothing to quell my longing for Andy. I was going to have to confront that issue sooner rather than later. My back burner of 'things to do' was becoming dangerously overcrowded, but I walked away from it nonetheless. 'Later,' I muttered to myself, 'later.'

I busied myself with a call to the hospital where the Lallys had been brought the previous night. After a few off-white lies about my position on the family tree, I was told that the three patients were comfortable and would probably be released the following day. This was positive and good, so I vowed that the rest of my day would match it, at least in intention. It was a tough call, though, and my body still turned towards the bedroom every time I held my breath. To put it technically, I felt like shit.

No. 4 chased the cats around, with much squawling and yapping. Then they ganged up on him and the positions were reversed. At least they were getting some exercise and amusing themselves at the same time. I decided to leave them to their own devices for the day, as I didn't think I'd be very good company for the dog if he was to come with me in the car. I dragged my sorry self upstairs and threw on the biggest, bulkiest clothes I could find. I was the spitting image of the Michelin Man as I made to leave on my errands. It was not a day I was looking forward to.

I had just loaded up the last of the unnecessary items I tote around in my bag when the landline rang and Barry's voice said, 'Yo, Coleman, any special requests?'

'Sorry to rain on your parade, Baz, but it's Leo here'

'Jeez, you're late going out. And you sound all croaky.'

'That's because I feel like shite and I'm mean as a taxman to go with it.'

'Oh, right.' I could tell he wanted to go away now, but I wasn't done with him.

'What made you think that Coleman, who didn't live in this house the last I heard, would be here? The answer's in the question, Barry.'

'Er, yeah. Well, we just thought we'd chill for the day, you know.'

'Oh, yes indeed I know. Now, one last question: does Coleman now have a key to my house?'

'Not as such. I gave him the spare, just for today.'

'Barry, I haven't the energy to tell you exactly what to do with yourself, but use your imagination and I think you'll end up in the territory I have in mind, doing what I think you're fit for. Gottit?'

'Yep. Sorry about that.'

'Don't say sorry when you're clearly not. You're just sore that I've caught you out. Now, I'm going to give you a top tip here, so listen very carefully. Sort out the key situation, or pack up and fuck off. Do I make myself clear?'

'Crystal.'

'Lovely. I really like it when we communicate.'

I could hear sounds in the background which registered somewhere in my gummed-up subconscious.

'Barry, where are you right now?'

'I'm in the video place, picking up a few movies.'

'Of *course*.'

'Ah, God, Leo, what's the harm in renting a few films?'

'No, no, it's not that. I just figured something out. And don't worry, it has nothing whatsoever to do with you.'

'Praise be for that.'

'Okay, you're dismissed.'

'Get well soon.'

'Sure.'

I met the cheddary Coleman coming through my front door.

'The very man,' I said. 'I've misplaced my key, so I'll take that back now.' I swear I thought he'd burst into tears relinquishing his ill-gotten pass to Funsville. 'Have a nice day,' I instructed.

My first stop had been chosen for me by the phone call. The sounds in the background of Maeve's nuisance calls were obviously from her local video rental store. Earlier, she'd reported the latest of them so if I was in luck the perpetrator would still be there. He or she was in for one hell of a roasting. In fact, anyone who crossed me today would know all about it. I liked this meaner Leo Street. Enough of the doormat, I wanted to be an ace shit kicker. My time had come.

Dublin was bathed in a wet, dreary mist, and looked as unattractive as any other city would under the circumstances. It didn't help that my vision was distorted by rock-solid sinuses pressuring my eyeballs. The journey took me to a small shopping centre, immortalised in radio advertisements with one of the worst jingles ever recorded. It was also insufferably catchy and impossible to forget. Whoever had 'invented' it could congratulate themselves on a job done all too well, and the resultant cack-ophony was a triumph of commercialism over art. I found myself humming the awful ditty and gave in to the fact that it would be with me for the next few hours, or until it was taken over in some drivelly cover by the newest teen pop sensation. I made a resolution to read the entire works of

Balzac to make up for the failings of modern culture. My head hurt something rotten now.

'Flix' was typical of its kind, a large, overlit emporium filled with a thousand good nights in. Or days, as in the case of Barry and Coleman who would pass these off as research. I approached the counter where a sign told me that the management was hiring staff. I glanced at the television screen above the desk to see a close up of remarkably pert breasts (two, female) and a slavering mouth (male). A ginger-topped employee drooled up at the image. He turned to me when I gestured to the sign in front of him, and I saw that his eyebrows were in danger of meeting any day now. They would then be a hairy orange boa above his hazel eyes. A pug nose pointed to the ceiling; under it a sparse moustache was trying hard to gain follicle hold. His mouth was full and effeminate.

'What're the hours like?' I asked.

'Grand, you know. Your basic eight-hour shift, but plenty of overtime at the moment 'cos of shortages.'

'So what time would you have started today?'

'About ten. Not too bad. Bit borin' in the mornins, but it livens up during the day.'

'And is it just you then, until the next shift?'

'Yep.'

'Right. Let me bring you up to date on a little situation I'm investigating.' I leaned my elbows on the counter, to show just how in charge I was. 'Someone from this store has been making unwelcome sick little phone calls to a customer. Not only is this a pain in the ass for that customer, it is also against the law. You with me so far, sonny?'

He indicated that he was, nervously looking beyond me to the entrance.

272

'The latest of these calls was just after noon today, from this number. And seeing as you were the only one here, it doesn't take a rocket scientist to figure out that you made it. Does it now?'

He swallowed air, glancing back at the door again.

'Of course, just to prove this, we could get a record of the hours you've worked in the last few months and match them up with the calls to my client, which we have been logging, you'll be comforted to hear. But you know, I don't think there'll be any need for that because these calls will never happen again. Sure they won't.'

He shook his head miserably, then lowered it.

'Good. Because, you see, if they were to continue, I'd have to bring the cops with me the next time I visit. And then we'd have to go through interrogating you, and charging you, and all have to spend a long time in court roasting your sorry arse. Still with me?'

He gave a jerk of the head which I took to be an affirmative.

'And there's probably no need for me to mention this, but I will, just in case you're thicker than I already take you for – if anyone else has this sort of trouble from you, I'll be back then too. We have very sophisticated methods of monitoring, get it? Good.'

No doubt about it, I could bullshit for Ireland. One down.

Then it was up again. I was about to swan out when I realised that the youngster was sobbing. Ah, shit, now I was going to feel bad, even though I had been on the high ground only twenty seconds earlier. I am a complete softie when it comes to tears.

'What the hell is all this about?' I asked him.

'I told a lie,' he whispered.

273

'Yeah?'

'I'm only minding the shop for a quarter of an hour, while Fidelma is on her break.'

'And Fidelma would be?'

'She's the boss. *She's* the one who's been on all morning.'

So why would she have a thing against Maeve Kelly? I wondered.

'Okay. Let's calm everything down here, shall we? Now, what's your name?'

'Pat.'

'Right, Pat. Fidelma is in a lot of trouble, as I'm sure you appreciate.' I was at a loss as to what to say or do next when my eye lit on the shop computer. 'Does that have a customer database?' I asked.

He gave an uncertain 'yes', more to do with not liking where this was going rather than being unsure of what the machine contained. I had no time to hang about.

'Here's what we'll do. I want you to call up the details of a Maeve Kelly.'

He hesitated, so I let out a loud 'NOW' and he jumped to.

Maeve's record as a customer was exemplary, in that she paid up on time and never incurred fines for non-rewinding of tapes. Her address and home phone number were listed. And then an intriguing detail, the note 'See also Rolands, Mark'. I felt close to pay dirt. We moved on to the second set of details, and Maeve's address and phone number were there too. But that was all. Just bare facts. My antennae were twitching now.

'Does Fidelma have a computer?'

'Yeah, it's in the office out back.'

'I'd better have a look at that so,' I announced, biting back my excitement.

Pat was sweating, and I could smell it. I ducked under the counter and made for an open door in the back wall, between a poster for *Alien* and one for *Hackers*, appropriately enough. Pat tried to follow me, but was distracted by a customer. I was sweating a bit myself now, keen to be finished before Fidelma returned or her assistant summoned up the courage to halt me in my tracks.

I sat before the screen and was delighted to find that Fidelma had logged on and all features were available to me. I punched in Maeve's name, and was rewarded with her standard details and a note telling me to look under 'Mission', which I did. The file here was very different from the ones for public consumption. Fidelma had downloaded articles about Mark Rolands, and any pictures she had located. These were almost lovingly rendered in sequence. This adoration was followed by information on Maeve, accompanied by on-line photographs and listings, but these had somehow been selected to seem less flattering. Then came the campaign of invective against my friend. All calls were triumphantly recorded, as were the preparations involved. There was a plan for the next few weeks which made the blood jitter in my veins. I sat in the synthetic light, mesmerised by the utter obsession of this woman, and her painstaking attention to detail. Yet nowhere was there any suggestion that she knew Mark Rolands in more than a casual way. Funnily enough, I thought it better to phone Mark on that one, rather than wait to enquire of Fidelma. I couldn't understand what she hoped to achieve, because clearly he could never be hers. Perhaps it was enough for her to know that she was unhinging the woman he wanted to be with.

I glanced at my watch and discovered that I had spent

four and a half minutes zipping through the files. This meant two things: one, that I had no time for ill-informed psychoanalysis, and two, Fidelma was due back. Even if she was a sick individual, and ultimately in a lot more hot water than me, I was still trespassing and didn't want to have to talk my way around that. I printed the relevant pages then saved the details on to a disk to verify my findings and sped back out through the shop, telling Pat that he needn't mention my visit just yet to his boss because that would get him into as much trouble as she was in. This last effort was a gamble. I wanted to buy time, and to guard against Fidelma wiping off her precious files before I had decided what course of action to take. Poor old Pat looked distraught; he had had a very bad morning indeed. I might have self-righteously told him not to tell lies in the future, but even I am not that much of a hypocrite.

I raced down the street, putting a good distance between myself and 'Flix'. Then I flipped open my mobile and rang Maeve to bring her up to date on events.

'I think it's time to let Mark loose on this,' she said. 'And I'll ask him about the Fidelma woman, but I can't say that I remember him ever remarking on her before.'

'People get obsessed for lots of different reasons. He may be just that perfect, unattainable stranger for a disturbed woman, the Mr Wrong who came around the right corner at the right time, depending on whose point of view you're looking from.'

'Do you know, I almost feel sorry for her.'

'Don't, Maeve. Remember, she was making your life hell.'

'I suppose you're right,' she sighed. 'Anyway, many, many thanks, and please send me a bill. I mean it.'

'I know you do. We'll see.'

As I hung up, I realised that not only was I buzzing with adrenaline, I was also famished. A reward was in order and no mistake so I loaded up on goodies in the delicatessen and returned to the heavenly dining room that doubles as my car. I had a quick Scotch egg behind the wheel before revving the engine and heading to the Model School to collect the children. I was hyper after my success so it seemed sensible to use that on Carmel Lally's behalf. The car stank of fart from my snack, but the fact that I could smell it at all indicated that my cold was lifting. I popped some more of the Aspirin-like sweeties from the glove compartment and crossed my fingers.

For all my lectures to Ciara about planning and facts, I operate a lot on instinct. Just then, I wasn't too sure of what I would do once I got to the school, but I was prepared to hoist a flag even if it ended up on my own petard. The yard was full of the usual specimens, with a Nolan brother bringing up the rear. No time like the present, I thought, unwilling to let my courage falter now. There was a lot of whispering and pointing as I made my way to the crèche door, where I took a deep, rasping breath and clapped my hands a few times for attention.

'Some of you will know that Carmel Lally and her children were evacuated from their burning home last night, and are lucky to be alive. It was the culmination of a horrible campaign of intimidation against her. Now, I know you all feel strongly about her claim for compensation but this is no way to go about things. Time and the law will settle all of that. The police take what happened last night very seriously indeed and if any of you knows anything about it, you'd be well advised to come forward. In the meantime, let me assure you that you have no idea of the complexity of Carmel's situation. Leave her alone.'

No one met my eyes now. It was as if the group as a whole was culpable. As it probably was. But I couldn't feel pleased with myself. In fact, I felt like a prig.

The bell rang for the end of classes, and I gathered up the small people and delivered them to their mother. They told me that the earth was round, according to their teachers, but that they felt certain that we'd all fall off the edge if we went too close: from the mouths of babes.

Back at the Indigent Sweeps' gaff, things were going my way. I travelled by elevator, no less, in great form that I didn't have to climb the stairs. The new proactive me was growing more bullish by the minute. I banged out of the cage and barrelled through the office door to tell Mick Nolan my exploits and findings to date. Then, I remembered that we had some unfinished business, which began with an apology from me to him.

I stood in front of the portrait photograph, not knowing where to start. That winded me. I looked into his eyes and said, 'I'm sorry. I didn't realise that it was me who was holding you. It's been me who couldn't let you go all this time. I thought you wanted me to hang around, but I realise now that I prevented you from going.' Tears welled up, but as always I was careful not to show them to him. 'The truth is that I was lonely without you. And I couldn't bear the missing of you, so I kept you here. I didn't know it till Ciara came on board and I let you have the rest you deserve. I'm going to put you by the filing cabinet now, seeing as how that's where you liked to perch in your own office and it always did throw the dynamics of the room off kilter and make people uneasy. You'll still have a role to play whenever you want. But you don't have to.'

I gently removed the photograph from the wall, and tugged out the self-contained leg of the frame to render it free-standing. I kissed the glass lightly and propped the picture on the metal chest.

'Thanks for everything. Don't be a stranger. Hope you haven't missed too many games of golf because of me.'

And we were done. For the time being at least. I knew he'd let me know if I'd missed anything important. We were still a two-way arrangement, and always would be, really.

I was stuffing my face with stodge in a most unladylike way when Kevin Mack appeared with an enormous bunch of blood red roses.

'These came for you when you were out yesterday, Miss Street, so I kept them in the tea room. Someone is very pleased with you, eh?'

The flowers were exquisite in shape, colour and present- ation, and they had a scent too which meant the bouquet had cost the annual turnover of a small African nation. The accompanying card simply read 'Call'. I may be cynical, but I didn't think they'd come from Barry and as I trawled through the extensive Rolodex of my suitors, the name I came up with was Andy Raynor. I sat down quickly, before my knees gave way.

'You've a bit of mayonnaise on your chin,' Kevin said. 'And just a little tomato on the side of your cheek. Eh, both of them.'

I had to do a Scarlett O'Hara on it, because I was busy, but boy, was I looking forward to tomorrow. First thing, I would go and see Andy, and if he gave me so much as half an inkling that he was interested in seeing me on a regular basis, say twice a year to begin with, then I was driving straight back to the northside to evict Barry and tell him we could still be friends. That was the crudely fashioned plan at any rate, and it was something to go on, I thought.

I couriered my booty from 'Flix' to Mark Rolands' office, then I dialled a friend in the Force to gently quiz her on the Michael O'Donoghue case. Sergeant Róisín Duffy snorted when she heard what I wanted.

'Leo, (a) that's another station, and (b) you know it's classified.'

'Does that mean you can't tell me anything?' I wheedled.

'You know it does.'

'Tell you what, Róisín, why don't we do the thing where I ask questions and you just answer yes, no or maybe?'

'Maybe.'

'Great. Are the police treating this death as suspicious?'

'Yes.'

'Is a post-mortem taking place?'

'Yes.'

'Is there another line of enquiry if toxicology comes up negative?'

'Yes.'

'Would this involve the nature of the accident?'

'Yes.'

'Might that be to do with the car?'

'Yes.'

'Any lead suspect so far?'

'No.'

'A lot of people wanted him dead.'

'That's not a question, but maybe.'

'Can I call you again on this matter?'

'Maybe.'
'I love you too, Róisín. Thanks.'
'Yes.'

I didn't see much point in calling ahead to Miranda O'Donoghue. With warning, she might try to divert me, and I wanted to be face to face with her. With that in mind, I typed up an interim report which loosely skirted the many facets of the case. I sorted out the bill, because I'm a practical person with a mortgage and a slew of dependants, and packed the lot into a large brown envelope addressed to the relict of the late Michael O'Donoghue. I grabbed the package containing the death threat, so kindly supplied by Tara, placed my roses in full view of the door and left. There are many who would say that this was not the perfect moment to be doing business with a grieving widow, but I wanted the props with me in case I needed more reason to call than to offer my condolences. 'Prepared,' I growled, to myself.

Second thoughts are the perfect partners to a false exit. I returned to phone Ciara. Her mother answered in a whisper and I explained that my assistant was to take the day off. We would review our situation the following day. I looked to Mick for approval and his silence gave it. Leo Street was properly '& Co.' now.

TWENTY-THREE

Low-scale dread filled me during the drive southwards. By the time I turned into the cul-de-sac in which the O'Donoghues' house stood I had residual panic ringing in my ears. I was not looking forward to the rest of the day, steeped as it was in uncertainty and gloom. But a yearning for closure and my own cussed stubbornness forced me on, even if a more natural inclination might have been to run home and bury my head in a pillow.

I was worried about a confrontation with Miranda simply because I knew that I would start my conversation with this woman from a position of inferiority. Always. I wasn't quite pinned down on the purpose of my visit, other than an amorphous hunch that I should check what was going on in the household. Right back to nosy me, then, complete with contents dripping out at intervals. I needn't have worried so much. The house was deserted and I spent an hour sitting in my car, with my buttocks going numb, then painfully

coming back to life in a spritz of pins and needles. I flexed
my feet, twisting the ankles in a circle, clockwise than anti.
A sluggish circulation is often better than none at all. I
shifted from cheek to cheek in the bucket of the seat,
looking for all the world as if I needed a pee. And eventually I did. I got out of the car and paced the street to return
a blood supply to my vitals and to take my mind off the loo.
It almost worked, and staved off the inevitable for a short
time. A reconnoitre of the neighbours' leafy properties
revealed several promising spots for any unfortunate emergency. What bothered me here was the notion that security
cameras would also record such an event. That was enough
to force a positive regression of my waste fluids; in fact, my
bladder shrivelled at the thought.

The estate was select and well-heeled. Each home was
similar to the next in size, which was at least five
bedrooms and all the rest, but the layouts had changed
over the years, with some residents opting for carbuncular
conservatories to the side and back, variously. High walls
protected large gardens, which ranged from finest
Gertrude Jekyll to minimalist Japanese. One individualist
had installed Tudor windows and attached a strange black
and white Elizabethan wood feature to the façade of his,
or her, house; it was nothing less than the cladding of the
upper-middle-class.

I had ample time to study the driveway of the
O'Donoghue house, along with a car port to the side, big
enough to hold two vehicles. Unsurprisingly, it was empty.
All ground surfaces were blemish free. If someone had cut
the brake cables on Michael O'Donoghue's car, and I considered this a possible cause of the crash, it had not been
here because there was no brake fluid to be seen.

I was leaning against my new blue bonnet when a sleek grey saloon purred around the corner, containing the lady of the house, Tara and a lad I assumed to be Tara's brother, Ben. My assumption proved correct, which was gratifying.

'Come to scavenge?' Miranda asked, and I was right back to square one. This woman knew a thing or two about power.

She was dressed to fit the grieving widow bill, with a hint of style guru and a pinch of image consultant. All her own doing too, I suspected. She swept up her driveway, with her children trailing miserably after her. The youngsters' eyes were hollow and red, their steps leaden with grief. Tara avoided eye contact with me, and I kept my distance. Ben hadn't noticed that I was there.

The interior of 14 Sea Point, Blackrock, was as I'd expected: tasteful and immaculate. I was familiar with the exterior and it held few secrets anymore. We shuffled down the hallway to a large kitchen which managed to suggest space as well as exhibiting every gadget and domestic fol-de-rol known to the late-twentieth century. I took a surreptitious look back along the cream carpet we had trodden to check that I hadn't brought any unwanted stains into the house with me; dog shit was number one on my list of worries. I seemed to have passed through without incident. Miranda flicked the switch on the kettle with a perfectly manicured hand. She posed by the sideboard and I had time to admire her expert hair cut and colour job. I did so in silence. When this had stretched to the required length, she announced that I would have a coffee while she fixed herself a gin and tonic.

'What a day,' she commented, which was as unnecessary as calling Mr De Beer a 'diamond geezer', I felt.

Tara stifled a sob and excused herself from the room, in a broken-hearted splutter of sorrow and dental steel. I hoped that some of her mother's mettle was embedded deep in her DNA as an underlay of resolve to help her through this awful time. Come to think of it, her father seemed to have had his fair share of strength too, even if he did use it to the detriment of others. Ben had disappeared silently, unobserved by the household. How would he deal with the decimation of his family? I would probably never know, even though I had crossed his path at this intimate time. The degrees of separation between us two ran deep and parallel to our lives; they mocked any notion of friendship or camaraderie, and underscored the evanescence of the casual encounter, the fragility of human relationships.

'I wonder if I might use your bathroom,' I said, realising that I wouldn't last too much longer. There is nothing worse than pissing yourself in public. Miranda waved me off to a small cubicle under the stairs. There, I perched on the seat trying to aim for the sides of the bowl in order to minimise the noise. A soft tinkling filled the tiny room, and I hoped that it was not travelling too much further. This was unlikely as I could clearly hear the sound of ice hitting glass in the kitchen next door, along with the liquid sounds of gin and the sloshing fizz of tonic. As I washed my hands, I noticed a plastic bag on the floor, full of men's accoutrements. Apparently, all signs of Michael O'Donoghue were due for quick obliteration.

'We'll go into the study and deal with your business,' Miranda said on my return. She made it clear that this was an unsavoury prospect, best dispensed with quickly. At that moment she was still paying, so I let her away with it. She was in no hurry to move and arranged herself like a frieze again, as cool as an Elgin marble and no less beautiful. Eventually she began to glide to a small room on the first return of the stairs. It had clearly been her husband's until a few hours before. A pen he had used was lying casually on a blotter, as if on 'pause' while he took a short break from his business. It looked lonely. Miranda sat in a swivel chair behind the desk and fixed me with her cool stare.

'How much?' she asked. 'What price have you decided on? What is the going rate for chasing up betrayal?' She was smiling now. I had no idea where to go with this, but I opened my mouth and hoped for inspiration to kick in. It did not, but words emerged and for this I gave thanks.

'I know this may not seem the ideal time for this, but I thought you might take some comfort from what I found out.'

'For instance?'

'Your husband was not having an affair.'

She gave a bored shrug. 'Zippideedoodah. Yes, that's a tremendous relief, I'm sure.'

If rudeness was a manifestation of her grief, she was very upset indeed. I didn't think so, though, and I was damned if I was going to let her use me as a punch bag to boost her own ego.

'There are some fascinating elements of this investigation that I think you may be able to shine some light on,' I said.

At least she had the decency to raise one well-plucked eyebrow at that.

'Such as?'

'I'd like to know why you were following your husband in your car?'

'Nice try,' she laughed. 'But I'm sure I don't know what you mean.'

Her fingers had drifted to the scar on her face. She saw that I had noticed.

'Michael gave me this, in a way, you know. I was so angry with him one night that I gouged my own cheek with a ring he had given me. It hurt like hell, and of course I regretted it almost immediately. But it scared the pants off him, which was what he deserved, and not just on that occasion either.'

She diverted her attention to the bureau and began to open and close various drawers. Finally she found what she was looking for, a packet of cigarettes and a gold lighter which she placed on the blotter. 'A filthy habit.' She grinned. 'But at this stage, who gives a fuck?' The unexpected coarseness echoed like a bullet from a gun; a small, modern and lethal weapon. She lit a cigarette with practised ease and inhaled with palpable relish. 'That's better.' She threw the lighter on to the desk without caring where it landed. Leaning back in the chair, she blew a long satisfied stream of smoke into the air.

I wanted to scream at her to continue talking. I willed her on, with as much brain power as I could muster in my disease-ridden skull. She did, and this probably counted as a third-class miracle, if such a thing can be quantified.

'He was a very vain man, you know.' A pot and kettle situation, then. 'And not half as clever or innovative as he would have had himself and everyone else believe. He was nothing without me.' Now she spat. 'Nothing.'

She looked around for an ashtray, seeming vulnerable for a moment as she balanced the long ash in mid-air. Then she was back to her power position as she tipped the waste contemptuously on to the desktop. In a measure of status, I would have to call this woman a red ten. She took up where she had left off with what seemed like enjoyment.

'Michael O'Donoghue was an amateur playing around with his Petri dishes. He had no idea of the potential he was sitting on. Every supposed breakthrough he made was known to anyone who uses the Internet properly. And he was negative in his approach, narrow-minded. He had no vision. But *I* do. I continually fed him information, brought him up to speed. But, of course, information is only useful if you know how to apply it. And he saw to it that I could not do that, that I was kept away from my rightful place. How dare he? Who the hell did he think he was to do that to me, of all people? I *made* the bastard, and he would have done better to remember that. Well, I suppose, he's finally realised it now, wherever he's frying.'

It was interesting to me that at no time did Miranda mention any religious objection to Michael's work. Tara had heard biblical quotations about fire and brimstone being hurled about when her parents had argued, but perhaps they had merely been Miranda's smokescreen. It made sense that she would be interested in her husband's research; she had worked with him on his projects when they'd met.

I didn't really know what to say so I put the envelope containing my report on the desk as another gambit. She barely acknowledged it.

'Where's the bill?'

I passed it to her. She gave the note a cursory once over before signing a cheque for the amount specified. It was from a joint account and had already been co-signed by her late husband. 'Handy, eh?' she crowed. As she ripped along the serrated edge, Miranda flashed me another of her frozen smiles. Her eyes were pale enough to take on the shades of her surroundings, like a lizard changing colour. Right now, they conspired to look brown, and almost warm.

'Thank you so much, Miss Street,' she said. 'You have been most useful.'

I shivered involuntarily. Why did I suddenly feel that I too had played a part in the death of Michael O'Donoghue?

'Was there anything else?' she asked, in a tone clearly intended to end our meeting.

'Yes. I'd like to ask you about the threatening notes your husband had been receiving. As I mentioned to you on the phone yesterday, I've come into possession of one of them. I have it here, actually. Police forensics will, of course, be testing it for DNA evidence and so on, but could you tell me if you recognise it?' I held the plastic folder well away from her grasp and let her read the note.

She reddened slightly, then barked a short laugh. 'They all looked the same to me. That might be one, but I doubt it.'

'What makes you say that?'

'We . . . he . . . Michael destroyed them all.'

'Not this one.'

She sat in contemplation for a moment, then narrowed her eyes. 'Of course. Tara gave you that, didn't she?' She waited for a response, but didn't get one. I clenched my toes in an effort to stay as still as I possibly could. This made both my feet cramp, and it took all my strength not to jump up and dance around the room in agony.

'Let me tell you something, Miss Street, my daughter idolised her father with childish tunnel vision and Michael was a big fan of such simple, uncomplicated adoration. I

290

sometimes think he took what she said to him about his work to be true, ridiculous as that was, because that was what he wanted to hear. He could not rely on me to be so deluded, or to give praise where it clearly was not due. I don't know what she thinks she has achieved by meddling in this way, but you'd be better off ignoring her and any so-called information she may have given you. She is just a hysterical little girl. All you have there is a worthless piece of paper – rubbish.'

'Hard to believe she could be so devious as to conjure this up.'

'Miss Street, I'm not sure what this cheap trick is supposed to achieve, but I would remind you that my husband was killed only hours ago and I should be allowed to grieve. I would thank you to leave now.'

'I'm interested to hear you say "killed" rather than "died", Mrs O'Donoghue.'

'Get out now, before I call the police.'

'Oh, I think you can expect to see them soon,' I said, as I rose to leave. 'And don't think you can threaten me,' I added. 'I know what you're up to, and I intend to do everything I can to aid the investigation surrounding your husband's death. Please stay where you are, I can see myself out.'

I think the last remark annoyed her more than anything else because of course she'd had no intention of going to the door with me. She was temporarily struck dumb as she searched for a retort.

At the top of the stairs, I turned. 'Your husband was said to have a God Complex,' I told her. 'It seems to me that you shared it.' That got her moving. I had reached the front door when she swept after me and roughly thrust forward her hand to grasp the folder containing the death threat. 'If that is as pertinent to my husband's death as you seem to think, I should pass it along to the relevant authorities,' she hissed.

'No need,' I said, wrenching it back from her. She lifted her hand to hit me, just as a tortured wail rang through the air. For a moment I wondered if I had made the sound.

'Randy, Randy,' cried a woman's voice. 'I came as soon as I heard. How *are* you?'

A screeching dervish in black weeds from top to toe bore down the driveway and into the accidentally open arms of 'Randy' O'Donoghue, who never managed to land that punch on me. Our visitor had the glazed eyes of one too many early-afternoon cocktails. Miranda's were filled with hatred and frustration, which she quickly veiled with more acceptable sorrow.

'Margaret,' she said, 'how sweet of you to call.'

'How will you manage? What's to become of you?' Margaret wanted to know.

'Oh, I shouldn't think she'll let a little thing like this hold her back for long,' I muttered as I hastened my exit. It took rather longer to remove the daggers from my back.

I was shaking badly by the time I got to my car. I reached beneath my voluminous jumper and removed the tape recorder nestled within. I rewound the tape a little, then pressed 'play'. I heard myself say, 'I'm interested to hear you say "killed" rather than "died", Mrs O'Donoghue.' 'Get out now, before I call the police,' came Miranda's voice. I rewound the tape completely, then packed it into its carton, with the date, time, and location on the label. I placed the cassette and the death threat in an envelope with a full report on my company's investigations and headed for the police station. I wasn't all that sure that I had anything of import to share with the authorities, but there was a stink about this case that needed pointing up, so the time had come to hand my information over to the Boys in Blue.

TWENTY-FOUR

My night was sleepless and not without incident. I presented my 'evidence' to the relevant Garda station, then quizzed Sergeant Róisín Duffy, by way of the telephone, for more information. Through our elaborate game of 'yes, no or maybe' I learned that, yes, the O'Donoghue vehicle had been tampered with, and yes, the brake lines had been cut, with a very sharp instrument. ('Perhaps a scalpel?' 'That is absolute conjecture, but maybe.') Yes, Miranda O'Donoghue was a suspect, but not the only one. ('Our nearest and dearest are often the deadliest?' I got a complete set of 'yes, no and maybe' for that). Yes, my help was cautiously welcomed, and no, she would not confirm any of the above.

I was attempting to breathe in the vapours of a menthol-based honey and lemon drink when I noticed the edge of a t-shirt sticking out from under the legs of the couch. I reached down to pull it free, and discovered that it was snagged on a loose spring on the underside of the seat. I placed the piping hot toddy at a safe distance because I am a prudent woman who hates being scalded. In general, pain and suffering are best avoided; something of which I constantly have to remind myself. I got down on all fours and reached into the murky depths. Amongst the old magazines and biros, I met with resistance and serious disapproval from No. 4. I tipped the sofa on to its back legs for easier access and surveyed the undercarriage.

Someone, or some creature, had been very busy. Through the torn webbing I could discern a cache of stolen goodies. They ranged from Barry's lucky underwear to a tea towel and a rawhide chew. I turned to my favourite choice as culprit and said, 'Is this where you hid the tie of my dressing gown then?' He had the grace to bark in the affirmative. I dithered over what course of action to take. It was clear that the little dog had been through a hard time, what with the death of his previous guardian and taking up residence in this unfamiliar house, so I suggested a compromise. 'How about I leave you the food, and I return Barry's stuff? And if anything goes missing again, we'll all know where to find it?' This was acceptable.

I took him on to my knee and cuddled him. 'I know you're probably worried about losing everything again, but don't be. You live here now, with me. And I love you,' I whispered. He licked me full on the face. Oh, yummy. What a way to celebrate acknowledgement of our feelings for one another. While I was vaguely ahead, I thought I'd chance a query. 'Did you have anything to do with my red glove ending up in the office loo?' He buried his snout in my armpit, without giving a definitive answer.

Barry fell in the door with the actor currently known as

Coleman Pearse. Even though they doled me a beer, I was not a feature of their evening. I felt fury begin somewhere deep in a place I had been ignoring for a long time now. They were taken up with the subject of piles, which led me to believe that one of them was afflicted. Barry dubbed them 'the devil's grapes', while Coleman preferred the notion of piles as 'the arse's answer to gravity'. As they continued their rant, I told Barry, 'I found your missing clothes, I'm going to throw you out of the house, and your fly is open.' Although all of these things were true at the time, he didn't hear, and most of all, he didn't care. I ran a bath, swiped another lager and soaked my aches away. I wanted to be clean for tomorrow as I had a lot to do. Tomorrow was Sorting Out Day, and I was excited and appalled at the prospect.

I am not a brave woman, I thought. And I'm not decisive enough. Or am I? I teased myself. But I had come to realise how precious life was over the last few days. And fleeting. And fragile. I didn't want to wake up at forty, trapped and feeling bitter. My destiny was firmly in my own hands. No one was to blame but me if I did not act to change my circumstances. I was sorely aware that I was hinging some key elements on the possibility that Andy Raynor would be available and interested in playing a part in my life, but I had to start somewhere. If he was the catalyst to all of this, so be it. I lay in bed later, staring at the ceiling and its Australia-shaped damp patch, and told myself that this time I was in the driving seat and things were looking up. Also, Australia's progress would have to be halted.

I came over all shy after my coffee the following 6.30 a.m. But fortune favours the foolhardy and all that, so I had a bracing shower and wondered at how squeaky I was from all the washing I'd done in the last while. I dosed up on drugs for my ailment, and ran a nit comb at length through my tresses. The results were satisfying. I very nearly passed for human. Lots of bits were up for swaps, of course; my nostrils probably won that particular bout, red and flaking as they were from days of rubbing. I tried a dab of foundation, but it clung stubbornly to the flakes, rather than smoothing away the blemishes. I cleaned it off with, according to the label, the kindest, gentlest, least perfumed remover on the market. It stung me like nobody's business; whatever that phrase means is beyond me, as I feel most things are, at the very least, *my* business, but it's acceptable parlance, and so it goes.

It was a ridiculously early hour to be leaving the house, but I was set on a course of action and knew that even the slightest prevarication on my part would result in going back to bed with a man I was about to ditch, and the avoidance of 'action'. So, I promised the cats extra long cuddles later in the day when I got back, then called No. 4 and together we bravely faced our destiny. The dog took up his regular stance in the Streetmobile; today, he was the canine Isadora Duncan. Minus the scarf, I'm happy to report. We headed into a darkness that was trying its best to suggest dawn and I took this to be a metaphor for our new life.

We were still inordinately early for a breakfast visit anywhere but a Trappist monastery so I brought us for a walk on the strand at Sandymount. As light encroached on the horizon, the wind whipped us mercilessly. Still, I threw driftwood and No. 4 chased it, like in the best television movies (I'm not sure what the musical accompaniment would have been, but I would have been happy with anything but the execrable 'Stranger On the Shore'). I stared at the curved patterns in the sand and made myself dizzy. No. 4 caked himself in muck. When I looked romantically into the middle distance, involuntary tears ran down my cheeks. It was me against the elements, among them the biting, chill air. Michael O'Donoghue had come here only hours before his death, and I wondered if he had been trying to sort out the big issues in his own life. If so, I'll venture he didn't get the result he was hoping for.

The time came when it was decent for me to release myself back into the community. We sheltered briefly by the Martello Tower while I tried to formulate a strategy, or at the very least a few plausible words. My brain was frozen in my head and my face was set in the rictus of a smile, not unlike an astronaut headed for the moon. I finally gave in to the inevitable, loaded up the dog and drove to Andy's house. I told No. 4 that this might take a while, but hopefully it would be worth the wait. He was too busy grooming the ends of his extremities to pay much heed. Without giving myself the option of any more time to reflect, I rang the bell on the Raynor gate, and walked through when the buzzer sounded. The climb to the front door was long, but eventually I was there and knocking on the door and feeling the stirrings of an excitement that was hard to fathom. I turned to look at Andy's garden, and when I heard the lock click open I turned back, smiling, to face a tall specimen of the female persuasion. She was drop dead you-know-what, and I found myself wishing that she would give in to fate and fall lifeless on the step. This was a setback and no doubt about it.

'Oh, hi,' I managed, cheerily. 'I was just passing by and

thought I'd call in. I'm an old friend of Andy's.'

She squeezed out a far from happy grin; more an ill-disguised sneer. 'It's very early, you know. We might have been . . . well, busy.' I noticed she was not wearing any shoes; feeling at home, so. 'Take a seat and I'll fix you a coffee, you look like you could use one.' Great, I looked every bit the bag of shite I felt. And worse, my heart had started a downward journey within my chest that was beginning to hurt.

The beauty didn't even have the grace merely to glide through the house, she clearly belonged there while I was a tub of whale waste that had accidentally been delivered to the wrong address. Before I could RUN AWAY QUICKLY, Andy appeared, in a towelling robe, looking sleepy and sheepish.

'God Almighty, Leo. Em, I wasn't expecting you.'

I bit back the 'clearly' that was on the tip of my venomous, disappointed tongue, and gave an energetic, 'Oh, I was just passing as I told, eh . . .'

'Ah yes, eh.' He looked from one to the other of us, then did the necessaries. 'Leo, this is Heather. Heather, Leo.'

I had reached some sort of limit. A light buzzing started up in my ears and white spots danced before my eyeballs. The room reeled and I put my hand out to steady myself. Instead of reaching a shelf or the back of a chair, I found that I was leaning on Andy's arm. I recoiled with all the elegance of a dancing pot-bellied pig.

'Is she all right?' Fern, or Frond, or Spore wanted to know, her delicate pink lips pursing into a classic moue of distaste. Scratch that, it was a clichéd pout.

'Are you, Leo?' Andy asked, almost passing for concerned.

OF COURSE I'M NOT ALL RIGHT, YOU STUPID

PHILANDERING BASTARD, I CAME HERE TO THROW MYSELF AT YOU AND NOW LOOK WHAT'S HAPPENED.

'Yes, yes, I've just had this awful cold, and it makes me unsteady. I think it's all settled in my ears and affected my balance.'

I'm sure I heard Mould or Compost Heap or Decomposition mutter 'too much information', but I wasn't confident enough to make something of it. To be honest, I think that the cold had got into my aurals somehow, and I wasn't sure of much in the way of sound, or smell for that matter. Unfortunately, there was no problem at all with my sight, and what I was seeing was far from ideal. I decided against starting a Bitch Fight, even though some bad angel inside me was saying that I could take her. But I was hanging on to my dignity by an extremely flimsy thread just then and I let reason win out.

I found myself staring into Andy Raynor's fabulous eyes and wanting to cry. I couldn't believe the depth of the pain inside of me, and the fact that it didn't seem apparent to the others in the room. Instead, I said, 'The dog's in the car. I've promised him a walk so I'd better keep my end of things up. You said to call, so I have. See you soon, I guess.'

By the time I had finished this speech, I was well into the process of fleeing as quickly as is allowed in polite society back to my point of entry, with my gracious host hot on my tail, in exactly the way I had not anticipated or wished for.

'Leo, there's no need to rush off.'

YES, THERE BLOODY WELL IS.

'Stay and have a coffee.'

OVER MY DEAD, GERM-FILLED BODY.

I had my hand on the door knob, on the cusp of freedom, when he grabbed my arm and swung me around. We stood there without speaking, listening to our own heaving breaths. Finally, he said, 'I'm delighted to see you, really I am. And this is not what it looks like.' He waved a hand back towards the kitchen. By now, I had a milligrip on my emotions and was determined to salvage something from this disaster.

'Andy, relax. It doesn't matter to me who you play Happy Families with. You're a big boy with a reputation to keep up. What you do in your own house is your business. I was just popping in to say hello, that's all. And now that I have, I'd better go. I have a very busy day ahead. I'll see you around.'

And with that I just ran out of the door and sped down the steps as fast as my fat little legs would take me. I was gulping back tears as I got into the car, fired it up and squealed away from the kerb. I drove for three or so streets then pulled over and sobbed till my body hurt. The sky was red that morning; I should have paid it more attention.

A good cry is a wonderful purge, not least because it leaves you too weak to think, or feel any more misery. I pulled a compact from my bag and checked the damage to my face. I would be lying if I said it could have been worse. My eyes were puffy and any soul that I could discern inside was bruised with humiliation, rejection and my own stupidity. My lungs were sore from smoke inhalation, the common cold and weeping, and my sinews, bones and senses were permeated with a good measure of the selfs – pity and doubt were playing blinders, with loathing on the street corner kicking an empty milk carton around. All present and correct.

There were two directions I could go now: up or down.

One of them wouldn't do at all, so I picked myself up, tried to dust myself off, with the added difficulty of a small, worried dog on my lap, and vowed to start all over again. Above all, I needed some sleep. A drizzle of rain helped a blob of grey and white birdshit to travel across my windscreen. It changed shape and size with each wipe of the blades, but never really disappeared. I limped us through the morning traffic jam of glum workers travelling into town.

When we reached Merrion Square I gave in to a whim and drove into the underground car park of the Fledgling. I snagged a space on the lowest level and walked back up to an area sealed off with official tape and burly policemen. A plate on the wall booked this section for Michael O'Donoghue. I looked high up from right to left to remind myself of the position of the security cameras when I'd first cased the joint. One pointed away from the taped off area and I calculated from its angle that the O'Donoghue space would have been its blind spot. But the other pointed directly at it and had a brilliant vantage point from which to record any activity in that parking bay. In a normal world, that is. Before someone had taken a hammer to it and rendered it useless.

The forensics team was dusting surfaces and collecting fibres and microbes and what have you. Smack bang in the middle of the fun was a dark greasy stain. I put my money on that turning out to be brake fluid. Before I could place my bet I was moved on by the cops.

I stepped out into the Dublin morning again. While I was here I might as well check out another hunch I was lugging around with me. I popped across to the florists opposite the hospital and bought a middle-of-the range bouquet of sedate flowers. Armed with these I was ready to blend in at the Fledgling, should the need arise. Instead, I approached the receptionist.

'I'm looking for my friend Miranda O'Donoghue,' I told her. 'I heard the terrible news an hour ago and I rushed over to her house but she wasn't there. No one was. So I assumed she would have come here. You know, a home away from home.' I sniffled and produced a handkerchief.

'She's not here,' I was told in return. The woman was sympathetic. 'We're all very upset too. We'll miss him. He was a great doctor.'

I gulped back my sorrow. 'I'll try a few of our friends. I just had this idea that she'd come to where she could be closest to him, to his work, his vision.'

'It's understandable,' the woman said. 'There are times when I have to remind myself that Miranda doesn't work here. She seems so much like a member of staff.'

'Yes. Some of his patients will miss her too, for that shoulder to cry on.'

'They will. She was an asset to Mr O'Donoghue's programme.'

So, Miranda had access to the hospital and the patients. Could *she* have been Kate Mulligan's mole in the organisation?

I left with my flowers and my information and rejoined No. 4 in the car. We took up our place again in the plugged up traffic lanes and seven days later Molly was looking critically at me, saying 'I think you're over the worst of it now.'

'I hope so,' I told him. We were more than certainly speaking at cross purposes.

My glove was looking jollier on the notice board, so I put

it in my pocket, and resolved to give it a new life far away from here. The post delivered at least one decent item; a cheque from a lawyer I work for from time to time. I let No. 4 race up the stairs, barking all the way to let everyone know that he'd arrived, while I sailed up in style in the elevator. As I approached the office, I heard a happy fugue of women giggling.

Ciara was sitting, legs a-dangle, on the edge of the desk and enthroned in the huge armchair opposite was the diminutive form of a returned Mrs Mack. Her husband was mopping the floor around them, and beaming like a man who'd won a million pounds. Perhaps he had, and he was one of those people who vow that it won't change their lives. It would sure change mine, I can tell you.

'Leo, fantastic. You're just in time to join us for the Lourdes Holy Water,' Ciara told me. She gestured to a child-sized statue of the Blessed Virgin held in Mrs Mack's arms. It was of white opaque plastic with a blue screwtop crown.

'After what I've just been through, it could do no harm,' I said.

'That's the spirit,' Ciara remarked, and Mrs Mack began to laugh.

What had brought about this rather unholy Entente Cordiale, and was it cause for concern?

'Who are the gorgeous flowers from?' Ciara asked, indicating the roses.

'Oh, just a thank you for a favour, nothing special,' I remarked, ultra-casually. For all I knew that was the truth; it was not Andy's fault that I had expected too much, was it?

'This is for our returned traveller,' I said, as I handed over the Fledgling bouquet. I had no other option, the look she was giving me.

Ciara put mugs on the desk and Mrs Mack undid Our Lady's crown and began to pour the contents of the statue into them. Then they were dispensed amongst us and we raised them in a toast, without knowing what the appropriate words were for such a blessed round. I knocked mine back, and it in turn knocked me into the nearest seat, Mrs Mack was beside herself with delight, and Ciara's eyes glittered with mirth. Only Kevin rushed to my aid, clapping me vigorously on the back, and doing quite a bit of internal damage to my already battered person. Eventually I persuaded him to stop and – painfully caught my breath. When I was confident that I would live, I said, 'Holy God, it's pure vodka, Mrs Mack. Have you smuggled that into the country from your pilgrimage?'

She nodded through the cackles. 'Amn't I a terror altogether?'

'You are that,' I confirmed.

When we had squeezed enough enjoyment out of the morning's ruse, the Macks left and Ciara and I got up to speed on events. She looked refreshed and rested, and seemed none the worse for her adventures.

'I bounce back,' she admitted. 'And I'm a cold-hearted cow, don't forget.'

'I won't,' I assured her.

'What's your best shot on who did what?' she asked.

'If I was pushed I'd pump Kate Mulligan for the name of her informant. I'm not altogether convinced that it was Maria Flood. It could so easily have been Miranda. As far as the crash goes she had every reason for wanting her husband dead. She hated what he'd done to her aspirations of medical advancement. And maybe she did think he was having an affair with Maria. I'd wager a tasty sum that he was well insured too. It's all academic now because the cops will take it from here.'

'That can't be right,' Ciara said. 'How can we just let this go?'

'We have to. This is the real world. It's in the public domain now, and our job is to help the police enquiry. We're off the case. It's one of the most frustrating elements of being a PI. I don't think I'll ever get used to it.'

'Not wanted on journey.'

'Precisely. Besides, the cops are all over the evidence, we'd never get near enough to figure any more out. Sometimes, though, you'll be delighted to pass the burden of proof on to the State. Unless you want to go legit and join the Force?'

'No way. There's far more anarchy on this end of things; that's more my bag.'

Ciara reached and handed me some Post-its. Two were orders for bread from ladies with posh addresses, and one said that Con had called and was due for his transfer to a Dublin inner city parish in five to six weeks. At least they raised a tired smile from me.

'That poor young fella in "Flix",' Ciara remarked. 'He'll never give himself airs and graces. You've probably put him off wanting to go into management. Stunted him.' She grinned as she shook her head from side to side.

'Stop, Ciara, I feel terrible as it is.'

'At least he'll think twice about fiddling with telephones, if he was ever to feel inclined in that direction.'

'I still don't feel like Social Worker of the Month.'

'No, and you shouldn't.'

We sat awhile in a comfortable uncertainty, gently sipping the last of Mrs Mack's treat.

'I hate being taken hostage to fortune on the O'Donoghue thing,' Ciara moaned.

'Yep. When I first started that used to burn me up. But there are times now when I feel an almost guilty relief that I don't have to go any further into some of the messes I've been introduced to. It's kind of "be careful what you wish for", I suppose.'

We let the silence return.

'So what now?' she asked eventually, giving voice to the question on both our minds.

'What indeed? I suppose we need to find more work for you to do.'

I had said the right thing. 'I've been thinking about that, and I have a few leads I'm going to follow up. So, if it's all right with you, I'm off out to drum up some business. You know, you're lucky I came along.'

'Tell you what, why don't you prove that to me?'

'I will.'

'I don't doubt it. I might have known you were up to something when I saw you dressed as one of the common people still.'

She snorted. 'And some advice now, okay?'

'Yeees,' I said, unconvinced.

'Get some sleep. You look wrecked.'

'Thanks, I think. I am, and I will.'

After she left, I put the roses behind my chair, because they were mocking me. I could have thrown the bouquet out, but where's the point in wasting beauty, even if it is the present of a total dickhead? I tucked No. 4 up in his box, but couldn't get settled myself. I had a way around this. If there's anything that sends me off, it's trying to do my accounts. Accordingly I started up the computer and by the time I had given my password and got to the spread sheets I was yawning and nodding. The warmth of the holy vodka was tingling through my veins, and my muscles were finally relaxing from the unwelcome spasms of early morning. My mobile rang, and I recognised the number flashing as Andy's, so I switched it off without answering. I refused to let my brain indulge in thoughts of what might have been. That was then, this would have to be now, and I was the only one who could look after me. As I drifted into the realm of crazed imaginings that heralds sleep, the computer system's Tip Of The Day repeated itself over and over: 'If you run with scissors,' it told me, 'prepare to be cut.'

EPILOGUE

The Fledgling saga wound its way through the pages of the newspapers, moving steadily backwards in vanishing column inches, stopping short of the classifieds and the puzzle page before disappearing altogether. An internal enquiry hedged its bets, praised the late Michael O'Donoghue, and effectively dropped his area of research, at least from the public eye. A file concerning the death of the obstetrician was sent to the Director of Public Prosecutions but no one was ever charged in connection with it.

Maria Flood never regained consciousness. Her mother, Bernadette, made the decision to turn off her life support after six months of waiting and hoping for a recovery. I have pictures of both of them in my files.

A body washed ashore on Dollymount Strand two weeks after the doctor's funeral. It was discovered by a family out walking their golden retriever. The woman was identified as Kate Mulligan, née O'Brien, only daughter of Mary and

Felim O'Brien, survived by her loving husband, Mark. Her clothes were found three miles along the coast, neatly folded and containing a note which simply said, 'I'm sorry'. As Ciara read the newspaper report over my shoulder, she pointed to the picture of Kate's abandoned car and said, 'She was following Michael O'Donoghue on the night he died. I remember that dent in the front bumper.' I don't really know what to make of that detail, and the only woman who could help me with it has taken her story to the grave. I think of Kate every time I look at the new paint job on my car, which is often, and I never fail to be stirred with regret at the waste of it all. She was thirty-two years old.

Mark Rolands sent the mother of all legal letters to the proprietress of 'Flix', a woman he had only ever met while renting out a movie, and Maeve's frightening ordeal came to an end. He has not moved back to his own apartment so I wonder if I should start shopping for a hat. They are both members of the 'Groovy Movie' video store now.

No one ever admitted to the intimidation of Carmel Lally and her family, but it did stop after the fire at their home. Her compensation case against the crèche is ongoing. I occasionally collect the children from school, and when I do, I keep my distance from my old pals. But sometimes I see Colette in town, at night, and we share a few words or a wave. Her Japanese man is still a regular, and has applied for government grants to set up an off-shoot of his factory in Dublin. Colette reckons this makes her a candidate for Irish Entrepreneur of the Year.

My own lucky numbers netted zilch on the lottery draw, but I won twenty quid on the computer's random selection. What can I tell you? You lose some, you win some.